AWAKENED ABYSS

FIREBIRD UNCAGED BOOK 2

ERIN EMBLY

THE METRO TUNNEL had its eyes on me, even as the train sped along so fast all I could see through the window was a blur.

Or at least it felt like that.

I glanced down at the six-year-old boy fully immersed in his schoolbook beside me and tried to ignore the oppressive weight of the world's expectations on us. With a sigh, I squeezed his hand a little tighter as the train raced through the tunnel.

He didn't look up at me, just wriggled his tiny fingers out of my grasp and turned the page of his book. He had a quiz today of some sort and had been obsessively studying all morning. Seemed a little intense for his age, but what did I know?

When it came to kids, the answer was next to nothing. I'd taken custody of my dead roommate's son two months ago only because I'd been in the right place at the right time. My legal claim on Noah was tenuous at best, and there was a whole line of very distant relatives just waiting for me to fuck something up. Considering the fact that Noah was just as likely to eat human souls as he was ice cream on any given day, I had a hunch that the distant relatives wouldn't have to wait long.

But I didn't want to fuck this one up. In part because that

would mean letting my friend's son become a monster, but also because I just liked having him around. You know, when we were at home—far away from anyone he might accidentally kill.

He's fine. This is fine, I thought. But I couldn't shake the feeling that we were being watched.

The walls had ears and eyes pretty much everywhere, sure. But not the metro tunnels outside of a moving train. My paranoia was getting to be problematic.

I ran my eyes over the other passengers in the car, wondering why my instincts hadn't suspected one of them of watching us instead of the speeding blur outside. That would be more rational, although they weren't a suspicious bunch.

An elderly woman met my eyes, a few seats down. She was sitting by herself, her spine rigid. That alone meant she couldn't be stalking me; no one doing so would be this obvious. She gave me a crooked smile and then let her eyes drift to Noah, her face softening. Yeah, everyone loved looking at that cute kid. If he did turn into a monster one day, he'd have a damn easy time catching his prey.

The lights flickered in the train, and I grumbled under my breath at the shoddy upkeep. People began to shift in their seats and look away from their phones and books and whatnot. The train slowed to a stop.

Noah smacked his textbook shut with a loud crack. He was already on his feet before he looked around and realized we weren't at any station. His eyes narrowed on me. "Why did it stop if we're not there?"

I put on my calmest face, the one I used to give everyone as a Guardian even when I was losing my mind with worry or frustration. Half my job as a bodyguard had been keeping other people from freaking out, and it felt like that was half my job as this tiny monster's pseudo-parent as well.

"Probably just waiting for another train to go through," I said.

"It means you get extra time to study."

Noah sulked. "But I already closed the book."

"Want me to help you open it again?" I couldn't help but chuckle.

He narrowed his eyes at me and plopped back down on the seat, and I didn't know whether to count it as a parenting win or fail that he'd clearly understood the sarcasm in my question.

"I don't need help to open a book," he said, but he didn't open it. Just sat there with his little fists clenched around the corners of the cover and his head tilted down.

"Okay, what's up?" I asked. "I know a kid with a problem when I see one."

"I'm not a kid," he said, but the usual playfulness in his tone wasn't there. "That's a goat . . ."

"And you're a fairy," I finished for him.

He looked up at me with only a weak smile, and I wondered how much longer that little exchange would work to brighten his mood. Not much longer, by the looks of it.

"It's Carina," Noah said, his face scrunching back into a frown. "She says she won't take me flying because I'm too dumb and don't know how to not fall off."

Yeah, that sounded like Carina. My demon goddaughter who'd turned out to be my dragon niece was quite the piece of work. And for some crazy reason, Noah loved her. It must start early, the whole thing where men see long eyelashes and lose all sense of reason.

"Okay," I said. "But what does that have to do with . . ." I tipped my head down to peer at his book cover. "History?"

"If I can get an A on the quiz, it'll prove I'm not dumb."

"Ah. And then Carina will let you ride her?" Bats, that sounded wrong. "She'll take you flying, I mean?" I corrected myself even though Noah probably had no idea what I'd just implied.

"She—"

The train jolted into motion again, and Noah reached for the metal bar to avoid slamming into me.

I was about to ask him what he was going to say when the train lurched back to a stop and I slammed into him.

Something screeched loudly, metal on metal, in a high-pitched wail that lasted too long and felt too violent to be normal braking sounds.

The lights flickered again, and when I peeled myself off Noah I could see other passengers getting restless. The elderly lady who'd met my eyes before was shaking her head almost frantically as she opened and closed her hands.

"Sorry," I said to Noah, but I didn't hear it if he responded.

I was too busy gaping at the old woman, who'd just grown claws so suddenly they'd pierced through the skin on the palms of her hands.

Blood dripped on the ground and blended in with the dark speckled pattern on the laminate flooring. The close air in the car filled with shouts as bodies migrated away from her, and I let out a sound of disgust.

Really, no one was going to ask the bleeding old lady if she was okay?

I stood up and made my way over to her. My healing magic hadn't been playing nice lately, but I at least knew basic first aid. And surprise claws didn't scare me. Although maybe they should.

The woman clutched the sides of her head with her bloody hands and let out a moan as she leaned over. When she lifted her head back up, blood dripped down her face from where the claws had dug into her hair.

This couldn't be good.

I crouched next to her and gently touched her wrist, trying to ignore the jeers and gasps from the panicked crowd around us.

"Hey," I said as I tried to get a good look at her wounds. "I like your nails. Where'd you get them done?"

I gave her a smile, hoping to break her out of her frantic state. The holes in the palms of her hands began to close even without my help as she looked up at me, but something felt wrong.

Despite the fact that she was clearly living and breathing and moving and healing, she felt . . . dead. Empty. And when she looked into my eyes, her stare was eerily familiar.

My heart racing, I gripped her wrist tighter and put out magi feelers for her soul. It felt like I was trying to drink from a empty glass—only it was one of those glasses with liquid in th sides, designed to confuse your senses.

A pit formed in my gut. I let go of the woman and glance back at Noah, who was watching me innocently with round ey He looked concerned, the sweet kid. But could he have done thi

Was it really a coincidence that someone nearby seemed to having soul issues? Could Noah even eat people's souls from distance?

I had no idea what he was capable of. And I could be im ining things. This woman's soul could be perfectly intact might just be a combination of my own fears and my ne wonky magic making me feel something off.

When I turned back to the woman, she had begun grow fur.

Okay, so the claws at least made sense now. She was a shi who had lost control. She still hadn't said anything to me, now she was moving her mouth like she wanted words to c out. For all her effort, I heard nothing but gasping silence.

She jumped out of her seat with more force than I w expect from anyone her age, and the bones shifted beneath skin as she opened her mouth to let out an inhuman roar. I about to tackle her, to keep her from hurting anyone, v she ran.

I ran after her, then hesitated when I saw her going for the door to the next car. If I weren't on this train with a six-year-old kid I was supposed to be taking care of, it would be a no-brainer. Follow her, restrain her, help her any way I could while keeping her from hurting anyone.

But I couldn't be save-everyone Darcy when I was parent Darcy—the latter couldn't just leave the kid alone on a train, especially when something so screwy was going on.

I growled in frustration and marched back to Noah as quickly as I could. Screams filtered over from the car next to us, where the woman had run.

I grasped Noah's textbook and forced it open in front of him. "Keep studying. You remember what to do if I lose you?"

He nodded.

"Good. Don't fuck it up, and I'll tell Carina how smart you are." I touched his cheek gently as I spun around, then ran down the aisle after the wacked-out shifter.

With the crowd of people all watching intently, I could only hope Noah would be fine. All these spectators now knew he was with me, so someone would intervene if anyone tried anything funny. And more importantly, he knew I hadn't abandoned him. He knew I was trusting him to look out for himself.

I sped down the aisle without looking back. I knew I would regret it if I did.

A gory mess greeted me when I made it over to the next car. A piercing wail, a woman clutching her bleeding gut, and a gurgling man trying to hold himself up by the railing while blood gushed out of his torn-out throat.

Yum, I thought with a grimace.

The old woman was gone entirely, a gigantic cat in her place. The kind of cat that prowled in the wilderness and had no business anywhere near people. Her paws and muzzle were drenched

in gore as she pounced haphazardly from seat to seat. She wanted out—she just no longer knew where that was.

Eerie laughter rang in my ears as the wailing died down, and I fought the urge to find and kill whoever thought this was funny.

I clenched my teeth. This woman would be much more difficult to restrain now that she was fully shifted. I didn't have any rope on me, or even any non-lethal weapons. Just the couple knives I always kept handy in my jacket. In these closed quarters, with all these people around and such a lithe creature with such pointy claws . . . attacking her here with my knives would be a recipe for disaster.

I ran past her instead. "Come and get me, Miss Kitty!" I yelled. Her predatory instincts should push her to chase me. I hoped I could outrun her long enough to get us off the train.

I had to stop to open the door to the next car over, and the cat-woman might have caught up with me had she not stopped to maul a large man who'd gotten in front of her.

"Hey! Cat-lady!" I called out to her from the next car, holding the door open.

The man grunted and stumbled back as too much blood ran down his leg, and the cat set her eyes on me, leaning back slightly as her tail moved slowly from side to side.

I cringed. That made at least two people already with fatal wounds in this car. But if I had my way, there wouldn't be any more.

Spinning around without closing the door, I yelled, "Everyone get the fuck out of the aisle!"

The cat pounced after me, the door slamming behind her. I kept on running. I probably should have yelled for someone to open the door I was currently running towards, at the other end of the car—the door that led off the train and away from the people in it—but it was too late now. I would be there before I could take a breath to say anything.

The people around me were a blur, bless their obedient souls, but someone came into focus just as I slowed to grab the door handle myself. Someone standing in my way.

His bright vest marked him as a Metro worker, and I had just enough time to be annoyed at how seriously he was taking *the one job I needed him not to do* before he opened his mouth.

"You can't—"

He might have said more, but at that point the snarling cat pounced on my back, claws tearing through my jacket sleeves and jaws snapping at the back of my neck.

I ducked my head and fell forward as soon as I felt her, letting her momentum guide me in a roll until she was flung forward off me—right into the metro worker.

He screeched and jerked away from her, his vest catching on the door handle as he did.

While she scrambled to her feet, all claws and snarls and twitching muscles, he nearly tore his vest getting the door open.

Grabbing onto the metal bar overhead with both hands, I braced myself and swung my feet up to kick the cat through the door.

My boots connected with her side before she could turn to face me. With a yowling hiss, she flopped through the open door into the dark tunnel beyond. I let out a breath and then jumped out after her.

Cool air filled my nostrils as the darkness washed over me, calming my racing heart. Clicks of cat claws on the concrete and metal echoed all around me, intensified by the tunnel walls just as the magic flowing through me was magnified by the dark.

The cat walked towards me slowly, limping just a little. A low growl came from her throat as drips of blood fell from her muzzle. She licked her lips and swished her tail, and I reached into my jacket for a knife.

I didn't want to kill her, not after seeing her unwilling transformation. The old woman under all that fur hadn't gotten on that train with the intention of going on a murder spree. I had no idea what had set her off or whether she could be brought back, but I wanted to keep her alive to find out.

If she was dead set on attacking me, that might be an impossible task. *I should start carrying tranquilizers or something*, I thought, and the walls around me seemed to laugh at the idea.

I narrowed my eyes and fought the urge to look away from the cat in front of me. Who the fuck was laughing now? Had some asshole with a death wish followed us off the train?

I gritted my teeth as the laughter echoed through the tunnel endlessly, sounding less and less human as it went. It was almost like a child's giggle, both innocent and cruel at the same time, mocking me and the cat both in our seriousness.

She moved before I did—but not towards me. Instead, she lifted her head and let out a high-pitched roar, then spun in a circle. Chasing her tail? Screw the tranquilizer, maybe I would have been fine with just a ball of yarn.

I pulled out my phone, eager to take the opportunity to call for help. The longer I was left alone with this deadly cat, the more likely I would have to kill her.

But before I could get a message sent, the cat stopped running in circles and dashed away from me.

I sighed. Nothing I could do but run after her. There was no one she could hurt in the tunnel, but it wouldn't be long before she made it to the previous station—and there would be plenty more people for her to maul there.

So I slipped my phone back into my pocket and ran. Taking a deep breath, I filled my lungs as my feet pounded the tracks and life flowed into my leg muscles. It felt fantastic. It had been too long since I'd had a reason to run like this.

I focused on the cat in front of me, pleased to be gaining on her. She was faster than me, no doubt, but not nearly as determined. She wasn't even running in a straight line—more like bouncing off the walls, snapping at invisible nuisances in the air around her.

That might be worrying if I had the space in my brain to worry about anything right now. All I could think about was how I was just a few moments away from being able to pounce on top of her—the only way I had any chance of taking her out without killing her. It would be easier if her movements weren't so erratic.

When I was as close as I was ever going to get, I had to act before she turned to me. This wasn't the kind of creature you leapt at while the pointy end was facing you.

I let the knife in my hand fall as I launched myself forward onto the cat. She yowled as I knocked her to the ground, my left arm wrapping around her throat while my right locked itself around her chest. I squeezed her hind quarters between my thighs as I rolled over, keeping her back pressed tightly to my body and her paws sticking up uselessly in the air.

She snapped her jaws and twisted her head as far as it would go—luckily not quite far enough to make contact with my face, which was pressed hard into the back of her neck. My instincts took over, and I let out a yell as I struggled to put more pressure on her throat.

After what felt like forever but was probably only seconds, she relaxed in my grip, air failing to go through her constricted windpipe. Shifters needed to breathe just as much as their human and animal counterparts . . . yet another reason I preferred dealing with them over vampires.

The back of my head went fuzzy as I released my hold on the unconscious cat. I had forgotten to keep breathing, myself. I closed my eyes briefly to let the dizziness pass, and the eerie laughter rang in my ears again.

A strong gust of wind pushed past me, knocking some of my

hair out of its tight knot. The unconscious shifter tumbled back as if kicked by something much stronger than a gust of wind. Then she began to float, rising in the air like a damn kitty balloon.

The laughter grew louder, bouncing around the tunnel haphazardly, no longer in any pattern resembling a natural echo. When the floating cat came to, she locked her eyes on mine and roared. And before I could even pull out my second knife, she hooked her claws into her neck and tore out her own throat.

Blood spurted out, pooling in the air for an eerie moment before everything fell to the ground. The laughter died down as soon as she fell, and silence filled the space.

I stepped forward and then stopped. I didn't know how well "suicide by own claws" worked to kill shifters—unless one had a silver manicure—but even if this woman could be saved, I couldn't risk touching her now.

I couldn't risk touching anything that might be dead or dying. Not after what had happened to my roommate Becca just a couple months ago, when I'd discovered that a rogue phoenix had somehow made my body half its home.

The last thing I needed right now—or ever—was to boop the dead cat that'd just been trying to kill me and then watch her be reborn in fire.

As I pulled out my phone again, a noise from behind me caught my attention.

The train.

It started up again and sped away from me, leaving me alone with the lifeless cat in the darkness.

I closed my eyes and let out a quick breath before turning around and breaking into a sprint. Whatever I was going to do about this . . . about whatever had just happened . . . I couldn't do it from here while Noah was still on that train.

2

THE BUZZING from my phone taunted me as I ran through the tunnel in the dark, chasing the train I'd been on just minutes ago.

When I made it to the platform, the train was still stopped there. *Right,* I thought, remembering all the bodies the cat had left in her wake. The train would probably be there for a while. Which at least meant no other train would come through anytime soon.

That was good, because someone who could safely touch dead things really needed to get in there and investigate the shifter's body, preferably before it got run over.

I stopped behind the train to catch my breath, shivering as I tried to process what had just happened. This wasn't just a case of a shifter gone psycho—something else was in this tunnel. Something else had made her do what she'd done.

And it was something I couldn't see. I'd been there with it, heard its laughter, felt it in the unnatural wind in my hair . . . but it hadn't been something I could stick my knife in, and that made me uncomfortable as hell.

I took my phone out to check whether the buzzing was Noah trying to get a hold of me. The train had stopped at the station where we normally switched lines, so we had a designated meeting spot here he should be waiting for me at, but you never know.

The light from the phone made me squint, my eyes having adjusted to the darkness of the tunnel. And when I focused on the words on the screen, heat rushed to my face.

Nope, not Noah. Adrian Crane. Apparently I *had* managed to get a message off while the cat had been chasing her tail, despite the chronically spotty cell service underground, and apparently my impulse text had gone to him.

He was the one cop I was still on friendly terms with and who might actually be inclined to help me deal with a crazed cat in a subway tunnel, so I supposed that was logical. But seeing his words flood the screen made me almost as uncomfortable as contemplating a killer I couldn't stab.

He was confused, asking where I was, blah blah blah . . . What had I even sent to him? I scrolled up to see that I'd actually *called* him. Well, fuck. So he would've heard the creepy laughter, a lot of running, me wrestling with a yowling cat, and then . . .

Ugh. He's not going to let me ignore him if he heard all that. Not that I should be ignoring him anyway. If he couldn't be the one to go look at the dead body I'd just left, he'd know who to call to take care of it. But I didn't want to talk to him. Didn't want to hear his soothing voice and let it calm me down. Didn't want to let him distract me for another minute from . . . from anything.

Dead shifter in Metro tunnel between L'Enfant Plaza & Gallery Place. Yellow line, northbound. Weird shit.

I sent the text and then stuffed the phone back in my pocket, climbing up onto the platform from behind the corner of the stopped train. The platform was still crowded, authorities not having been able to corral the peanut gallery just yet. But it looked like the passengers had emptied the train—the live ones, at least—so Noah should be upstairs.

I pushed my way through the mass of onlookers, thankful no one had spotted me and stopped me. Did I want to talk to the train conductor and ask why they had started and stopped all those times? Yes. I also wanted to turn right back around and run through the tunnels until I could find whatever invisible laughing creature had caused all this. But Noah would kill me if I made him late for school, so I zipped up the escalator and put the mysterious violent episode behind me.

Say what you will about kids, but at least they make you get your priorities straight. My life span had probably gotten a lot longer having Noah around, what with all the walking away from crazy danger I was doing on his account. Curiosity may have killed the cat, but it wouldn't be getting at me anytime soon.

I took a deep breath when I got to the upper level of the station. After the tunnel I'd just been running around in, this felt like open air. Gallery Place was one of the biggest stations in DC, right in the center of the city, and from the upper platform it felt far bigger than any subway station should feel. The domed ceiling was so high it made the space look cavernous, like it had been made for something far bigger and grander than trains.

I made my way to the end of the Red Line platform where Noah and I usually switched lines on the way to his school. There was a big round column here that I'd told him to stand by if we ever got separated—and sure enough, he was there now.

He was facing the column with his back to me, his nose probably deep in that book he was obsessed with this morning. I walked up to him and put my hand on his shoulder.

"Come on, kid. We should—"

He turned around and I gasped, jerking my hand away from him.

The skin on his face was sagging, wrinkled, shriveled. So distorted it didn't even look like him.

It wasn't him.

An old man's head on a child's body, his smile slowly growing until it was inhumanly wide, and then a familiar laughter . . .

The phone buzzed again in my pocket, and in a blink the man was gone. Flies buzzed in wild circles in the space where he'd been standing as the eerie giggles faded out of earshot.

I stood frozen for a moment, my insides churning from disgust and horror in a way they hadn't minutes ago when I'd witnessed the death of a stranger. This wasn't bloody or violent, but it was *Noah.*

Had someone cursed him with accelerated old age in the short time we'd been separated? Had he stumbled into some kind of fae decay nightmare world?

My breath quickened, heart racing again. I never should have left him. Not even if it meant more people would have had to die without my help.

The buzzing in my pocket seemed to get stronger, and I snapped back to my senses. It might be Noah calling me.

I nearly declined the call by accident with my frantic, fumbling fingers before I managed to answer it and put the phone to my ear.

"Ma'am?" The voice of the woman on the other end was sharp and filled with disdain. "Did you hear me?"

"I . . . who is this?"

"This is Doreen Jackson from the Metro Transit Police Department. We have your son in our custody."

"Noah?" I asked, relief washing over me.

She didn't bother to answer me, just said, "You have fifteen minutes to collect him at our 5th Street location. After that I'm calling CPS."

The phone clicked, and I was left with my pulse pounding and my eyes still focused on the empty spot where I'd just thought I'd seen Noah.

"5th Street," I said to myself, then turned on my heel and

pushed through the masses waiting for the next train to get to a station exit.

I ran up the lengthy escalator and emerged into the sunlight with burning thighs. Only stopping briefly to check for directions on my phone, I hurried across the few short blocks to the office.

When I pulled open the door, my t-shirt was damp underneath my jacket and sweat was dripping down my neck. A woman I assumed was Doreen sat behind a desk with her eyes raised to me in a condescending glare.

Shit, was I bleeding? I'd been so distracted I hadn't bothered to check. A quick glance down had me cringing. No blood, but my jacket sleeves were torn to shreds. They'd done their job protecting me from the cat's claws.

Possibly even worse, the t-shirt I was wearing underneath displayed the logo for the strip club I'd been working at for a year and some change: Bawdy Baz's Bits & Bats. I wasn't ashamed of it or I wouldn't be working there, but I'd been on the receiving end of enough glares like Doreen's to know other people had some crazy opinions on what this said about my ability to take care of a child.

I opened my mouth to offer her a greeting, but Noah tackled me before I could, wrapping his arms around my waist in an uncharacteristic show of affection.

The corner of his history textbook dug into my side, telling me he'd been studying right up until the second I walked in. He was only happy to see me because it meant I could take him the rest of the way to school, but I didn't care. I put my hands on his shoulders and let myself enjoy the immense relief of knowing for sure that he was okay.

He looked up at me. "Can we go now?"

"Yeah," I started, but Doreen let out a loud huff that made me pause.

"I'm going to need you to fill out some forms," she said.

"Sure." I cringed again, wondering just how much of a pain in the ass this was going to turn into.

As I walked over to the desk, a high-pitched sorrowful wail erupted behind me, interrupting my thoughts.

I turned to see a woman gaping at me between sobs as a Metro officer awkwardly tried to comfort her, patting her on the back with one hand while leaning away with the rest of his body.

Her face was streaked with tears, and she let out another shriek when my eyes met hers.

"It's like you don't even care!" she whined at me. "You left him all alone and I brought him here for you—and you don't even care! Do you know what could have happened?"

I clenched my teeth, willing myself to not lash out at her. This woman *had* done me a favor if she'd gone out of her way to make sure Noah was safe, and if she wanted to scold me about leaving him in the first place I would be the first one to agree that it was probably a bad call.

But instead, she was scolding me about my emotions, and how dare she even presume to know how much I cared? Turning into a sobbing mess had never helped anyone in any situation, and there was no way I would do that even if the kid died. Even though just thinking about that possibility sent a hollow feeling through my insides.

"Thank you for looking after him," I said, just trying to get this over with. "It won't happen again."

The woman let out a groan and dropped her head and shoulders into her lap, and I gave Noah a questioning glance. Had he done something to her emotions? This was not the kind of reaction I would expect from a Good Samaritan witnessing the happy ending she'd just brought about.

Noah shrugged at me. But he was already bouncing from foot

to foot, clearly eager to get out the door and back on his way to school.

I probably should have left well enough alone, but something made me walk over to the sobbing woman and kneel down in front of her. I touched her shoulder lightly, and she looked up at me with puffy eyes.

"What happened?" I asked. "Why are you so upset?"

With a sniffle, she pulled her phone out of her purse and held it up so I could see a picture of a young boy around Noah's age. He had darker hair than Noah, but they had the same chubby cheeks and the same sweet smile.

"My Brady's still missing," she whispered, and then it all made sense.

"How long?" I asked.

"Six days." She lowered her voice even further. "They stopped looking after two."

I jerked back at her words, not sure why anyone would stop looking for a missing little kid so soon. "Who's they?"

"The police. Of course, they tell me they're doing everything they can, but I know he's not their priority anymore. They haven't called me with an update since Monday." She shook her head at me, face swelling as another sob built up in her throat. "No one even cares. He's lost and alone and he's going to miss his piano recital and he's allergic to eggs—what if they try to feed him eggs?—and no one even cares."

She was getting frantic again, and I shook off the moment of wonder that piano and eggs were the biggest things she was worried about. They weren't, though. These were just the worries she was distracting herself with to keep her mind away from the more likely horrors of abuse and murder.

I touched her knee this time to get her attention. "I care," I said. And I did. The panic I'd just felt at the thought of losing

Noah made me care a lot more than I normally might have. "What's his full name? Brady . . . ?"

"Lee," she said. "Brady Lee."

"Got it," I said. "I have some friends who might be able to help. I'll ask them to look into it for you."

She stared at me blankly for a moment, and I didn't blame her for not jumping for joy at my offer. Too many people had made her false promises already, and I'd just been proven neglectful in leaving my own kid alone. But I hoped I could help her anyway. Even though Noah should have been fine without her, I was grateful she had cared enough to step in.

And for her to see him abandoned, a little boy around the same age as hers . . . her emotional breakdown for today at least was clearly my fault.

"Can I have your number?" I asked. "In case I find anything?"

She nodded without saying anything, and I handed her my phone to add her information to.

"Ma'am?" Doreen piped up from her desk, sounding even less amused than she had the first time.

"Forms, yeah," I said through gritted teeth, my patience wearing thin. I took my phone back from the sniffling woman and walked up to the desk, where Noah was almost running in place in his anxiousness to get going, his book clutched to his chest.

Doreen piled a stack of papers as thick as my thumb in front of me and placed a pen atop it, giving me a smirk as she did.

"All those?" I asked, eyes wide. "I'm picking up a kid, not buying a house."

I regretted it as soon as I said it and saw Doreen's face harden. This woman could report me and probably have Noah taken away from me if she felt like it. If there was one time to be polite no matter what, this was it, and I couldn't even manage that.

I tried not to groan as I said, "I'm sorry."

But before I could even pick up the pen, Noah said, "We don't have time to buy a house, Darcy."

He handed me his book and I took it without thinking, then watched him walk around the desk so he could get close to Doreen.

Lowering his head, he pushed himself forward and bumped up against the arm of Doreen's chair with his skull. "Baaaaaaaaa," he bleated, then stood up and erupted into a fit of giggles.

It was his goat impression, which Becca had taught him originally when he'd first learned what a "kid" was. Doing it always made him laugh, and he'd been busting it out more often lately now that he'd been spending more time with Carina and her livestock.

Normally I thought it was cute as hell, but what was he thinking doing this *now*?

It didn't take long for me to find out.

In mere seconds, Doreen had thrown her head back and erupted into laughter along with him. A crazed-sounding wheeze made me turn around to see the previously sobbing woman overtaken with laughter as well, along with the man who'd been trying to calm her down.

I could maybe understand Doreen finding Noah's display hilarious. Who knew? She might have a great sense of humor when she wasn't dealing with neglectful parents like me.

But the two behind me hadn't even seen what Noah had done. They couldn't, not from where they were seated and with him behind Doreen's desk.

Feeling like I'd been dropped into crazy town, I let the creases in my forehead deepen as the laughter only got louder around me. Then suddenly Noah was tugging on my hand, and I looked down to see a heavy dose of sobering impatience on his cute little face.

"Come on, it won't last long," he said as he pulled me to the door.

And if I hadn't felt like enough of a horrible parent yet today, I certainly did now, with the little kid I was supposed to be taking care of using his manipulative fae magic to get me out of trouble.

Bats. I'd spent so much energy trying to make sure this kid wouldn't kill people to eat their souls that I'd completely neglected the dangers of his other capabilities. Honestly, I hadn't even known he'd learned to control this shit, and now I wondered if he'd been using it in other ways he shouldn't.

My thoughts raced with all the horrifying possibilities before I remembered that he was still studying in frustration to get smarter so a girl would like him when apparently he could just as easily do something like this to *make* her feel whatever he wanted.

Simeon's face took shape in my mind, his dark eyes and intoxicating smile that had made me feel so many things I shouldn't. With one look full of vampire magic, he had taken away the control I'd worked so hard to cultivate in my training, made me prioritize our fun over the work I'd chosen for myself so carefully, stolen my identity and then had the audacity to die on my watch.

I blinked myself back to the present. I was letting my past color my fears. Noah hadn't crossed any truly horrible lines yet, to my knowledge. I'd just need to sit him down and explain the importance of . . . emotional autonomy, I supposed.

I was so lost in my thoughts that it wasn't until we stepped into the shade near the down escalators that I realized Noah was leading me back to the Metro.

I stopped short, squeezing his hand to make him stop with me.

He turned to me with an exasperated sigh. "Come *on*—I'm going to be late."

"No you're not." I pulled out my phone. "We're taking a car the rest of the way."

His face brightened immediately, and he actually hopped up and down in his excitement. "For real?"

"Mmm hmm," I said, although I could practically hear my bank account bitching at me as I requested the ride on the app. "But we need to have a talk on the way about what just happened."

That would be a fun conversation for our lucky driver to overhear.

It wasn't ideal, but it needed to happen. And there was no way I was going to take Noah on another train until I knew just what I had witnessed down there with the giggly murder ghosts and the creepy doppelgänger.

3

I TOOK my ruined jacket off as I jogged home from the Metro stop nearest my apartment. After all the running around I'd done this morning, it felt nice to let the cool spring air rush over my damp skin.

With Noah safely at school and probably acing his test, I'd almost hoped to see something weird underground on my way back. Anything to help me make sense of what had happened with the out-of-control shifter and the awful Noah doppelgänger.

But nothing out of the ordinary had happened, unless you counted the wacky old man I'd sat next to who had snuck his pet lizard on the train and fed it crickets while it curled up under his sweater. No one had paid him any mind.

Just a regular Friday morning, apparently. Whoever had said weirdos only came out at night had it backwards, as far as I was concerned.

When I got to my apartment, I rushed up the steps and tossed my jacket over the sofa, kicking my shoes off and leaving them wherever they landed as I made a beeline for the shower. I only stopped to plug in my phone, which had died during one of my many failed attempts to get it to pick up a signal from deep underground on a moving train.

Annoying that the spotty service had only worked when I'd been too distracted to make use of it.

When I stepped out of the steaming shower not five minutes later, the phone's screen was bright and filling up with missed calls from Adrian.

Groaning, I decided to walk away from it just long enough to put on some clothes. I wanted to hear whatever Adrian had to say, of course—especially if he knew something about what had happened. But that didn't mean I wanted to talk to him.

I'd been trying hard to avoid this man ever since he'd let it slip after the debacle in January that I didn't need to use magic to make him want me. Not that I'd ever done that intentionally in the first place. But it had happened . . . and worse, my own physiological responses whenever he was around were clear evidence that I wanted him too.

I still barely knew the guy, and I had no idea if he had any sort of actual feelings for me. But I didn't want to find out. I could feel the danger with every tingle of warmth that ran through me at his touch, with every moment I caught myself staring as I tried not to imagine running my fingers through his light sandy hair and pressing myself into his strong chest . . .

That was how it always started. I knew the signs. So if I had to talk to this guy, I at least wasn't going to be naked while doing so.

I finally answered his latest call as I was slipping on my boots, putting him on speaker and then dropping the phone beside me.

"What's up?" I said flatly while I attempted to lace up the boots with hands that were shakier than they should be.

"Not much," he said after a brief pause. Even through the shitty phone speaker, his voice sounded rich and warm. And even though I could tell he was frustrated with me, my hands steadied and my heart slowed a little when I heard it. "Just trying to figure out how you managed to get a shifter to tear her own throat out."

"Didn't you get my text?" I asked.

"What? Was 'weird shit' supposed to mean something specific?"

"It means something weird was going on, and I don't know what."

"Right, of course. That's great. Maybe you could have elaborated on that an hour ago so I could have convinced the transit police to rule you out as a suspect."

I pursed my lips, glad he couldn't see my annoyance. I should have at least sent him another text, true, but I'd been kinda distracted by losing Noah and then trying to teach him not to hijack other people's emotions without getting consent first. And then my phone had died.

"What do you mean?" I said instead of apologizing for my lack of communication. "Isn't your department working the case?"

"No. Not unless I can find a connection between this and the bodies I found yesterday in the basement of the mall just outside the Pentagon City station in Virginia. I don't have jurisdiction in DC proper, and even if I did, the Metro crosses state lines and has its own police."

"Damn," I said, a tiny bit of dread starting to build in my chest. Whatever it was down in the tunnels, it was no joke. And if Adrian was talking about more bodies he thought were connected, it probably wasn't a one-and-done kind of thing. This wasn't the kind of case I wanted to see hampered by jurisdiction nonsense. "What about the DSC? Any of their people on it?"

"I brought Miriam to the crime scene you fled. She was my ticket in, but besides her I didn't see any others. Doesn't mean they're not on it, though."

"They work in aggravatingly mysterious ways, right."

More like aggravatingly incompetent, I thought to myself. But then that was probably why the Department of Supernatural Crime had started stationing their agents, like Miriam the psychic Barbie swamp monster, with local police departments. There was too much on the line politically for them to disband, but they just didn't have the organizational structure or strategical skills to effectively do their job. That was what happened when you hired people based on their supernatural abilities rather than their aptitude for the work, which the DSC was notorious for doing. It was why Adrian, a mere human, hadn't been able to get a job with them. And it was why the Guardians, the private security company I'd started out with, had a much better track record when it came to protecting people from all the things that went bump in the night . . . or the day.

"So are you going to tell me what happened?" Adrian asked. "Or am I going to have to come over there and make you coffee first?"

My lips creased in something that wanted to be a smile. He knew I was avoiding him, and this was his way of pressing me into some kind of corner. Coffee sounded nice, but I'd rather make it myself. "There was something down there in the tunnel," I said. "Something I could hear but not see."

"Okay . . ."

"It had a strange sense of humor. One minute, innocent old lady sitting there making eyes at Noah like they all do. Next thing I know she's growing claws, slicing into herself, then runs wild and starts tearing up anyone who gets in her way. Something made her do it while it watched and laughed."

"Did it say anything?"

"Just creepy giggles. Like horror-movie doll-child creepy. And after I cut off her air supply to knock her out, she started levitating."

"Is that when . . ."

"Yep." I made a croaking noise in my throat to signal that it'd been the end of her.

I could hear Adrian scribbling it all down, probably eager to start researching. He loved that shit, whereas a good mystery just made me want to throw a grenade at it. That'd be a bit difficult to do in this case, which was why I was a little glad my non-thinking self had accidentally called him.

"Is that it?" I prompted, uncomfortable with the warm fuzzies I was feeling not even five minutes into a phone call with the guy. "I've gotta go to work."

"Isn't it a little early for you to go to the club?" he asked.

Yes, it was, theoretically. It was barely nine am right now, and if I had my way I'd still be asleep. But Noah was a morning person, and the school he went to started early, so I'd started opening the club early to make our schedules align. "I'm trying to get a day shift going, bring in more business," I said. "Got any coworkers who could use a nice view on their lunch break?"

"Dirk's on leave, so probably not."

Ah, Dirk . . . Adrian's asshole of a partner who was also now secretly my Guardian handler. Not my favorite person to be around, and apparently also a shit handler since he hadn't said anything to me about taking leave.

"Well, ask around," I said awkwardly, fighting the urge to tell Adrian to come by himself.

"Um, okay." He paused, and my fingers twitched as I tried to decide whether to just hang up on him. "I'll call you if I need anything else," he said, his voice hardening. "Answer your damn phone. It's not cute making me waste so much time listening to your voicemail recording."

"I'm not trying to be cute," I snapped back, but he said nothing. And when I looked at the screen, the call had ended. *He'd* hung up on *me*.

Heat rushed to my face and my fingers clenched tightly

around the phone before I realized it was ridiculous for me to be angry. Everyone had their limits. It made no sense for me to be a jerk to him and not expect the same in return. But I had less sense than I should whenever he was involved, and that was the whole problem.

After dating the vampire I was supposed to be protecting and letting him turn my mind to mush in the process, I wasn't interested in feeling anything similar ever again. Or at least not anytime soon. And honestly, even now it was hard to tell just how much of the mind mush was because of Simeon's magic and how much of it was because, like everyone else on the planet, I got dumb when I was in love.

I shook my head as if it would shake loose the troubling thoughts and headed into the kitchen to make coffee.

The cabinet creaked when I opened it to get my travel mug. I'd been having coffee out more often these days, and a layer of dust had built on the animal mugs Becca had gotten for me and Etty. Yet another thing I didn't want to think about. It was great having Noah around, but I felt a hollowness inside me whenever I remembered the roommates—the friends—I'd lost in January.

Somehow it was worse knowing that neither of them were truly gone. Theoretically, Becca's soul was resting happily inside of Noah, and Etty was still alive in the fae realm. But they were both gone from my life, even if they still existed somewhere. And that made me feel even lonelier than I would have if they'd just been dead.

I filled my plain travel mug with coffee and took it out the door, letting the steam keep my face warm in the air of the cool spring morning, which felt significantly cooler now that my heart rate had lowered. Tiny pink buds were starting to form on the cherry trees outside my building, and the signs of life moving on made the hollow pit in my insides feel a little deeper. It shouldn't, I knew. I should be strong enough to look at those buds and see hope or new beginnings or some shit like that. But apparently, for today at least, I wasn't.

I lowered my head away from the trees as I made my way down the stairs. Only then did I notice the streaks of blood on the white railing near the bottom.

I stopped, lifting my foot and pretending to adjust the laces on my shoe so I could listen to my surroundings without tipping off anyone who might be watching me.

It was quiet, not even much wind rustling through the branches, so I looked up as I kept walking and slowly slipped my fingers under the sleeve of my jacket where I had a knife at the ready.

When I reached the bottom of the stairs, I spotted a few drops of blood on the pale yellow petals of the daffodils in the flower beds.

Well, that certainly couldn't be a good sign when it came to new beginnings and hope and all that.

I walked up to the flowers and peered over at a limp arm sticking out from behind the tall bushes. Crouching down, I carefully stepped around the plants to see a mutilated severed head that couldn't be human. Its tongue looked human enough, except that it was hanging out the side of a mouth rimmed with long, pointed teeth. They seemed more like vampire fangs than fae teeth, as they were fewer and thick at the base—like a whole mouth full of canines. And the jaw was unhinged, with massive lips that were just as plump on the sides as they were on the top and bottom, creating an evenly round opening.

I tried to resist the urge to nudge it with my foot because just next to it, Dirk was lying either unconscious or dead, his blood slowly seeping into the mulch.

"Fuck," I whispered. "This is your idea of a vacation?"

My fingers found a weak pulse at his neck, which would have been more reassuring if not for the deep puncture wounds just above his clavicle. Probably a bite mark from the severed head, before it'd gotten to be severed.

He was losing far too much blood—and who knew how long he'd been in this state? He might have been here when I'd gotten in twenty minutes ago; I had probably been in too much of a hurry to notice.

I closed my eyes and gently placed my fingers around the wound, trying to feel for magic to close it. But the daylight was too bright for me to get a good hold on any of the ambient magic around me, and the magic inside me . . . Well, the magic inside me wouldn't even begin to play nice unless Ray was around, my other half when it came to the phoenix whose invisible talons were perpetually clutched around my scrye these days.

With a sigh, I took off my t-shirt and pressed it to Dirk's wound as I pulled out my phone to call my evil half-brother.

"Ray," I said when the phone stopped ringing. "I need you at my place, now."

I hung up before he could say anything, knowing he would come without asking questions. He might not be happy about it, but he would come. And the faster I could get Dirk inside, out of the sunlight, the better a chance I had to save him.

It was a good thing this nutjob wasn't as tall or as bulky as his partner. Or as sexy. I slipped my arm underneath his shoulders and lifted him into a sitting position, then bent over so I could sling him over my shoulders fireman style. It would have been easier if he were conscious, but as a woman who'd worked as a bodyguard protecting men for four years, lifting unconscious bodies bigger than my own was one of the things I had spent far too long training for.

Blood dripped down my shoulder and onto the steps as I carried Dirk up to my apartment. I took him into Etty's room, which was still just how she had left it, and dropped him onto her bed as gently as I could. Feeling better already behind the drawn curtains and out of the sun, I set my hands to his wound again and lost myself in the effort of trying to patch it back together.

Something like this would have been easy for me to heal before I'd met my long-lost brother, but I'd basically had to relearn magic from the ground up since he'd come into my life. And with only two months plus a full-time job and a kid to take care of, I hadn't had much time to dedicate to the relearning.

By the time Ray rang the doorbell, I had mostly given up on healing Dirk's wound and was just applying steady pressure to keep him from losing any more blood. That was the most important thing. With Ray around, I would be able to close the wound, but I couldn't magically create blood out of thin air if Dirk lost too much, and I didn't keep a fridge full of O negative lying around for transfusions. I had IV fluid we could give him once he was patched up, but that was about it.

I could always take him to a hospital, but I didn't want anyone else asking questions before Dirk could tell me how he'd ended up bleeding in my flowerbeds.

"Come in," I yelled from Dirk's side.

Luckily, I felt Ray's presence as soon as he walked through the door, like a tingling spark in my scrye. The magic inside and around me slowly started to flow through me again, waking up my nerves and clearing away the fog from my mind.

The part of me that controlled magic was just like any other muscle in that when it was strong, I couldn't remember the way it felt when it was weak, and vice versa. I'd always thought this was a product of how gradually those changes usually occurred, but the effect of my brother's presence felt just as inevitable and just as baffling every time I experienced it.

"In here," I yelled so he wouldn't wander through the apartment looking for me.

He popped his head in from behind Etty's door and frowned,

probably wishing that just once, his newfound sister would call him for a game of cards instead of a medical emergency.

"Ay," he said as he sped over to us, shaking his head at me.

I held out a bloody hand to him without saying a word, and he knelt down beside me to take it. As soon as his fingers touched mine, the spark in my scrye ignited into an effusive inferno—not so much hot as it was overflowing with energy. With life.

Using the methods I'd learned from my adoptive coven to channel magic for healing purposes, I let a small bit of it flow through my other hand into Dirk's skin, and the tissue repaired itself in just a few seconds.

Dirk didn't burst into flames at the touch of the phoenix's magic, so I had to guess that meant he would live. Yippee.

I sighed, slumping my shoulders as I turned to look at Ray. "Thanks."

"What happened, hermana?" he asked. "You get a little too rough in some role play?"

I chuckled. It was only funny because it was so far from the truth. There was nothing like that going on between me and the unconscious asshole on my roommate's bed, and there never would be. He was a liar, and downright unpleasant. But since he was also my Guardian handler, I couldn't just let him die outside my apartment without ticking off more of the people in charge of my life.

"I have no idea what happened. Found him outside like this. I need him to wake up and start talking."

Ray followed me to the linen closet, where I kept my first aid equipment. "Hey," he said as I grabbed an IV kit and smelling salts. "You can't expect me to just drop everything and come every time you need to heal someone. Not with the life you lead . . ."

"This is the first time I've needed you to drop everything," I said.

"But it won't be the last." He followed me back to Dirk and hovered over me as I positioned him appropriately and stuck a needle in his arm. I'd wait a few minutes at least to use the salts, see if he'd wake up quickly on his own.

"No, it probably won't be the last," I said, looking up at Ray.

"If you'd only—"

"No," I snapped, not interested in having this conversation again. Not now.

If I'd only accept Ray's god into my heart and become a good, devoted witch like him, he was going to say, then we would both have much better control of the magic inside us and I could go back to healing people on my own whenever I pleased.

Yeah, I fucking knew that. He'd been telling me so almost every day for the past two months. But I wasn't about to sign up to be some god's slave. I already had the Guardians bossing me around; the last thing I needed was someone else expecting me to bow to their whims.

Luckily, I didn't have to fend off any more of Ray's proselytizing because Dirk blinked his eyes open then.

Ray made a frustrated sound at the back of his throat and clapped his hand on my back. "We'll talk later," he said before letting himself out of the apartment. Whatever drama Dirk was about to unleash on me, Ray was smart to not want to be a part of it.

I didn't turn my head to look as he walked away, frustrated with myself more than I was frustrated with him. I shouldn't be asking for his help if I wasn't willing to help him in return. But I hadn't *needed* his help before he'd forced his way into my life . . . It was a whole tangled up ball of crazy, and I'd need to find my way out of it soon.

I felt weaker as soon as the door shut behind him, a sluggish chill creeping over me to add insult to injury. We were stronger together, like he'd always said. But this work, I needed to do alone.

Dirk licked his lips as he focused his eyes on me. "Good to see you found me, pretty lady," he croaked.

"Oh, I'm pretty now?" I asked. "Wasn't I just little before?"

He squinted at me and raised an eyebrow. "Well, you're kinda blurry. How much blood I lose?"

"Not enough to kill you, unfortunately." I shrugged. "Why'd you decide to lie down in the flowerbed with that lopped-off head? You were in the stairwell—I saw the blood."

"I don't remember flowers." He groaned. "They were fucking with my head."

"Who was?"

"Vampires, must be. I was after one and . . ." He paused and looked around. "I've been here before."

"Um, nope. You have not." I'd never brought Dirk to my place, and we'd only communicated indirectly since he'd shown up at my club all smug with his Guardian badge to re-recruit me.

"Shit, this is your place." He struggled to prop himself up on his elbows. "You find me here?"

"Just outside," I said, a little disturbed that he seemed sure he recognized the inside of my roommate's bedroom. I frowned, making the connection in my head a little too late. "Seriously, Dirk? You were here with Etty? You knew her for less than a week before she was whisked away to fairyland."

"Yeah, well . . ." He shook his head, refocusing his eyes on me with a scowl. "That's none of your business. I need your help."

"No shit," I said. "Is it my group of vamps?" Per his instructions, I'd been casually socializing with a small circle of blood-suckers for the past couple months, whom I'd met through Kat, the only vampire who danced at the club. I still didn't know what the end goal of the mission was or if there would ever be one, but in this stage of the game it was safer if I only knew what was absolutely necessary.

"No—at least I don't think so—but they might be able to help." He sat up all the way and then swayed a bit, his eyes glazing over for a moment.

I pushed him back down and nodded my head at his elevated feet and the needle in his arm. "You're not going to be getting up anytime soon, so don't push it. Just tell me what's going on."

He closed his eyes and took a few breaths before focusing in on me again. "A couple months ago, we started noticing heightened vampire activity, and not in the usual places. Drained humans no one bothered to hide, more blood on the black market, an uptick in botched jobs."

I shivered involuntarily at the last thing he'd said. Botched jobs. They were rare, but I'd seen one at the clinic when I was just a teenager.

One of the girls I'd gone to school with had binged on stolen vampire blood in an effort to become immortal without paying the hefty fee. Only problem was, vampire blood didn't exactly have a shelf life. Its magical properties began to degrade as soon as it left the body of a live vampire—so unless you were drinking it directly from a pumping vein, it just didn't work like it was supposed to. And the half-state this resulted in was not pretty by anyone's standards.

Best-case scenario, it meant you'd become a bloodsucking vegetable, cursed to shrivel for eternity with your consciousness trapped in your body unless some kind soul decided to bring you a bloody breakfast in bed. Worst-case scenario, you'd lose your mind and all sense of control, becoming a psychotic predator who would end up dead or in jail sooner rather than later. Most cases were somewhere in between, with a sprinkling of gruesome side effects you could never really predict. "Wait," I said, making the connection. "Is that what bit you? The head out there, with the crazy mouth—a botched vamp?"

Dirk rubbed his head, then looked at his palms for a moment as he opened and closed fists. "Yeah, I think. I think I had a knife . . ."

I shivered again. "An uptick in botched jobs" was one thing, but a dead one in my flowerbeds made it hard to think of the matter in terms of statistics. It made my skin crawl to know something like that had been here, so close to my home and the child that lived in it, and in broad daylight no less.

Swallowing my discomfort, I tried to refocus on what Dirk had been telling me. "So there's disorder in the vampire ranks."

Dirk nodded. "And then, last week, we got a call from a local client with a lost daughter. Little girl, missing with no rhyme or reason, and they didn't trust the cops to find her."

I got quiet again, shifting my jaw as I thought about the sobbing woman I'd just met and her missing kid.

"They didn't trust the cops, but you're a cop . . ." I said, narrowing my eyes. I still wasn't entirely clear on how Dirk's job worked as both a secret Guardian and a police officer.

"Yeah, but I never saw this case until the Guardians handed it to me. Police don't have the same resources we do; they can't always afford to investigate every lead in every case."

"So you're like a dirty cop that's secretly for hire to give a damn when you normally wouldn't?"

He glared at me but only said, "Sure." After briefly rubbing his temple, he continued, "So, I start comparing this girl's case to every other missing child report I can find in the area in the past month, talk to all the families and I notice a connection. Eight of them went out to eat the day of the disappearances, and the restaurants they went to are owned by the same group."

I pressed my lips together. *Eight* missing kids, then. I pulled out my phone and brought up the sobbing woman's number, trying to refresh my memory. It said: Brady's mom.

"Brady Lee," I said, and Dirk raised his eyebrows.

"Yeah, that was one of 'em. How'd you know?"

"Just met his mom. Told her I'd see if I could help."

Dirk chuckled. "That was a dumb move, but you're in luck—you're damn well going to help. Just won't be able to take the credit."

I frowned, then put away my phone. "You said the disappearances were all linked to the same restaurant group. Which one?"

"Soma Hospitality."

"Huh." The name rang a bell, but I couldn't figure out where I'd heard it before.

"Which is owned by vampires," Dirk added. "The head of the company is rumored to be the oldest in the city. Soma himself."

"So you think the odd vamp behavior is connected to the missing kids?"

"Yes, and I need you to get close to Soma. I don't want him to know we suspect anything, but I need someone on the inside to find out what he's up to."

"Okay . . . except if these vampires just tried to kill you outside my apartment, they'll definitely suspect something when I show up suddenly wanting to be friends."

He shook his head. "They didn't try to kill me *here*. I . . ." He sighed. "If I'm here, it's because of this." Reaching into his pocket, he pulled out a small pouch. The fabric was black, and the way it glimmered in the light gave it a strange sense of depth, like my eyes might get lost in it if I looked at it too long. It was the same feeling I'd gotten whenever Becca or Etty had put on an especially over-the-top fae glamour.

I frowned, amazed at how great this guy was at finding new ways to piss me off. "That's Etty's." I wasn't sure exactly what it was, but I'd seen it in her room before. "How do you have it?"

"She gave it to me. Fairy dust." He shrugged. "Said she might as well leave some behind because she was screwed anyway and I'd probably need it."

"*You?* Why would she care if you needed it?"

"I mean, she might have meant both of us. Or all us sorry mortals. You know how she is."

Dirk was lucky he was effectively my patient right now, or I'd have been tempted to hit him. Yes, I knew how Etty was. But how did *he* know? I hated this guy, would have given anything to have my roommate sitting here with me in her room instead of him, and here he was telling me Etty had invited him here and given him a bag of fae dust before she'd gone away forever? She hadn't left anything for me besides an empty room. She hadn't even said goodbye.

I took a deep breath to clear the emotional chaos out of my head. "Well, don't get addicted to the stuff," I told Dirk levelly before standing up. "If you used the dust to get here right after cutting off that thing's head, then at least you weren't followed. You can stay until you're feeling better."

"Where are you going?"

"Work. I'm already late because of you."

"Don't forget—"

"I know. Go after Soma, make friends, be a good little spy," I said, already texting Kat out of the corner of my eye to see if she could make an introduction. "But my job is my cover, remember? And in this case, it's perfect. He owns restaurants, I run a club— I'd bet anyone in my position would want to schmooze with him."

"He owns clubs and bars, too." Dirk flashed me a grin, his near-dead expression brightening for just a moment. "Including one of the best strip joints in DC."

I put my phone away, hoping Kat would see the text before coming in for her shift tonight. I had a feeling Dirk would be sticking around until I could get him the information he needed, especially if my apartment wasn't currently on his attackers' radar. And I wanted him out of my hair as much as I wanted to take down any vampires that were nabbing people's kids.

"Here." Dirk fetched something else out of his pocket and handed it to me, a small box.

When I opened it, one of Miriam's pink squishies stared back at me, the jelly-like translucent lump pulsing subtly with life.

Gross. I'd hoped to never see one of these things again.

"That one goes the other way," Dirk said when I looked up at him. "Doesn't read your thoughts. More like an information injection."

I wrinkled my nose, not sure that sounded any more pleasant than the mind-reading thing.

"That's everything we know about Soma so far," Dirk added, gesturing at the squishy. "You're lucky you don't have to memorize the file."

When he put it that way, I didn't mind quite so much. At least it was smaller than the alien monstrosity Miriam had stuck to my neck the first time I'd met her.

I pulled the tie from around my knotted hair, letting the curls fall free in a chaotic mess. After sticking the squishy behind my right ear, I gathered my hair again and twisted it into a bun at the side.

"How do I look?" I asked Dirk, flourishing my hands around my face with an exaggerated smile.

"Well-informed," he said. "Now get out of here so I can sleep."

He didn't have to tell me twice.

4

By the time I got to the club, an hour late, the new chef I'd hired a week ago was waiting by the door with her hoodie pulled tight around her face. It was easy to forget I wasn't the only one who needed to show up early these days. I should probably give Kiri a key of her own.

"I'm gonna need a key if you want to see me here again tomorrow," she said as soon as she saw me.

I smiled at the way it seemed she'd read my thoughts, then snapped my serious face back on. "You got it—sorry. Should've thought of that before."

I might technically be the boss here, but Kiri had all the power in our relationship. That was fine by me. When Baz had been running the place, we'd had an empty kitchen doing nothing but attracting cobwebs. And with him gone, along with whatever mysterious magic he must have been using to keep the business afloat, I needed someone in there making food who knew what they were doing. Couldn't attract a lunch crowd if I had no lunch to offer.

But there was a shortage of good chefs in the area, and not many of them were interested in putting a supernatural strip club on their resume. Although she was human, Kiri had been a dancer before she'd become a cook, so finding her had been miraculous.

She disappeared into the dark depths of the club as soon as I got the door open, and I turned on the stage lights to kick off my opening ritual. It was different, now that I was more of a manager than a bartender.

The bar called to me, enticing me with gleaming glasses to be polished and fragrant citrus to peel, a world of new recipes waiting to be concocted. But today I didn't even have time to make myself an espresso and soak in the violet lights glinting off the chrome poles before I had to hurry into the back office, with its white walls and buzzing electronics and creaky rolling chair.

I grimaced as I sat in the fuzzy torture device, my head already starting to ache. Baz the bawdy genie still owned the club, but he couldn't actually run anything from prison. And he'd set it up so I was the only one authorized to act in his name—with a whole boatload of limitations and a ridiculously small operating budget, of course. I could barely afford to pay myself for my time after all was said and done, and I needed more money than ever now that I had a kid to feed and no roommates to help with the rent.

Could I just wash my hands of it all and get a better-paying job elsewhere? Yeah, sure.

But I didn't want to. The club would have to close if I abandoned it, by Baz's orders, and I couldn't let that happen because of me.

As imperfect as it was, this place had been a refuge for me when no one else would hire me, and I knew it was the same for many of the dancers. Clubs that didn't discriminate based on species were still few and far between, and there were a lot of shifters and fae who worked here that couldn't hide what they were—not in this day and age, when any human who cared would know exactly what to look for to see through a glamour.

Trying to keep a broken business afloat definitely kept me busy, but it took so much of the fun out of bartending and made it even harder to feel like myself where no weapons were involved.

As much as I resented the Guardians forcing me to work for them covertly, and as much as I wished they'd pay me with cash instead of untraceable "investments" I couldn't touch for years, at this point I knew I needed them to keep me sane—probably more than they needed me.

An hour went by before I stood up and stretched, what with all the answering emails and placing orders and crunching numbers that had to get done. I was about to head to the bar and finally treat myself to that espresso when Kat came bursting into the office.

"Hey birdie," she said, giving me a wide smile. With her hip cocked and her eyes sparkling, she seemed even more self-satisfied than usual today. The tips of her fangs gleamed behind her lips, putting me on edge. She normally kept those well hidden unless she was playing to someone's kink.

"Did you get my text?" I asked.

"Yep, and you'd better load up on the coffee, cause you've got a long night ahead of you." Kat's smile widened even more.

I narrowed my eyes at her. "What—"

She tossed a fancy paper bag at me, but not before reaching in and pulling something out of it.

When I looked up at her after catching the bag, she had a silky G-string dangling from one of her absurdly long red nails. After a couple twirls, she threw it at my face and giggled. "You like?"

"I'm . . . confused." I peeled the lingerie off my face as I looked down to see more black silk in the bag.

"I had to guess your size." Kat shifted her head back and forth as she peered at me, her eyes traveling a bit too much for my comfort. "So you should go try it on. I have enough time to get you something else if I go now."

"Sorry, I don't have any . . ." I grimaced into the bag, trying to resist the sudden urge to run my fingers over the smooth fabric. It was clearly some high-end stuff, the kind of thing I'd never worn in my life and probably never would. "I don't have any occasion for this sort of thing, so—"

I stopped, unnerved by the way she wouldn't stop smiling at me, her fangs still visible.

"Kat, did I accidentally put on the 'fuck me, vampire' body spray today? Cause you're really giving off that kind of vibe right now."

She giggled, and her smile grew wider. "No," she said. "But if you have some, I'd suggest putting it on when you wear that tonight." She leaned in close to my face and opened her eyes wide before saying, "I got you an audition!"

I looked at her blankly, trying to process what she could possibly mean by that and failing utterly.

She tsked a little as her fangs drew up behind her lips and her smile faded. "An audition at Bite."

I shifted my eyes, realization dawning on me. That was the club Dirk had been referring to, the one owned by Soma Hospitality. One of the most exclusive clubs in DC, it was run by vampires and catered only to vampires and humans. They'd been advertising it as a place where the two species could play on the same level—the dancers were a mix of both, and the clientele were a mix of both. But as someone who'd spent more time than I'd like around vampires, I knew that had to be a carefully crafted illusion.

"You told me you wanted to meet Soma, right?" Kat prompted, taking my silence for a protest.

"Yes," I said slowly.

"The club is your best bet. It's practically the only place he leaves his crypt for anymore."

"He . . . lives in an actual crypt?"

"No." Kat shook her head at me like I was a child. "Ever heard of sarcasm? He's just really old."

"Okay . . ." I held up the bag of lingerie. "But is this really the kind of thing their bartenders wear?"

Kat actually snorted at me, then burst into full-on laughter. When it subsided, she wiped a bloody tear from her face and said, "Girl . . . since when does anyone *audition* to be a bartender?"

"Kat, I can't dance."

"Why, because you have morals or something?"

"What? No. I literally can't dance. I was raised by people who thought good music was a regular EKG rhythm."

"If you survive tonight, I'll help you fix that," Kat said. "But really, it doesn't matter." She leaned in close to me again. "You've got a hot body and hot blood underneath all that delicious . . . mmm. Just try not to fall in your heels and you'll be fine."

She stood up straight and ran her tongue over one of her fangs before retracting them back into her gums. Then, with a tiny shake of her head, she spun around and left me sitting in the office alone with a bag of lingerie.

This really does look expensive, I thought, my frown deepening. I doubted I could get the Guardians to reimburse me for whatever Kat had paid for it anytime soon.

And if I hadn't been worried about my mental state before, I started to worry when all I could think about was how I'd better not get any blood on this lace tonight.

I STARED down at my phone from behind the bar a few hours later, fingers scrolling through my address book so quickly the names all blurred together. Not that there were many names in there.

I'd been through the whole thing too many times in the last few hours and had yet to find anyone who was willing and able to look after Noah tonight while I went to my "audition."

Dirk was the first one I'd called, since he was at my apartment anyway and at least I wouldn't have to lie to him about what I was doing tonight. But he had failed to pick up his phone, probably napping off the blood loss, and in any case I supposed it would be best to leave Noah with someone who didn't have botched vampires gunning for him.

I thought about calling Miriam since she apparently had a finger in every damn pie and was a secret Guardian too, but she was working the Metro case with Adrian right now. And if I didn't want to bother him, it meant I didn't want to bother her.

For the thousandth time in so many minutes, my finger hovered over Etty's name on the screen. Calling that one would just be masochistic. I missed her too much—more than I'd actively missed anyone before, even Becca. I still wasn't entirely sure *why*, but it probably had something to do with the fact that she might be the only person in the world I'd ever really trusted.

I'd thought she hated me all through the first year we'd lived together, because she'd never hesitated to pick fights with me about all the little ways I made her life hell as an inconsiderate roommate. But looking back on it all now, after she had broken fae laws to save my life, ruining hers in the process, I knew she had never hated me. She was just honest. As allergic to bullshit as I'd always been. And I loved her for it. Even if she'd apparently had some kind of tryst with Dirk instead of saying goodbye to me . . . I couldn't hold something like that against her.

It was why I still hadn't moved out of our old apartment, even though I could barely afford the rent on my own. I was still holding on to some hope that Etty might find her way out of the fae realm, and I wanted to be somewhere she could find me if that happened.

I felt my eyes start to sting, so I turned around to face all the bottles of liquor instead of the few people having a late lunch in the club.

I was pretty much only standing here for show anyway, considering how little business we had at the moment and how little they were drinking at this time of day.

"Got any good tequila?" someone said behind me, and I rushed to wipe away the wetness from my eyes.

When I turned around, Ray stood at the other side of the bar. Great. I'd already seen enough of him for one day. "Yep," I said. Without any elaboration, I poured him a shot of the cheapest tequila I had on the shelf.

He shook his head at me when I slid it over to him, but he downed it all the same and had the gall to not even give me a grimace.

"Why are you here?" I asked. "We agreed it was too dangerous for us to meet in public, remember?" It wasn't because we couldn't be seen together or anything like that. We'd been meeting regularly at his glass workshop, once a week on my day off while the kids were in school, trying with minimal success to figure out how to get the volatile phoenix spirit living inside us under control. The thing got more powerful whenever we were together, so it was risky if anyone else was around. Last time he'd come in here for a drink, we'd accidentally turned my dying friend Becca into a pretty fae torch.

"I remember," he said. "But I've had a rough day, no thanks to you. And this hardly counts as public." He nodded his head to the side to emphasize how empty the place was, which didn't exactly make me any happier to see him.

"Okay, sit down," I said with a sigh. "Thanks for coming when I called. I do appreciate it, and I'm sorry if I ruined your day."

"Actually, it was a good distraction. Today was rough before you called."

"Oh?" I perked up a little, intrigued now. "Is it girl problems? Anyone you need me to kill?"

He chuckled. "Maybe . . . Carina's mother is coming to town."

"The dragon?"

"That's the one." He motioned for me to pour him another shot of the shitty tequila, and I obliged.

He shook out his hand before picking it up, a small gesture to protect the sleeve of his crisp button-down shirt, drawing my attention to his rough fingers and strong forearm that moved with the elegant precision of a craftsman.

I shook my head slightly, not surprised that this man had managed to attract a dragon. Was that a weird thing to think about my brother? I was still getting used to the idea of having a brother in the first place, so I had no idea.

"Is she coming to visit Carina?" I asked.

"Of course not," he said. "Dragons are . . . not very maternal. Or paternal. They never raise their own children, and they don't acknowledge lineage. They grow up orphans and turn into emotionally unavailable adults who are terrified of commitment."

I pursed my lips, sensing some hard feelings about that last part. It wasn't difficult for me to imagine Carina eventually becoming such an adult, but she was only half-dragon, so at least she had the luxury of being raised by her father.

"I don't know why she's coming," Ray continued when I said nothing, "but it's not good for us."

"Why not?"

"Because Popo isn't going to let us play around out here forever. So even if he had some other reason to send someone . . . he chose to send someone who has a history with me, which means he's losing patience with me. And with you."

Ah, so that was really why Ray had shown up here. To make

yet another attempt at getting me down on my knees and worshiping some god I'd never heard of until a couple months ago.

Supposedly, this god had been the facilitator and benefactor for the ancient phoenix that had claimed us as its newest corporeal ride when we were just kids. I had been too young at the time to remember any of that, but Ray was a few years older than me and had told me the story in bits and pieces during our weekly meetings.

We had different mothers but the same father, and when the panic of the Opening had hit shortly after I was born, our devoted witch dad had easily convinced both our scared human mothers to gift us to his god, who would surely make us strong enough to survive the supernatural apocalypse they thought was coming.

But the apocalypse didn't come, and vampires were great at public relations even back then, so it didn't take long for my mother to regret her decision and steal me away. Knowing what I now knew about the mage mark my adoptive family had given me, the tattoo that functioned as a way to suppress my connection to the god who thought he owned me, I could understand why my mother had brought me there. But I still had no idea why she'd *left* me there. Why I'd never met her—why I'd always thought my parents must be dead.

I had a feeling I'd need to take a trip to California if I ever wanted to find out.

Until then, and maybe even after, it would be crazy of me to consider crawling back to the god so many people had worked to keep me away from throughout my childhood.

I shook my head. "What part of 'No' do you all not understand?"

"It won't take much," Ray pleaded. "You've already lost your mage mark—"

"Because you had your daughter rip it off my ankle!" I started to yell at him before I remembered where I was. Lowering my voice and drawing out my words, I said, "I'm going to get my tattoo back as soon as I have time to figure out how."

But my unwillingness to accept Ray's god and become a full-blown member of his witch family was probably the reason we'd only had minimal success controlling the phoenix inside us. That aggravating bird had chosen to align itself with Ray's god long before the two of us were born, and it was the god's power that had allowed it to attach itself to us. Until I could get my mage mark back and block the god's influence for good, I wouldn't be able to control magic like I used to.

For now at least, that felt like a small price to pay for my freedom.

Ray dipped his head and curled his shoulders forward, staring into his empty glass. "If you don't . . ."

With a sigh, I brought out another glass and poured myself a small shot along with his.

Ray ignored the liquid in his glass and looked up at me with eyes filled with dread. "I'll lose her if you don't join us," he said.

I downed the mouthful of awful tequila, closing my eyes so I wouldn't have to look at him. He was talking about Carina, his daughter, whose dragon-shifting abilities were an obvious boon to their god. Ray's abilities, on the other hand, were useless without me by his side. And their god was apparently not the most generous when it came to freeloaders. Did I want to be responsible for my half-brother being separated from his daughter? No. Of course not. But it wasn't fair of these strangers to come into my life out of nowhere and expect me to become a slave to their god just so they could stay together.

I opened my eyes and gave him a hard glare. "You won't lose her," I said, and I meant it. I wouldn't sacrifice myself to a god to keep their family together, but that didn't mean I wouldn't fight for them. "We'll find another way to keep her with you. I'll find another way." I forced a smile onto my face. "Hell, I need Carina around more than you do at this point—the way Noah worships her."

Ray still hadn't picked up the shot I'd poured for him, but he swallowed down whatever he might have wanted to say to me, and I could see him try to match my forced smile. It struck me then that he must trust me, to some extent, even though he didn't have much reason to. Even though, had I been in his shoes, I probably wouldn't trust me.

But he'd known he had a sister his whole life, so I wasn't a stranger to him the way he was to me. And more importantly, he *needed* to trust me. If I couldn't help him, no one could.

That realization made it a little easier for me to trust him in return. "Tell you what," I said. "I'll do whatever I can to help you, short of worshiping your god, if you do me a favor tonight."

"What kind of favor?"

"Watch Noah while I work a late shift."

Ray lit up instantly, sitting taller as his eyes brightened. He'd been trying to get me to let him spend time with Noah since our first meeting. And I'd been resisting since then because he wanted the same thing of Noah that he wanted of me—another "creature of fire" to add to his god's devotees. But he didn't *need* Noah like he needed me, so at this point I felt like I could at least trust him not to steal the kid away.

Indoctrination was another story, but Noah was smart, and how much damage could one night do?

I immediately regretted asking myself that question when Ray said, "That's perfect! Tonight is our spring rain festival ceremony, and Noah will love it." At my icy glare, he threw up his hands. "Calm down, it's nothing gruesome. We won't make him do anything he doesn't want to do."

"You know he'll do anything Carina asks whether he wants to

or not." My tentative trust definitely did not extend to Ray's daughter.

"This is true." Ray smiled. "But Carina will do anything I ask, and I'll make sure she doesn't take advantage of your boy." Probably trying to keep me from changing my mind, Ray changed the subject. "What are you doing working late tonight anyway?"

"Something I very much don't want to do," I said, even though it was only partially true. I didn't want to put on Kat's outfit just so I could take it off again in a room full of overexcited vampires, but I did want to get a lead on whoever had been making kids disappear. I wanted to be useful, to help take down a bad guy, to feel like myself again.

"Sounds like you need to worry more about yourself and less about the boy," Ray said.

He wasn't wrong, except that it was too late for me. Noah hadn't signed any documents stating that he had to jump at Carina's every whim, but I had done so with the Guardians years ago. They would own me for as long as they wanted me, and tonight that meant getting naked and flirting with vampires.

Flirting with death.

5

THE ROSE GOLD light of early dusk shone in my eyes as I stepped off the escalator from the Metro where Noah and I had stopped this morning.

I shifted uncomfortably in my jeans as I walked up to the entrance to the club. I was still wearing my comfy boots, for now, but Kat's lacy nightmare was itching me in all the wrong places underneath my clothes, and I had a pair of Etty's heels—the shortest I could find—in a bag slung over my shoulder.

I had gotten ready at Ray's place to save time and avoid Dirk, since I'd had to take Noah there anyway after picking him up from school. It was a miracle my evil half-brother had steadier hands than I did, because if I'd had to put on my own eyeliner evenly after nearly killing myself in the shower shaving places that had never before seen a razor . . . I let out a short breath, in more awe than usual of the women who went through this routine every day.

More than anything, I was lucky to have had his help healing all the places I'd cut myself shaving. At a vampire club, going in with even a tiny nick was the kind of amateur mistake that could be the end of me. Bleeding was the one thing you didn't do around vampires unless you had a death wish.

When I opened the door to the club, I was met with darkness. I walked forward blindly, taking small steps, until a creak ahead and a sliver of dim light indicated a door was being opened for me. A man stood stiffly holding it open, more like a soldier than a bouncer at a club. His eyes never moved, and he said nothing to me.

I tried to imagine Mitch with all his bad jokes standing at the door unmoving, unseeing at our club while customers filed in, and the thought simply did not compute. I'd been hoping to pick up some useful business tips while I was here, but maybe this place was just too different for that.

I walked down a dimly lit hall, slightly more comfortable with every step as my eyes adjusted. I tried to look more nervous than I felt as the hallway opened up and I walked out onto the empty floor of the unfamiliar club.

Looking around the open space, I saw no one. Just the gleam of an especially tall pole and plush seating all around. The ceiling was so high that I could see the railing on the second floor, where customers could probably sit to watch the same show as those below. I'd bet there were VIP rooms up there too. Off to one side was a bar much bigger and shinier than the one I tended.

I walked over to check it out and someone called out from behind me, "Can I help you?" I swiveled around to see a young man—he almost looked too young to be in a place like this. "We don't open for another hour," he said, looking into my eyes.

I remembered I was supposed to be nervous and wrapped my arms loosely around my chest. "I'm here for an audition. At seven, I thought."

He walked up closer to me, allowing me to get a better look at him. His skin was smoother than mine, and he was only a couple inches taller than me. I doubted he was an actual teenager, judging by the expensive-looking jacket and flashy neck scarf he was wearing. Probably a vamp.

"Are you Kat's?" The way he said it made it feel like he was implying I was her property. Normally, I would have corrected him, but then normally I wouldn't even be here.

"Yep."

"She said you were a baby . . ." He walked a full circle around me, eying me with skepticism. "And a human."

"That I am—both things." I tried not to cringe at him calling me a baby. He meant it as in baby stripper, a term that had taken a while for me to get used to when I'd first started working for Baz. But when in Rome . . . "I've been bartending for a while, but I've never danced. Kat said I should learn from the best, so here I am."

He smiled then, showing me his fangs, and extended his hand. "Well, you're in the right place . . ."

"Birdie," I said as I took his hand, biting my lip a little and casting my eyes down. Not an ideal stage name, but at least I was already used to responding to it.

"You're in the right place, Birdie." Taking me by surprise, he snatched my hand and pulled it to his face, inhaling deeply. His fingers were cold around my wrist, much colder than any other vampire I'd touched. He dropped my hand and looked at me with hard eyes. "But you don't smell entirely human."

"I . . ." Bats, the magic bird inside me just kept finding more and more ways to make my life difficult. "I really am human," I insisted. "I can do a few magic tricks is all."

Closing my eyes, I brought my hands up and created a tiny amount of wind, enough to blow my hair gently out of my face. It required so little effort that I knew I would be able to do it without Ray at my side. Plus, it made me feel glamorous, which couldn't hurt here.

"Cute," he said, not sounding an ounce like he meant it.

"Alright, up you go." He gestured to the stage behind him and then snapped his fingers at a dark corner where the sound controls must be. An eerie melody filled the space, low and slow despite the vibrations it sent thrumming through my ribcage.

I dropped my bag on a chair and rushed to change out of my jeans and into Etty's shoes, stumbling just a bit in the process. By the time I'd made it onto the stage, I was already a little sweaty, the cool air blowing over my exposed skin making me feel more naked than I'd expected. And I wasn't even naked yet.

I was starting to feel nervous for real now. After watching countless other women get up on stage at Baz's and do this—after seeing the power in their movements and the way they were showered with cash for their efforts—I hadn't thought it would be too difficult for me. I wasn't planning to try any challenging moves, and I'd never been squeamish about nudity. I was expecting the hard part to be the *actual* work, a full night of nodding and smiling at uninteresting human men and dodging the fangs of excited vampires without offending them.

But there was something about the silky lace moving over my skin as I walked, far more comfortable now that my jeans weren't pressing it into me. The low lights energized my spirit, the heels and the stage lifting me up to tower over the whole room . . . it felt amazing, and my enjoyment of it made me feel vulnerable.

I had to remember I was behind enemy lines here. I needed to be focused if I was going to deceive an old, powerful vampire into incriminating himself in front of me. This was not the time for me to be having fun, but standing up here I could tell how easy it would be to lose myself in the moment.

I'd barely touched the pole when the music shut off and the vampire said, "That's perfect. I'm putting you on for your first set at midnight."

"Huh? I didn't do anything yet." I turned to look at him and brought my hand up to block my eyes from the lights that had suddenly gotten brighter.

"You don't need to. I have a VIP who loves the awkward first-timers. You look great and you can barely walk in those things." He nodded at Etty's shoes on my feet. "You're perfect."

Well, if I'd needed something to take my ego down a notch, that certainly did the trick. "I can—"

"Just get downstairs and fill out your paperwork. You can be on the floor when we open, but don't dance for anyone until your stage set. Trust me—it'll be worth it to wait."

"So I'm just supposed to sit around and look pretty for four hours?" I asked, getting a little irritated. If I saw Soma before my set, this guy would just have to deal. I hadn't left Noah with Ray so I could waste the night doing nothing in fancy lingerie.

"You can chat, let customers buy you drinks, but no dancing. Soma will pay more than you'd normally make in a week if he can see your first dance."

Ah. Soma was the VIP who loved baby strippers? Suddenly I was feeling a good deal more persuaded to do nothing for four hours.

"Here," the young-looking vampire continued, reaching behind him to grab something off the bar. It looked like some sort of chalice, with a shape similar to a wineglass but opaque.

The base of the thing was thicker than I would have expected, and I turned it over to see two little tabs that looked like they could be pulled out. "What is this?" I asked.

The vampire took it back from me with a sigh. As if explaining something to a child, he said, "We don't allow physical contact here. Of any kind." I was more confused than before until he pulled one of the tabs and out came a blade. "You can bleed, but only into this cup." He slid the knife back into the base of the chalice and then pulled on the other tab. The thing that came out looked almost like a tube of lip gloss.

"Vampire saliva," he said. "To dull the pain and heal the wounds."

I tried not to grimace at the realization that bleeding would actually be expected of me here. They must either have some amazing bouncers or amazing ways to hide bodies if this was the case, because it was a rare vampire that could control itself around a bleeding human.

"Um . . ." I asked tentatively. "What happens if . . ."

"No need to worry, Birdie. We take security very seriously. We'll keep you safe." He said it far too quickly, too lightly, too practiced for my liking. I wanted to ask what their turnover rate for human dancers was, but something told me that question would not be quite so well received.

At least I wouldn't have to bleed directly into anyone's mouth. Hopefully, that meant I wouldn't have to deal with any of the mind-warping side effects that usually came with blood donation. Blind devotion, memory loss, fabricated feelings of love—all the bullshit I'd already allowed myself to go through during my years with Simeon. I hadn't ever let him take blood from me directly, but I supposed other bodily fluids could be just as effective.

I eyed the tube of saliva as the vampire in front of me slid it back into the base of the chalice, and I wondered whose it was. Regardless, I didn't think I'd be using it tonight.

He handed it to me and ushered me across the room, where he opened a door that led to a staircase down. "Off you go. Tell them Gary sent you."

"Gary?" It was a name more ordinary than I would expect from a vampire in a place like this.

"First rule of dancing, Birdie—don't question anyone's name."

He had me there. Still wobbling in Etty's shoes, I gripped the railing and slowly began my descent. For a moment I dared to hope these stairs in these crazy heels might end up being the worst part of the night, but no . . . my life was never quite that easy.

I FINGERED Miriam's small squishy behind my ear as I sat at the bar sipping orange juice. No alcohol for the dancers in this club —or at least, not for the ones who wanted to survive the night. Anyone who might end up bleeding in front of a vampire would need electrolytes and iron and vitamin C more than any liquor.

Soma's face took shape in my mind as I focused in on the information stored in the squishy. It was strange. I normally had no issue recognizing people after seeing them in photographs, but for some reason the image of this man's face kept fading from my memory. Kat had said he was ridiculously old, so it might have something to do with elderly vampire magic. Folklore said vampires had no reflections in mirrors and wouldn't show up in pictures, but I had never met a vampire for whom that was true.

There's a first time for everything. But I didn't like the idea that a vampire could influence the way my mind worked just by existing when we'd never even met.

I scanned the room, trying to match the foggy image of Soma to one of the faces of the men in here. Gary had said he usually showed up before midnight, when I was scheduled to go onstage. That was still an hour away, but I wanted to get this done as fast as possible.

I nearly choked on my orange juice when I saw a face that was a little too familiar.

"Motherfucker," I muttered as Adrian walked over to me, dressed in what must be a new suit.

The crisp lines of dark blue fabric did nothing to hide the bulk in his chest and arms, although the color brought out a tinge of azure in his eyes that were normally a dusky gray. His face was even freshly shaved, a first since I'd met him, and he looked polished enough that he might have been able to pass for a vampire if not for the fact that he towered over everyone born more than a century ago.

I tensed, squirming in my seat. I wouldn't have been happy to see him anywhere, but this was probably the worst place and time I could have possibly run into him. It was hard enough to avoid accidentally flirting with him when I wasn't wearing a lacy set of lingerie, and if I tried too hard to *not* flirt here I'd probably blow my cover.

"Hello to you too," he said, his mouth twisting like he was trying to hold in laughter. "I'd ask what you're doing here, but your outfit kind of gives that away." He took care to keep his eyes on my face despite his comment about the rest of me, which somehow annoyed me more than if he'd ogled me outright.

"Seriously?" I asked him. "Two months ago you could barely handle sitting at the bar at Baz's without dying of embarrassment, and now you're what—a regular here, and not even breaking a sweat?" I reached a finger out and poked him in the cheek, half expecting him to be made of plastic or something. But no, his skin was warm and soft, just like I remembered. "Who are you and what have you done with—"

"No touching," said a gruff voice behind me, and I turned to see a tiny gremlin standing on the bar with arms crossed and chin raised, like a doll-sized bouncer.

Okay, so Gary hadn't been kidding about them taking the rules seriously here. That should be relieving, but it also meant I was being watched more closely than I'd anticipated.

"Sorry," I said to the gremlin as I pulled my hand back to my lap, and the little angry creature disappeared behind my drink.

I didn't think this night could get any weirder, but then Adrian shrugged and leaned his back against the bar, propping his elbows on it. "I'm not a regular here," he said. "It's my first time, and I have you to thank." He looked over at me. "You showed me there's no reason to be embarrassed about coming to a place like this."

"You're welcome, I guess." I took a sip of my drink to hide the look of disdain I was sure he could read on my face. "But aren't you supposed to be working? Did you figure out what's going on in the—"

"I'm here with my wife," he said, cutting me off.

"Your what now?" I couldn't hide my disdain at this point, so I put my drink down and turned to face him with raised eyebrows.

"My wife. She's always wanted to come here with me, and you helped me realize there's nothing wrong with that."

I didn't know what unnerved me more—his words or the easy smile he wore while saying them. He might have secretly gotten married since I'd last seen him or he might be babbling nonsense, but the truly weird part was how confident and collected he was acting about the whole thing.

"Here she is now," he said as I gaped at him, and a statuesque woman appeared at his side from behind me. Her white-blond hair hung loose around her ageless face tonight, but the rhinestones on her glasses gave her away. *Of course.*

"Hi Miriam," I said, leaning back in my seat and trying not to groan. "Congratulations on your marriage or whatever." If they were here together, it meant they were here on police business, and Adrian had been trying to keep me from tipping anyone off. Well fine, I'd play along.

"Thank you, dear." Miriam pushed herself awkwardly up against Adrian's side and pressed the top of her head against his neck. It looked like something a dog or cat might do rather than a loving wife, but at least she was trying.

He stiffened—finally—his eyes bugging out a little before he coughed and said, "How was your dance? Did you learn anything you want to try out at home?"

"A little, but I'd like to stay longer."

I had no interest in listening to them speak in code if they weren't going to tell me why they were really here, so I gave them a polite fake smile and stood up with my orange juice, ready to find a seat somewhere I could go back to scanning the crowd for Soma.

Caught off guard by how tall I was in Etty's seven-inch heels, I paused for a moment and looked down at Adrian. *I could get used to this*, I thought. He quickly stood up straight, and I smiled when I saw his eyes were almost level with mine. I might have to practice wearing these shoes more often, because this was awesome.

"Darling," Miriam said, her hand on Adrian's shoulder. "You should tip the pretty lady for keeping you company."

"Yes, you should," I agreed, popping my boobs out a little as I held out my hand. I could *really* get used to this.

Adrian fished out a crisp bill from his jacket and handed it to me, and I felt a little better when I saw the familiar reticence creep back into his eyes. I didn't know *why* it made me feel better, but it did.

"Thanks a bunch," I said with a sultry pout, tucking the bill into my wristband like Kat had shown me earlier. I had no pockets, after all. "Have a nice honeymoon, you two."

I had just barely stepped away when I felt someone grab my arm. I spun around to see Gary, a look of relief on his face. No gremlins appeared to admonish him, so I supposed the "no touching" rule didn't apply to the club's employees. "This way," he said. "Your VIP is here early and wants a private dance."

He thankfully let go of me when we started walking, because I might have stumbled in my shoes trying to keep up with him otherwise. "Soma, right?" I asked from behind him. Soma was technically the owner of the club, even if he was functionally a customer, so I wasn't sure I could count on all the rules applying to *him* if they didn't apply to Gary.

"That's right. And remember, he loves the new girls, so don't try too hard."

"Got it," I said as he led me upstairs.

It was mostly private rooms up here, aside from the seating directly in front of the railing where people could watch the show from above. A great setup, I thought. They either had some subtle magic working or a very intricate air conditioning system, because the cash that was dropped over the railings always floated perfectly down to the center of the room to land on the stage.

When we reached the room all the way at the end of the walk-way, Gary turned to me and looked me over thoroughly. With a frown, he snatched the bill Adrian had given me out of my wrist-band. "You'll get this back later." He knocked on the door twice and walked away without another word.

"Yes," called a low voice from inside.

That was my cue. I fingered the tiny squishy behind my ear again quickly before pushing the door open, solidifying the image in my mind of the man who sat before me now.

Soma was as difficult to describe as he was to remember. He appeared ageless almost in the same way Miriam did, his posture and facial expression indicating an elderly demeanor despite the lack of wrinkles on his face. His skin had an unnatural sheen to it, multifaceted despite its utter smoothness, and because of that it was difficult to pinpoint what color it might have been when he'd been human. Thick, luminescent black hair fell in chunky waves over his forehead, and black eyes stared straight into mine as I closed the door behind me.

This might be the first time I'd seen a vampire who actually *looked* like a vampire. Immediately, I could understand why I'd had to go through all this trouble to meet him, why Kat had said he didn't get out much. A being like this would attract far too much attention walking down the street, and it wouldn't be the kind of attention the vampires wanted at this stage in their collective career. To someone already on the hook of immortality, nearly ready to pull the trigger, Soma's appearance might be encouraging—miraculous, even. But to the majority of humans in the world, it would only be terrifying.

Even I was having trouble keeping my heart from beating wildly in his presence, and I was well practiced when it came to keeping my cool around vampires. Remembering Gary's comments, I realized that was probably a good thing. I was playing a role here, and Birdie the baby stripper *should* be terrified right now. Perhaps Darcy the trained killer should as well, if she knew what was good for her.

I inched my way towards him, keeping my head down and my arms crossed in front of me. With the low sofa he was sitting on, I felt like a giant standing before him. It was a strange sensation to be so tall and so powerless at the same time when I was used to being the very opposite. "You wanted a private dance, sir?" I spoke with a higher pitch than usual, and a softer tone.

"Indeed." His voice reverberated through my whole body even though it was barely more than a whisper. My ribcage shook and my fingertips tingled. Not an unpleasant sensation, although unsettling.

The skin on my neck and shoulders was beginning to feel hot under my hair, and I lifted my arms to adjust my curls as I attempted to move my hips in a seductive manner. There was no pole in here, so I didn't have to pretend to be wobbly. With nothing to hold on to, I was sure I looked like an uncoordinated baby deer—this predator's favorite snack.

"Chin up, please," Soma said, and I lifted my head to look at him. Involuntary fear coursed through me when our eyes met, but it was quickly overtaken by confusion as he smiled and then broke into mirthful laughter.

I didn't get a chance to ask what was so funny, because

another vampire pounced on me in the same moment. In these shoes, I couldn't brace myself for the impact, so we were both knocked to the ground where he attempted to pin me underneath him.

Batty fucking hell, this was awful. The lacy lingerie might have been comfortable for dancing or lounging with a drink in my hand, but it was the last thing I wanted to be wearing in a fight. Too much of my bare skin was pressed up against the cold, gritty floor, and the thin strips of lace pulled and shifted and cut me in all the wrong places. I was sure this bloodsucker was getting a free show of something or other, although I couldn't tell specifically what.

Vampires were fast fuckers, and I only managed a quick hit to this one's face with my free hand before he grabbed it and pinned it to the ground along my side. With the weight of his legs on mine, I couldn't move much except my head, which I turned to avoid the blood that threatened to drip from his nose onto my face.

My right arm stretched under his grasp until my fingers reached the chalice at my thigh, which I'd thankfully strapped on with the base up. The small blade slipped out easily into my fingers, and I brought my forearm up behind his to slice him in the elbow—the only place I could reach.

He snarled in surprise and loosened his grip on my arm for a moment, just enough time for me to lift the blade and shove it up between his ribs. It might have pierced his heart if the blade were longer than a couple inches and if I'd been able to aim properly. But with the limited leverage I had in this position, it hit too low and went in too easily.

He coughed up blood almost immediately, his face now dripping red from more than one place. But he only licked his lips with a smile, staring down at me like a cat who'd just been squeaked at too loudly by a mouse. I'd only pierced his lung, which wouldn't hurt him.

There was no way I could kill him with this knife, even if I'd managed to get his heart, since vampires needed to be decapitated or burned to really die. But so much of their power came from blood that I could have at least incapacitated this one for a while by messing with his heart. Lungs were nothing more than vestigial organs on a vampire.

Maybe I couldn't kill him, but I wasn't going to give in. I made a fist and swung it hard at the elbow of his arm that was still pinning mine. It gave a nice, satisfying crack and before he could react, I hooked my arm under his shoulder and yanked him forward.

With his weight off my thighs, I could finally bend my knees to plant my heels on the ground and lift my hips. I was just about to flip him over when he lifted up off me of his own accord.

I blinked in confusion. Was this motherfucker levitating? I didn't think that was a real thing vampires could do. Scrambling to sit up, I saw Soma standing next to us, holding the vampire up by the back of his neck as if he were a naughty kitten.

"That wasn't necessary, Ellis," Soma said. "Darcy won't hurt me. We're old friends." With a flick of his wrist, he threw my attacker at the wall, which he smacked into before sliding down to a heap on the ground.

Lifting his head, Ellis muttered, "That's the Guardian who was charged with Senator Drake."

"I know, I know," said Soma, still looking at me. "But she didn't kill him, and she won't kill me. Like I said—old friends."

I swallowed and slowly stood up, resisting the urge to adjust my outfit. Doing so would let him know I was uncomfortable, and I wasn't sure that was a good idea anymore. I had no idea why Soma was acting like he knew me when we'd never met, but off the top of my head it didn't point to anything good.

"Darcy," he said. "I see you've found a new calling. Or did you just miss me? You could have picked up the phone instead of going through all this trouble . . ." He gestured at my torn and twisted getup, and I took the opportunity to adjust it. I did so decisively, only moving the fabric enough to make sure the important bits were covered, and I didn't look away from Soma while I did it.

It at least gave me a chance to think, which I needed because I was absolutely baffled. I couldn't think of any reason a vampire this powerful, both physically and socially, would have to pretend he and I had a history. There was no one in the room with us but his guard, so if this was a show then who was the audience?

"Not that I'm complaining," Soma continued when I failed to answer him. "I'd always wondered what you looked like under those unflattering suits." He chuckled to himself and then tilted his head, his expression far too friendly. "You know I would never touch you, though. Simeon may be gone, but you'll always be his."

My heart jumped into my throat unexpectedly at his words. It was real. He wasn't pretending. No one could have known about my relationship with Simeon if they'd never met me. We had hid it well, since I would have been fired just for that if I hadn't let him get killed first.

And the way this man said it—it was what Simeon had loved to say to me, that I would always be his, in a tone that forced me to believe it even though it made no damn sense. Hearing it now, it terrified me how much I still believed it. How unerringly true it sounded coming out of this stranger's mouth. Soma had to know me . . .

The real mystery was why I didn't know him.

6

"It's been too long," Soma said as he watched me, sitting up straight with his hands entwined around his knee. His legs were crossed, slacks lifting just slightly around his ankle to reveal socks with a pattern I couldn't quite make out.

I sat across from him and stuffed a cracker with decadently soft cheese into my mouth, then washed it down with a mouthful of floral white wine. Walking in these heels all night had been hard work, and if this guy wanted to sit me down and feed me instead of watching me attempt to dance, I wasn't above enjoying it. "I have to be honest," I said once I'd finished chewing. "I don't remember you at all. If we met while I was working for the senator, well . . . I don't think I was myself at the time."

"You don't seem much different now." Soma's cheeks lifted, and his eyes gleamed a little too brightly. "Except for the outfit, of course."

I nodded my head in conceit, shifting involuntarily. Despite how comfortable this getup actually was, I suspected it would take a long time for me to get used to the feeling of a plush sofa squished against my nearly bare ass.

"I don't like it." Soma snapped his fingers in the air.

The vampire who had attacked me appeared at his side obediently.

"Give the lady your jacket, Ellis," Soma commanded.

He did as he was told, although he didn't look happy about it. His nose still had smears of crusted blood lingering beneath it, and the crooked angle indicated I might have broken it. It would heal—vampires always healed, unless you cut off their heads—but bones took longer than flesh wounds, and he would still need to get it reset. That wouldn't be fun.

I stood to wrap his jacket around myself, then sat back down, not sure a stranger's dress coat was an improvement when it came to something pressing against my ass. Soma looked more comfortable, though.

"Much better," he said.

I almost laughed. "Do I look that bad in lace?"

"Not at all. But you belong to another, and it isn't appropriate for me to see you in such a state."

Gag me with a bloody chalice. That kind of attitude would have made me sick even if Simeon were still alive. It was bad enough for men to act like any of them could claim ownership of my body in any circumstance. But in this case, it was even worse. Soma was giving off a strong vibe that the only *appropriate* course of action would have been to bury me with my dead master.

His use of the present tense did not go unnoticed. The only way to still "belong" to a dead person was to follow them in death.

"I don't belong to anyone." I intentionally let the jacket fall open to comfortably expose my skin underneath. Taking a gamble that he would appreciate it despite his words, I picked up another cracker, spread it with the delectable soft cheese, and leaned back as I munched on it.

"You are exactly as I remember," he said, averting his eyes. "Bold, to the point of stupidity. You might have been able to kill

Ellis had I not stopped you, but you would stand no chance against me."

I couldn't let him see just how much I believed him. I would play the perfect little demure widow if I had no choice, but my goal here was to establish an ongoing relationship. Become someone he confided in—or someone he let close enough to sneak around when he wasn't looking. Allowing him to categorize me as the untouchable property of a dead friend was not likely to get me there.

"And yet you antagonize me," he said. "Is that why you're here? To provoke me to kill you so you can be with him again?"

I froze for a moment, struck by the idea. It made no sense, of course. I knew dying wouldn't bring me back to Simeon, or to any of the people I'd lost. But on some deep, primal level, it sounded appealing. I could almost feel the tingling warmth in my bones that I'd always felt whenever Simeon had held me, when we'd slip out of our public roles at the end of the day and into his sheets. The feeling that I could truly relax, leaving all my responsibilities in the light of the day and becoming someone different —someone I liked better.

That feeling was the reason he was dead, though. The reason I hadn't been doing my job properly when his killer had come for him. And it was probably the reason I'd been raised to never turn off my phone, even when I was sleeping. When your responsibilities were of the life-and-death variety, you couldn't shed them with your bra at night and expect everything to be okay.

"No," I said. "I have no interest in dying. And I'd appreciate it if you didn't use your mind tricks on me." The emotions I was feeling were grounded in my past experiences, but it wasn't only his words that had triggered them. I was far too good at burying useless feelings like this to be caught off guard by them now. No, he was doing what Simeon had always done, playing my mind like a musical instrument without my consent.

He cocked his head and the feeling subsided, that alluring suicidal pull vanishing to leave a chill in my bones instead. I fought the urge to wrap the jacket tighter around me.

"I'm here because I've taken up a new career path. I'm the operations manager for a club in Old Town, and I'm trying to learn from the best." I gestured around us with a nod of my head, figuring a compliment might take the edge off my disobedience.

"Well . . ." He poured a little more wine into my glass while letting the silence linger. "That is a shame."

I tensed, chewing at the inside of my cheek. I didn't think he was going to try to kill me, but it was a real possibility. You never really knew when it came to vampires outside of the public eye.

"If you were still working in security, I might have a job to offer you," he said instead. "You did good work for the senator, before . . ." He smiled and held his hands out in a gesture that seemed to say what's done is done.

I swallowed, unable to put my finger on what sort of game he was playing. It made no sense for anyone to want to hire me for *that*. To work for yet another vampire in the same role I'd failed in so badly . . . I was, quite literally, the worst possible person for a job like that.

I understood why the Guardians had wanted me to work for them again in a different capacity, because my outcast status made me uniquely qualified for covert work. But this? Soma was either insane or just toying with me.

"Before I let him die on my watch," I said. "Yes, before that, I was great at following him around everywhere looking menacing. You'd be better off hiring an actress if that's what you want." I knew I shouldn't have said it as soon as the words left my mouth. It was tough to remember that I *wanted* any job he was offering me—that this wasn't a damn therapy session. It wasn't about me; it was about finding the missing kids and stopping whoever had been taking them. But his presence alone was like a drug, making all my emotions more volatile even if he wasn't doing it consciously.

He surprised me again, leaning forward with softness in his eyes and touching my arm gently. "Darcy . . . you did do great work for him. No one could have saved him; it was simply his time, and you know that."

No, I didn't know that. Did I? Soma was looking into my eyes with such genuine care and such determination that again, I was inclined to believe him even though it made no sense.

He must be able to see how shaken I felt, because he leaned back again with a smile. Part of me wondered if this whole conversation had been an act to knock my confidence and make me into the meek, nervous creature Gary had told me Soma had a taste for.

But then he reached into his pocket and drew out a card, which he handed to me. "Report to this address at dusk tomorrow if you'd like the job. I hope you will, because you really aren't suited for this one." He gestured around us and then clapped his hands. "Please leave now. It was wonderful to see you, but I'm here for a reason and you are not my type."

I stood in a bit of a daze, almost slipping his card into a pocket before I remembered the jacket wasn't mine. Instead, the card went into my bra and I shrugged off the jacket as I walked across the room.

Ellis met me at the door, holding out a thick bundle of cash. Gary hadn't been wrong about this being worth my time. I traded the jacket for the cash, ignoring the look of disdain on Ellis's broken face and not looking back as I walked out the door into the busy club.

Taking a breath, I tried to compose myself. I had come here tonight with a clear mission, and with Soma's baffling job offer I had apparently accomplished that mission. So why did I feel so completely in over my head?

The fact that Simeon had fucked with my mind wasn't news to me, but the extent of it was. That I'd just walked into a room with a stranger I had no memory of at all only to discover he knew me quite well . . . this was beyond what I'd expected, and it was beyond reasonable. Even worse, he seemed to think I knew more about Simeon's death—that I should know somehow that it wasn't my fault.

I couldn't continue to live like this. Not knowing how much of my memories were accurate, how much was missing, how much might be entirely fabricated.

I needed to get to the bottom of it, and fast.

I marched back down the stairs to the main floor of the club, gritting my teeth against the pain that was beginning to worsen in my feet. Gary wasn't around—probably off finding Soma a more appropriate snack—but I spotted Adrian and Miriam sitting at a table in a corner of the room, a little too conspicuously watching the other patrons rather than the dancers on display. I'd accuse them of cramping my style, but after what had just happened I wasn't sure I should be throwing stones.

I approached them from behind, and Adrian jumped a little when I leaned over him to let my hair brush against his smooth cheek. I bit my lip and moved in closer to whisper in his ear, "Hey sweetheart."

I didn't even care that I was taking advantage of the opportunity to flirt with him when we both knew I was only playing a role. Getting out of that room with Soma had made my fears about Adrian feel insignificant.

This play-acting felt safe somehow, just like when I'd teased him at my bar when we'd first met, and I relished the shock in his eyes and the catch in his breath at my words. I knew things would go back to normal as soon as we were out of this place and in different clothes, that I would go back to my cowardly avoidance and him his resigned distance—but for tonight, I was in control and unafraid.

"What are you—" he started involuntarily and then stopped, probably remembering where he was.

I walked around the chair to face him and bent over again, resting my hand on the plush surface behind him. "Do you know what I would love?"

"What?" It came out as a whisper almost, his whole body tensing as I hovered above him.

"Some time alone with your wife." I winked, trying to resist the urge to tap him lightly on the cheek. "Why don't you go sit at the stage for a while so us girls can have fun?"

It took him a moment to process my words, and then he looked down where I was discretely holding out part of the wad of cash I'd earned during my strange encounter with Soma. If Adrian was going to be here, he should be spending, and I knew he and Miriam couldn't have much of a budget for this kind of thing.

It hurt my soul to give away money when I'd been struggling so hard to pay my bills, but I wasn't doing it for him; I was doing it for the other dancers who didn't deserve to be shorted by his cheap cop ass.

He let out a sigh and took the cash from me. "Yeah, okay. But you need to let me up first."

"Of course." I obediently stood tall and then enjoyed the view again when he stood next to me, not towering over me like he usually did.

I took his seat once he was gone, finding the warmth of the chair oddly comforting despite the fact that I was still sitting on plush furniture with bare skin. "Hello beautiful," I said, smiling at Miriam. "Would you like to buy me a drink?"

Miriam adjusted her glasses as she waved over a cocktail

waitress, who took my order of orange juice and soda water before leaving us.

"What's your name, dear?" Miriam asked me, only really looking at me out of the corner of her eye.

"Birdie."

"Well, Birdie, I'm not really in the mood for talking at the moment."

"Don't worry, I'm not interested in what you two are doing here," I said, and she looked at me fully.

"Oh?"

"Everyone has their kinks; there's nothing to be ashamed of." I crossed my legs and shifted in the chair to attempt a more alluring position as the cocktail waitress returned with my drink. Miriam tipped her, and once she was gone I said, "I need your help."

"Is everything all right?"

"I don't know. Do you have any experience with lost memories?"

"I'm not sure what you're asking."

"You know, the way you got inside my head before. Could you do it again and look for memories that have been erased, or messed with?"

"Has someone been tampering with your mind?" Miriam sat up in her chair and leaned closer to me.

"Maybe. I've had some foggy spots for a while, thought it was a side effect of . . ." *Bats,* I thought, hitting the ingrained mental block that kept me from divulging my affair with Simeon, even now that he'd been dead for over a year. I'd already lost the job, so it wasn't like there would be any real consequences if that particular scandal were made public. At this point, I didn't think anyone would even care. But I cared. I was ashamed of it, and I didn't want it to be common knowledge among the people I interacted with regularly. Who knew what secrets Miriam might relay to Dirk . . . or Adrian. "Promise you'll keep this to yourself?" I asked her.

"Not necessarily," she said in a stern tone. "But I won't say anything unless I need to."

I sighed. That would have to be good enough. "Okay. I had a *relationship* with a vampire."

"Oh, really?" she asked. "Yes, well, you're certainly dressed for it."

"No. I mean a long-term relationship—all the works, for several years."

"Oh . . ."

"And he fucked with my head." I nodded with her as she seemed to make the connection. "I didn't think there was much of a lingering effect, but I just met a complete stranger who was *not* a complete stranger, and I'm a little freaked."

Miriam brightened in recognition. "You mean like that nice English girl at the coffee shop? She said she knew you but you didn't remember her."

I paused and frowned slightly, caught off guard. It took me a moment to remember what Miriam was referring to because I'd assumed that girl at the coffee shop—some kind of fortune-telling barista—had only been pretending to know me so she could rope me in as a client.

"Wait . . ." My eyes focused back on Miriam. "She told *you* she knew me? And you didn't think to tell me that?"

"You were a bit busy at the time," she said with a tilt of her head.

"Right," I said. When Miriam had been at that coffee shop, I'd been trying to keep a crazed ifrit from demolishing an entire city block.

"Anyway . . ." Miriam pointed at my forehead. "You should come see me in the morning so I can take a peek in there."

I was about to agree, but then I remembered Dirk at my place and figured it would be a good idea to get the whole secret Guardian squad together. Maybe we could braid each other's hair while we shared notes on what the hell was going on. "Can you come see me instead?" I asked. "I'll make those cinnamon rolls you like." They were just the ones from the can, but she didn't need to know that.

"That sounds splendid."

I saw Gary walking towards us out of the corner of my eye and raised my voice a bit. "It'll be so hot and sticky and sweet . . . and then I'll . . ." I frowned a little, running out of naughty things to say about cinnamon rolls. "Then I'll show you my tits."

"That also sounds splendid, dear," Miriam said without a hitch.

"Alright." I picked up my drink, feeling the need to end this conversation. I wanted to leave early so I could pick up Noah and get some sleep in before our morning meeting, but I was sure that would ruin my chances of ever being allowed to dance here again, and even with Soma's new job offer I wasn't sure that was a smart play. Jiggling my bra to push my boobs back up to the top, I stood up and swished my hair.

Gary was behind me when I turned, a look of approval on his face. Soma must have said nice things, despite his insistence that I made for a shitty stripper. "I canceled your stage set. You've already racked up a long list of requests for private dances." A slow smile crept up his face. "Everyone wants the new girl."

Excellent. Leaving early was out the window, but at least I'd make back some of the cash I'd handed to Adrian. And with all the crazy in my life about as taken care of as it could be tonight, I might even have a little fun.

It was a good thing I was so tired at the end of the night, because if I'd been more alert I might have attacked the strange woman in the dressing room mirror whose eyes were darkened with liner and whose curves could only be described as poppin' under all that black lace.

Instead, I gave her a little wave before I collapsed into a chair and wrenched my feet out of the torture devices I'd stolen from Etty's closet. Wiggling my toes in the cool air, I sighed in relief. Then I pulled together all the bills I'd made in tips—minus what I'd paid the house—and stacked them neatly before stuffing them in my bag. I couldn't help the weary smile on my face. This was damn good money, and the occasional shift here might be exactly what I needed to make ends meet while I was funneling most of my bartending cash back into the club.

Okay, maybe not *here*, I thought as I grimaced at the small cut I'd made earlier on my outer thigh. I hadn't gotten through the night without a little bleeding, and that wasn't sustainable since I refused to use the provided vamp saliva for healing. It would be fine once I made it to Ray's and had his help, but in the meantime I could use a bandage.

I got up and relished in the feeling of my bare feet on the cool floor as I made my way towards the bathroom, where there would at least be some paper towels I could tie around my leg before putting my jeans on. It was nice to get away from the laughter and loud voices of the other dancers getting ready to go home. My head was pounding, and I couldn't wait to be somewhere quiet.

But the silence in the hallway was broken by a giggle that rang in the back of my head, making the pounding worse.

I stopped, recognition taking hold. I'd heard that giggle before.

It sounded again, faintly, seeming to echo and vibrate in the walls around me. Was I imagining it? Could be, as tired as I was. But I didn't think so.

Stepping forward, I moved past the door to the bathroom and

followed the eerie vibrations of weak laughter down a dimly lit corridor. A sickly sweet, rotten scent made its way to my nose, and it only got stronger as the giggling got louder.

It led me to a door that looked ordinary. I tried the handle—locked. Of course. Licking my lips, I fought the urge to start kicking. The last thing I needed was to be caught destroying property in a fancy club run by vampires that I might want to keep working at. Instead, I grabbed the chalice that was still strapped to my thigh and pulled out the tiny knife.

It just barely fit inside the lock, so I wiggled it around hoping to hear a click. No luck.

Sighing, I pulled out the blade and slid it in between the door and the jamb, then worked at the bolt until I managed to push it back inside the door.

With a creak, the door cracked open, and my stomach turned as I inhaled the stinking air inside the room.

So this must be where they keep the dead bodies. I reached in and slid my hand up the wall to find a light switch.

When I flicked it on, I was more convinced than ever that I must be hallucinating. There were no dead bodies in sight. Instead, it looked like someone had built some sort of creepy gnome shrine.

A terracotta figurine of a child-sized goblin-like creature stared at me with a demonic grin on its face. Flies swarmed around it, some perching on it only to get stuck in the shiny, sticky substance that was smeared all over the thing. In its arms, a shallow bowl was crusted over with dried blood—and what looked like some fresh blood pooled in the center.

"What the . . ." I walked up to it and ran the tip of my finger along the top of its head, then pulled my hand back along with some of the sticky substance. I rubbed it between my fingers. The golden color and slightly granular texture looked familiar, as did the scent when I brought it to my nose.

Honey.

The rotting meat smell was probably from whatever had been drained for the blood.

Well, gross. This was not what I'd expected to find in the basement of a swanky strip club, even one owned by vampires.

The figurine looked eerily alive as I wiped my fingers against the wall, despite the fact that it was unmoving.

"What are *you* looking at?" I said, and then I heard the laughter again, echoing all around me.

My instincts were telling me to find a way to burn the thing, even though I had no clue what it was or why it was here. But then I heard voices in the hall along with footsteps drawing close.

I ran back to the door and shut off the light, then ducked behind some boxes that were stacked up against the wall. A key turned in the lock on the door, and the lights went back on as Gary walked in, followed by another person I couldn't see.

"The blood," Gary said, turning to his companion and holding out a chalice like the one that was still strapped to my thigh. Liquid splashed against metal, and then Gary turned around and poured it from the chalice into the clay statue's bowl. He muttered a few phrases in a language I'd never heard.

The eerie laughter came back with a vengeance, ringing throughout the room loudly before fading into the walls as an echo.

"How many more?" said a raspy voice from behind Gary. It felt somewhat familiar to me, but I couldn't place it.

"I can't say . . . not yet. But soon." Gary paused. "Do you hear something? I think . . ."

I held my breath, hoping that neither of these bloodsuckers were old enough to hear my heartbeat from across the room. If they were, my blood would be the next thing fed to the rotting honeyed fly goblin over there. At least the pungent stench in here probably masked the scent of my blood.

"Nothing but your excuses," said the raspy voice. "Come. We have work to do."

"Of course." Gary followed the mystery man out through the door and shut off the light again.

I started breathing again slowly, immediately regretting it as the rotten smell filled my nostrils. Not only was this unpleasant to say the least, it was also unnerving to be stuck in here in the dark with this horror show and the familiar laughter. How long would I have to wait to ensure no one caught me? And how long *could* I wait here before someone noticed my stuff was still in the dressing room without me?

After a few minutes and nothing but silence outside, I decided to chance it. I slipped out of the darkness into the empty hallway and all but tiptoed back to the bathroom, where I futilely pressed a bunch of paper towels against the crusted-over wound on my thigh.

I texted Adrian as soon as I got back to the dressing room, knowing there was no other course of action at this point. I had seared the image of the honey goblin in my mind, remembering every detail so I could relay it to him accurately. Not only was this probably connected to what I'd witnessed in the Metro tunnels this morning, it was also just the kind of random-ass crazy bullshit that he might know something about.

"Huh," Adrian said after I'd finished explaining what had happened in the basement of the club. "I have no idea what that could be. Are you sure you can't remember any of the words he chanted?"

"It was a language I'd never heard before. Not exactly easy to process. Sorry."

He shook his head, looking away from me and stuffing his

hands in his coat pockets as the wind picked up around us. We were standing on a street corner a few blocks from the club, waiting for a car to pick us up. Since we both lived across the river, he'd agreed to ride with me to Ray's so I could grab Noah before going home.

"I'll hit the books tomorrow and see if I can find anything. There's no use arresting anyone until we have some sense of what they're up to."

"Right," I said, but I was only half listening to him at this point. The familiar giggle was bouncing around in my brain again, making my stomach sink.

I turned around, looking for the source even though I knew I wouldn't see anything. There was a Metro entrance just a little way behind us, the glow of the lights underground carrying out of the stairwell. The laughter seemed to carry with it, beckoning me to descend.

"Darcy?" Adrian touched my shoulder.

I turned to see him standing in front of our ride, which had pulled up by the curb.

"Do you hear that? The laughter?"

He shook his head slowly, looking behind me, his frown deepening in confusion.

"Just . . . can you ask him to wait? I want to check something out." I walked away before letting him answer, following the trills of laughter to the descending stairs.

Was the Metro even open still? The gates weren't closed yet, but I was sure they would be soon, at this time of night.

Not worth it, I thought, ready to turn back around and climb into the car with Adrian. Like he had said, there was no point in going after something if I didn't know what it was or how to kill it.

But then I saw a figure standing at the bottom of the stairs, its back to me.

Noah. With his light-blue school uniform and his curly mop of blond hair that was getting a little darker every day.

More giggles reverberated up the walls of the stairwell, getting crueler as they climbed.

I gripped the railing, trying to tear myself away. Rationally, I knew that thing down there probably wasn't Noah. But could it be? Unless the actual kid was here to hold my hand, some part of me had to wonder.

Then the figure turned, just like it had when I'd seen it before, with wrinkly, sagging skin surrounding dull eyes that looked nothing like Noah's. And this time, flies swarmed around it, some crawling on its cheeks and creeping into its mouth as it grinned at me with crooked yellow teeth.

The giggles turned into screams, and for a moment I thought I saw faces stretching out at me from the walls around the creature—faces of the dead, their eye sockets hollow and lips cracking as they stretched open impossibly wide.

The faces retreated back into the walls, and arms reached out at me in their place. Skeletal and spectral at the same time, they stretched up over the flight of at least a hundred steps in an instant, wrapping their cold fingers around my extremities and pulling.

It didn't hurt; in fact, I couldn't feel much at all. It was like I was dreaming, all my senses muddied and detached. I tried to pry myself away from them, but the message didn't go through. No part of me moved except my tired feet, which calmly stepped down the first few stairs.

A strong hand closed on my shoulder, stealing my focus, and suddenly I was at the top of the steps again, as if I'd never moved.

I blinked and the spectral arms were gone, the faces along with them. Only the creature with Noah's body remained, still grinning at me as flies crawled out from between its teeth. A swarm of the black bugs grew around it, engulfing it far too quickly before the whole vision disappeared altogether.

I stood stock still, swallowing the bile in my throat and trying to work out whether all that had really just happened.

"Hey." Adrian's voice finally made its way to my ears as my grip on reality returned. "Darcy, what the hell? Can you hear me?"

"Yeah," I said, turning around and dislodging his hand from my shoulder.

"Uh . . ." He narrowed his eyes at me. "What just happened?"

A car horn sounded, and I turned my head to see the ride we'd called flashing its lights.

I held up a finger, graciously not my middle finger, hoping the driver would wait. "Did you see anything? Just now? Down there?" I asked Adrian, trying to keep my voice from shaking.

I needed to know. Was I having creepy visions of Noah because he was somehow involved in this crap, or was I just going completely batshit crazy and projecting my nightmares into full-on hallucinations?

Adrian shook his head at me. "No, why? Did *you* see something?"

"Did you *hear* anything?" I asked, ignoring his question.

"You mean aside from our angry driver?"

Fuck. Batshit crazy must be my answer, then. "Yeah, must've been that," I said, doing my best to chuckle. It came out as a pathetic choking sound, but I shrugged it off and turned towards the car. "Come on, can't keep him waiting."

"Wait." Adrian moved his body in front of mine, looming over me without touching me, blocking my view of the car. "What just happened? Seriously. If you saw something I didn't, it could be important."

There he went with his reasonable thinking again, and my own head cleared a little as I focused my eyes on the reassuring expression on his face. His lips were parted slightly, soft and inviting, and his eyes held mine with an unwavering sharp intensity that told me he wanted to listen to whatever I had to say.

He was right; it could be important. But that didn't change the fact that it was *Noah* I'd seen. And if it was anything other than all in my head, that meant the kid was somehow involved. I'd taken him under my wing with the knowledge that I'd have to be wary, constantly watch him for signs of . . . hunting people and eating their souls. Baz and his murderous auntie had clearly warned that it was a common thing to happen to any of his kind who got a taste of the good stuff.

So if Noah was involved, I'd have to treat him like a suspect. And so would Adrian.

I didn't want the kid to have an official record, didn't want him held in police custody, didn't want to see him in cuffs. Even if he truly was killing people, if he truly was a monster—I wanted to handle it myself. If I needed help taking him down, then I'd ask for it; but I wouldn't subject him to any of that cruel treatment until I knew for sure it was necessary. My responsibility as the kid's guardian would come before my responsibility as a professional Guardian every time.

I shook my head, knowing I needed to tell Adrian something. "I saw faces in the walls. Dead things with hollow eyes, laughing and then screaming. They reached out to me and pulled, and it only stopped when you touched me. Did I move? Because it felt like I was walking down."

"No," he said. "You just stood there."

"I think I'm going nuts," I said, telling him as much of the truth as I could.

He sighed and softened his stance, his shoulders lowering as he looked down at me. "You should sleep more. Don't you get up early these days?"

"Tomorrow's Saturday," I said.

"That's not the point. Why are you working two jobs?" He dug into his pocket and brought his hand out with at least half of the stack of cash I'd handed him earlier. "If you need money, you shouldn't be giving so much away."

"That's—" I stopped myself, letting the urge to yell at him pass. "Why do you still have that? It was for spending on the dancers."

Adrian finally broke his eyes away from mine, looking down to the side as he held the cash out further to me. "I was saving it," he said.

"What the hell for?" I asked as I swiped it from him, flipping through it with my thumb to see how much was left.

He shifted on his feet when I looked back up at him, a tightness in his jaw that hadn't been there before. "I thought you were going to dance." He said it so quietly I almost didn't hear him, and part of me wished I hadn't.

I froze, unable to look away from him, swallowing to avoid saying something I might regret.

He cleared his throat, steadying his posture as I stared at him. "I was *hoping* you were going to dance," he said, louder now. "I wanted to make it rain for you." He cracked a smile, uneven in its hesitance, and it made me want to catch his crooked lips and right them with my own.

I bit my tongue instead, hoping the pain would snap me back to my senses. This beautiful bastard had been a lot easier to deal with when he'd been too shy to actually flirt with me. Now that he was getting more comfortable . . .

I shook my head at him. "If you're going to make it rain for me," I said, enunciating every word as I skirted around him towards the waiting car, "it had better be with your own cash."

He reached around me to grab the door handle before I could, his face coming dangerously close to mine as he pulled it open for me. "I'll remember that."

7

I WOKE up the next morning bursting with excitement. For the first time in a very long time, I sat straight up in bed and threw the covers off before I could even get my eyes open.

The crisp air engulfed me and sunlight streamed in through open blinds as I cracked my eyelids apart. I didn't know why my blinds were open, but I didn't care. The light was beautiful, casting dramatic shadows behind my furniture and making the dust in the air sparkle.

My stomach growled at me and I put my feet on the floor, standing up with a big stretch. Today was cinnamon-roll Saturday! My favorite day. My . . . *Batty hell, this isn't me.*

"Noah!" I yelled, and he popped up with a mischievous grin from behind the other side of my bed. "We talked about this. Keep your emotions to yourself, please."

"It was the only way to wake you up!" he whined happily, but then he closed his eyes and scrunched up his face and made adorable little fists with his adorable little hands. As he breathed out, all the excitement drained away from my body and was replaced with pain.

My blood might as well have been the texture of molasses for all it was doing to keep me upright with open eyes, and my feet had to be standing on knives instead of carpet. I looked down, resisting the urge to collapse back in bed. Nope, that was definitely carpet and not knives.

"Thanks," I managed to say in a voice I hoped didn't sound too unpleasant. "Now, what do we need before we use magic on anyone?"

"Consent," Noah said. "But I knew you would want to wake up."

"That doesn't count." I took a breath, trying not to raise my voice. "You can't actually know what I want without asking me first."

"But Miss Miriam can, right? She told me so."

Oof. This was too difficult a topic to handle before coffee and on only a few hours of sleep.

"Miriam is here?" I rubbed my head, remembering that I'd asked her to come over for breakfast. "Good, okay."

Noah sped out of my room like a little squirrel, screeching, "She's awake!" at the top of his lungs. I pulled on my robe and stuck out my tongue at the raccoon eyes that stared back at me in the mirror. This right here—this was why I hated wearing makeup. Trying to take it off was worse than putting it on.

When I came out of my room, the spicy sweet scent of cinnamon rolls met my nose. "Noah, did you use the oven without me? That's another thing we've talked abou—" I stopped when I walked into the kitchen to see Dirk in Etty's apron, standing over a pot on the stove while Miriam messed with my coffee maker.

I groaned, not ready to deal with whatever was going on there and already wishing I could just get back in bed. I usually worked the night shift at the club on Saturdays so I could spend time with Noah when he was home from school. So at least I had all day to maybe sneak in a nap before I had to be somewhere. I let that thought calm me as Miriam came out of the kitchen and handed me a cup of coffee.

"You were out almost as late as I was last night—how are you not dead right now?" I asked.

"I don't sleep," she said sternly. "But if I did, I would have made time to wash my face before bed." She shook her head at me as I glared daggers at her over the rim of the coffee mug. "You'll get wrinkles and clogged pores like that, you know. And your sheets must be a mess."

"Do you even have pores? You look like a giant doll." I took a sip of coffee, fully recognizing that was the kind of thought I normally would have filtered out before it could make its way to my mouth. "Sorry, what I meant to say is you have very beautiful smooth skin for a . . . swamp monster."

"Oh, this?" She touched her cheek. "It's not skin, but thank you. And I prefer amoeboid."

I sighed into my coffee and let the steam billow up against my cheeks. "Okay."

Miriam held her hand out with the palm up, where an orange gelatinous blob emerged from underneath her not-skin. She gave it a tickle, and it hopped up slightly with a jiggle.

Trying not to cringe, I put my coffee down.

"Come closer, please," Miriam said. "You still want me to look inside your head, yes?"

"Yes," I said even though my gut answer was no. I didn't want that squishy on me, but I did want to find out just how crazy I was. I couldn't keep going around not knowing what memories I was missing or whether I was hallucinating.

I leaned forward for her and held up my hair.

"Oh, no need for that," she said. "We can put this on your forehead since you won't need to hide it."

Wonderful. "It won't take long then?"

"Just a few hours. You don't need to be anywhere, do you?"

"Not until this evening."

"Perfect." She pressed the squishy to my forehead, and I was surprised at how cool and refreshing it felt. Maybe I could nap for the few hours this thing would need to stay on. "Just go about as you normally would," Miriam continued. "I need to lie down so I can concentrate. I'll be in your bed." She sauntered off to my room, taking my hopes and dreams of getting any rest today along with her.

I picked up the coffee mug again and gulped the rest of the warm liquid down just as Noah bounced his way out of the kitchen with a plate of cinnamon rolls stacked tall. Icing oozed down the sides of the golden-brown buns, and the sweet scent made my mouth water.

"Are those . . ."

"I made the real kind," Dirk said, coming out of the kitchen behind Noah and untying his apron.

Noah had already sunk into the sofa and begun stuffing his face, and the blissful light in his eyes made me swallow all the rude comments in the back of my throat. They did look delicious.

"You didn't have to," was all I could get out before I stuffed one in my own mouth.

"Yeah, well, you didn't have to be so loud when you came home at that ungodly hour. I was awake anyway, and this guy kept going on about cinnamon rolls, and you had all the ingredients. Yeast was expired but still kickin'."

"This is amazing," I said involuntarily. The sugar was making me feel slightly human again even where the cup of coffee I'd just downed had failed.

"I've had practice." He smirked. "Whoever said the way to a man's heart is through his stomach must'a been thinking about women. For us, it's actually our—"

"That's okay," I said. "I can guess."

Dirk shifted his eyes and cocked his head in a gesture that

told me he doubted I could guess. Then he rubbed his hands together and said, "Alright, spill it. What'd you find out last night?"

I raised my eyebrows. "Noah, go wash your hands."

"Can I have another one first?"

"Sure, but take it into your room. We have grown-up stuff to talk about." And maybe I could get Dirk to clean up the aftermath of the sticky fingers later.

Noah usually wasn't allowed to eat in his room, because I'd kept as many of Becca's rules going as I could manage. She was still watching me through her son's eyes, after all, even though she was technically dead. I knew I'd never be perfect, as evidenced by this moment right here, but I owed it to my friend to at least try.

The kid jumped up and grabbed the biggest, gooiest cinnamon roll off the plate before running off to his room.

"You shouldn't let him eat in there," Dirk said, and I shook my head.

"Sorry, did you come here to give me parenting advice? Cause last I checked you needed my help not dying."

He threw up his hands in defense. "Okay, okay, just tell me what happened last night."

"Soma and I have a history, apparently," I said, getting right to it. "And he offered me a job. I start tonight at dusk, if I can get someone to cover for me at Baz's."

"You work quick."

"I'm not sure if I should go," I said as I licked my fingers.

"Why not?"

"I have no idea *what* our history is, for one. That's what Miriam's trying to help with." I pointed to the orange blob on my forehead. "And I think our case might be linked to their case." I gestured to my bedroom. "Miriam and Adrian's, with the people going crazy and the killings in the Metro."

Dirk raised his eyebrows and picked up a cinnamon roll, then sat back in his seat and motioned for me to keep going.

"They were at Soma's club last night, too, so they must have gotten a lead that pointed them there just like we did. And . . . I found something creepy in the basement of the club." I kept going, explaining in detail what had happened when I'd found the clay statue, how the vampires were feeding it with blood, how I'd heard the same laughter there that I had in the Metro. Even if my visions of Noah were hallucinations crafted entirely by my own paranoid mind, the rest would be suspect.

"Huh," Dirk said when I was finished.

"That's exactly what Adrian said."

"You *told* him?"

"Just about the stuff I saw. Not about us. He totally bought my cover; I was there last night to get ideas to liven up my business."

Dirk sighed, putting his head in his hands. "This is worse than I thought."

"Why? Are you going to tell me now why you're still hiding out here? And why are you on leave anyway? You couldn't tell me what to do while working your regular job?"

"Look, I thought it was just vampires. Vampires acting squirrelly, maybe some rogue young ones misbehaving we'd need to feed back to the elders for discipline. But it sounds like at least one elder is in on it, and it sounds like they're working with something else . . ." He scowled. "A honey goblin statue, really? That's not a vampire thing, far as I know. And I'm not hiding out here. I just don't want to go home until this is taken care of. I showed the vamps my badge before they attacked me, so they'll know where I live."

"Why would you show them your badge?"

"Because I was poking around asking questions at one of the restaurants where a kid disappeared. They jumped me outside after I left. I'd be dead if not for Etty's dust."

I let out a long breath. I really might have to solve this case entirely before I could get Dirk out of my apartment. "Well, Adrian's looking into it. Maybe you should just go back to work and get his help officially."

"No. It's too hard to keep shit from him. He knows my tells."

"If he doesn't already know you're a Guardian, I find that hard to believe."

"That little tidbit's never come up between us. Never had to lie about it to his face."

I wanted to suggest that we just loop Adrian in all the way, tell him we were doing covert shit and trust him to keep our secret. But I knew what the Guardians would do to him if they ever found out. Plants like Dirk and Miriam were too useful, long-term investments they wouldn't want to give up.

Tensions had been rising between the police force and the DSC, with official structural change looming, and it was bound to erupt in chaos at some point. I didn't know whether the Guardians wanted to prevent that chaos or capitalize on it, but either way they needed their secrecy to do it. "Okay, well . . . we can at least use Miriam as a go-between," I offered instead.

"And you. You could lie to that boy all day."

"Uh . . ." I twisted my face in confusion, not sure how to respond to that, but he didn't wait for me to figure it out.

"Where are you supposed to meet Soma tonight?" he asked.

"Some address in DC. I didn't check yet. It's on a card in my room." I got up to go get it, then turned when the doorbell rang.

Dirk sat up straight. "You expecting someone?"

"No," I said, my empty hands already reaching for knives that weren't there because I was still wearing my pajamas. "You sure they couldn't track you here?"

"No," Dirk said with a shrug.

"Go—get in my room." I hit him on the shoulder to emphasize I meant now.

The doorbell rang again while Dirk was standing up, and this time Noah ran out of his room. "Someone's at the door!" he chirped as my eyes widened in panic.

"Noah—wait!" I whisper-yelled, practically leaping over the couch to stop him. But he got there before me anyway, with his energetic little legs that had gotten a full night's sleep and loved mornings.

The kid pulled open the door, and I was caught standing in my living room wearing a weaponless robe, like a sleepy raccoon in the headlights, when Adrian appeared in the entryway. His hair was messier than usual and the stubble starting to show again on his face, although his eyes were clear and he was wearing the same decently nice clothes he normally wore to work.

"Hi Noah," he said before his eyes lifted and landed on me. "Did you just wake up? I need to talk to Miriam."

I stayed frozen, my relief that it wasn't some vampire here to murder us all quickly giving way to the realization that Adrian couldn't know Dirk was here. I looked behind me to see if he'd made it to my room, and Adrian's eyes followed mine to see Dirk smiling at us as he jiggled the doorknob.

He shook his head at me and said, "She locked it."

"What are you doing here? I thought you were on vacation." Adrian shifted his eyes back from Dirk to me. "What is he doing here?"

Noah grabbed Adrian's hand before I could answer and said, "They're doing grown-up stuff. Come on, we have cinnamon rolls!"

I groaned internally, my sluggish mind unable to come up with a good way to elaborate on "grown-up stuff." Dirk was quicker than me, coming up behind me faster than I could move anywhere and putting his arm around me.

Oh bats, what the hell was he doing? I shimmied away from his grip and said, "Why are you touching me?"

"It's okay, baby. He's gotta find out some way." Dirk put his arm around me again and pulled me against him harder this time.

I closed my eyes and wished that I could be literally anywhere in the world besides here right now.

"Find out what?" Adrian said a little too calmly for my liking.

Feeling sick to my stomach, I followed Dirk's lead. It was the only thing that made sense, as gross as it was. I tried not to cringe as I said, "We're dating."

Adrian said nothing for a moment, just stared at us while I stared at him, his eyebrows slightly raised and his mouth partly open. Then he shook his head a little, turned to Noah, knelt down and said, "Do *you* know where Miriam is?"

Noah pointed to my room. "But the cinnamon rolls are out here," he whined when Adrian started walking in that direction.

Something sank in my gut, uncomfortable heat rising in my throat. I wasn't sure why, but I hadn't expected Adrian to be so completely unaffected by Dirk's lie. Maybe I was wrong; maybe he hadn't actually been flirting with me last night. Maybe the months of me avoiding him had worked as intended and he'd lost interest.

Before I could think about what I was doing, I removed Dirk's arm from around me and followed him. "You could have called before showing up, you know."

"I did. Miriam didn't answer. Did something happen to her?"

"She's fine, just busy. I meant you could have called *me*."

Adrian gave me a pointed glare and then reached into his coat pocket. He pulled out my phone and handed it to me. "You left it in the car last night. Might want to take some time off. Seems like you could use the rest." He shifted his eyes, trying not to look at Dirk behind me as he said it.

"How are you not as exhausted as I am right now?" I asked.

Whatever inexplicable force was pushing me to antagonize him, my groggy brain wasn't equipped to fight it.

"I can't afford to be tired today. There's been another incident." He turned to my closed bedroom door. "She's in here?"

I reached out and grabbed his hand before it could get to the doorknob. "I said she's busy." I pointed to the orange glob of Miriam on my forehead. "Can it wait for just a little?"

"Can you let go of my hand?" Adrian said, and I looked down to see my fingers were still curled around his. "No, it can't wait," he said, his voice getting snappier. "Did you hear me? There's been another incident. That means people are dead. And more will die the longer we draw this out."

I took my hand off his and pressed my fingernails into my palm, needing the pain to knock some sense into me. What was that I'd been thinking just yesterday? About how I knew the signs? And here I was, letting my lusty lizard brain get in the way of a murder investigation just because I'd expected a jealous reaction from a man and hadn't gotten it.

I needed more coffee. And a very cold shower.

I sighed and lifted my fist to knock on my door, but Miriam opened it before I could do so. She took her glasses off to rub her eyes before she said, "Alright, I heard you. Let's go."

Adrian stepped out of the way to let her through the door, and I followed as they made their way through my living room. "Hey." I pointed to the blob on my face. "What about this?"

"We'll have to finish later," Miriam said. She reached out and reabsorbed the orange squishy into the not-skin of her hand, which left me feeling strangely empty. "I did find something interesting, but I need more time. I'll call you."

"Hey, wait," I called out as they walked towards the door, realizing I really wanted to go with them. Now that I suspected their case was also my case, the urge to insert myself everywhere relevant was almost too strong to suppress.

Adrian turned around to look at me, and I saw now that the harsh set of his jaw and the pain in his eyes were much bigger than whatever I'd expected him to feel at seeing Dirk and I playing house. Whatever had happened this morning, it must have been worse than what had happened already. Worse than a deadly shifter going on a murder rampage inside a train and then slitting her own throat on the tracks. Worse than the other bodies he'd found before that.

"Never mind," I said softly. "Good luck. Call if you need help." I fingered my phone in the pocket of my robe, already itching to plug it in so I could text Miriam for the address and follow them discreetly.

"Thanks," Adrian said. Then, with one last glance at Dirk, he and Miriam headed out the door.

As soon as it shut, I dashed to my room to throw on real clothes and wipe the rogue eyeliner from the night before off my face.

"Hey," Dirk barked at me when I emerged. "Where do you think you're going?"

I stopped in my tracks, one shoe half dangling from my foot, and tilted my head at him. "It's not obvious? I want to see this crime scene. I think our cases are connected, remember?"

"Oh, I remember. But you don't get to make decisions like that without consulting me first."

If we were really dating, I would have punched him right about now. But unfortunately, as my handler and the one reporting on me back to the Guardians, Dirk was right. I needed his approval before I went meddling in any police business.

"Miriam's there," he went on. "She'll tell us anything we want to know, and we need to work on a plan for your job with Soma tonight."

"Right, but I need Miriam's help for that." I pointed to my

head. "Remembering whatever I've got locked in here about Soma is my best chance of going in prepared tonight."

Dirk frowned as Noah came up behind him and tugged on his apron for attention.

"Plus," I added, trying to bombard him while he was distracted, "if this really is a huge case, it might be best for both Miriam and I to check out the scene. Two heads, better than one, you know . . ."

"Can you teach me to make more cinnamon rolls, Uncle Dirk?" Noah asked, tugging on Dirk's apron again. "I want to bring some to school on Monday for Carina."

I bit my lip, not sure about the whole "Uncle" thing but still wanting to hug Noah for inadvertently helping my cause. A chance to teach my adoring kid a lesson and help him woo a girl? That would be hard for this guy to pass up.

Dirk huffed a breath out at Noah and said, "Sure. Go wash your hands."

I smiled as Noah ran into the kitchen, stuffing my foot all the way into my shoe and picking up my bag. "Thanks!" I said. "And don't worry; he'll be ready for a nap soon after all that sugar."

I was out the door before Dirk could protest, only a little bit jealous that there was no afternoon nap in the cards for me today.

That was okay. The invigorating feeling of having a killer to chase was just as good.

8

Red brick walls loomed over me as I stood outside the address Miriam had given me, unsure whether I should go in. I'd hoped for a window or something, at least, to do some sneaking, but this was apparently a basement bar, and the only entrance was a door that opened to a dark, narrow stairwell down.

I paced up and down the sidewalk a couple times, thankful no one outside recognized me, then ducked into an alley and decided to wait until they left so I could break in and take a look at the crime scene on my own.

I eyed a pile of broken-down cardboard boxes, the fleeting desire to sneak in a nap tugging at my senses. I leaned back against the brick wall instead. If I let myself lie down, I didn't know when I'd manage to reenter the world of the living.

Something blinked at me. I only noticed because I was trying so hard to keep my own eyes open. I squinted, focusing in on the two glittering gold orbs in the brick wall across from me. They blinked again as I tilted my head, then shut completely and vanished in a thin puff of sparkling dust.

A fae glamour.

If I hadn't spent so much time around Etty and Becca, I might not have recognized it at all. But why was a hidden fae watching me? Was it even watching *me* specifically, or was I just intruding on its space in this alley?

My phone rang, and I filed away the strange encounter as something to worry about later.

"Miss Pierce." Miriam's voice came through in a tone that was overly formal, even for her. "We could use your help. Come to the address I sent you."

"Okay . . ." I said to myself; she had already hung up the phone. It *was* exactly what I needed, but if Miriam had convinced the others to let her call me, I wasn't sure that was a good thing. It meant they might think there was a connection to me—or to Noah.

I made a quick lap around the block and then walked in, only to be greeted by Adrian at the base of the stairs saying, "You got here fast." His face was paler than usual, glistening with a bit of sweat that seemed out of place for the way he was dressed.

The air smelled only faintly of death, which meant they'd either carted out the body or the incident was recent. Someone walked past us up the stairs with a camera around her neck and gloves on her hands, and a bustle of noises indicated there were more people taking photos and bagging evidence further in.

"I was already on my way to see Ray," I lied, peering around Adrian to try to get a glimpse of what had happened. But I couldn't see anything from here, just the host table and a decorative wall.

"Hey." He put his hand on my arm to keep me from walking around him. "Don't go through just yet."

"Why not?" I asked, resisting the urge to look at his hand. Even though he was touching me through a few layers of sleeves, it still set my nerves on edge.

"It's . . . bad," he said. "Worse than anything I've ever seen."

I raised my eyebrows, curiosity officially piqued. Adrian wasn't the toughest of the tough, but he'd seen plenty of death in his line of work, and I would have guessed he'd passed the point of losing his lunch at crime scenes. Apparently not. I looked to his left, where his arm was propped against the wall holding him up, and saw the entrance to the restroom he'd probably just come out of. "Sorry," I said, not entirely sure what I was apologizing for. "Wanna tell me why I'm here?"

"We think the killer was fae. Whole place is covered in dust. That's why it doesn't smell as bad as it should."

My heart nearly stopped beating. He'd said "fae" as if that was a clear connection to me. But the only fae still in my life was Noah. And aside from that minor issue of emotional autonomy, it hadn't occurred to me to worry about his fae abilities in the same way I worried about the soul-sucking ifrit part of him. I had never met any fae who were murderous and out of control, though, so I supposed I had no idea what they were truly capable of.

Perhaps I was about to find out.

I pushed past Adrian into the bar, where Miriam was standing at the center of a glittering massacre.

No, not a massacre, I thought as I took a closer look at the bodies slumped over tables and splayed on the ground. *A mass suicide.*

I could hardly see the floor through all the blood. Broken glasses littered the space, jagged shards gripped in the rigid fingers of so many of the dead patrons, uneven gashes over their throats where the glass had cut.

Other patrons lay still with long, metal drink stirrers shoved up their noses or in their ears. A bartender had fallen over the bar with a blowtorch by his hand, his whole face a melty, charred mess. I didn't want to think about what the kitchen looked like, if there was one.

There was no one killer, no one weapon—every person in this full bar on a busy Friday night had stopped what they were doing at the same time and offed themselves with whatever was most convenient.

And Adrian hadn't been exaggerating. The whole place was covered in fae dust. The blood on the floor should have been crusted over by this point, but instead it looked fresh and luminescent. Sparkles shone throughout the space in every direction, settling in the hair of the deceased and floating in the air around them. It was more dust than I'd seen Etty or Becca use in the entire time I'd known them, and it was far more than Etty must have used to get herself permanently banned from our realm.

"How many fae were in here?" I said softly, not really expecting anyone to answer.

"Just the one," Miriam said, pointing behind me.

I turned around, and Adrian motioned me over to the restroom. A gentle push was all it took to swing open the door, which was missing its handle. The air inside was so filled with dust I could barely see through the glitter.

Waving my hands in front of my face to try to clear it, I stepped forward and found a body on the ground that didn't look human. Aside from the pointed ears and the long, sharp nails and teeth, the man's flesh was shriveled to the bone. He looked dessicated, like a skeleton covered with just a thin layer of skin. Which made it easier to spot the unnatural shape jutting out from his throat.

"It's the door handle," Adrian said from behind me, and I was grateful I wouldn't have to pry the man's jaws open to figure that out for myself.

"Iron?" I guessed.

"If it's the same as all the other handles in the place, yes."

I backed out of the restroom, against all odds preferring to be with the blood and gore over what I'd just seen.

"All this dust . . ." I said, "from just the one?"

"Yes," Miriam said. "There are no signs that anyone made it out alive."

"Fuck." I swallowed to try to keep the cinnamon rolls in my gut from doing anything they'd regret. It wasn't the blood that got me, not even the sheer number of bodies—which was higher than I'd ever seen in one room—no, it was the horror of the idea that they'd all done it to themselves.

I'd always known, going into the line of work that I had, that I'd probably be killed for it one day. I'd never been afraid of dying, but I'd always assumed I'd at least go down fighting. None of these people had fought, not even for a moment. If they had, they wouldn't all be dead in their seats. The only people on the ground between tables were waitstaff, and not a one had attempted to make it to an exit. The only person who hadn't killed himself instantly was the fae in the restroom.

The one who had caused all this.

I thought of what had happened on the train yesterday, the way the woman had completely lost control of herself. I'd thought that was bad, but it turned out the damage an out-of-control shifter could do didn't hold a candle to an out-of-control fae.

No wonder the fae courts were so strict with their laws, so controlling of their people. For the first time since Etty had been taken away from me, I could kind of understand the reasoning behind it.

"Any thoughts?" Miriam asked me, and I almost laughed. Of course I fucking had thoughts.

"Can you be more specific?" I shot back.

"We don't exactly have any fae experts on our roster to consult," she said.

Is that why they called me in? I breathed a relieved sigh through my nose. It didn't have to do with Noah, not specifically. I was just the most convenient person to call who had some experience dealing with the fae. "And I'm really the best you could dig up?"

"This is unprecedented." Miriam gestured around the place. "I'm sure the fae courts will give us a statement when they find out about it, and I'm sure it will be the most roundabout nonsense they can manage. None of their people will talk; all our laws that govern them are moot because they only hold sway in our realm. Anyone who gets out of line is pulled back to theirs, and quick. So yes, the best we can do is a mortal with personal ties to the fae, and you're the only one whose number I have in my phone."

I bit my tongue, slowly nodding. "Well," I said after a moment, "First things first, I spotted a fae hiding out in the alley on my way in. Gold eyes and dust. Might not be related, but you should check it out."

Adrian jotted down a note before eagerly saying, "What else?"

"I can tell you that the use of dust is heavily regulated, and there's no way this much would have been approved for anything. So either he knew he had to die going into it, or he completely lost his shit and had no idea what he was doing." I took another look around. "If this is related to what I witnessed on the train yesterday, I'd assume it's the latter. Have you IDed him yet?"

Adrian held up a plastic bag with a wallet inside. "The picture on his license doesn't match what he looks like now, so it could be a plant, but that's unlikely."

"And?" I asked.

"Finn Everette, lived in Silver Spring, worked for an environmental non-profit."

"This bar doesn't look like it would be a hotbed of people who hate the environment, but you never know." A part of me wished there would be a motive this simple, even though I knew there wouldn't be.

"And how does . . . how does dust work?" Adrian asked. "If this wasn't premeditated, is it feasible he would have had so much dust just lying around wherever they keep it?"

"Probably," I said. "Every fae produces it. They can't regulate who *has* it, only how much they use. It's rare that they ever store it outside of themselves." I thought of the small bag Dirk had and the significance of Etty giving it to him. "This is just a hunch, but I doubt the shriveled state of him has much to do with the iron he swallowed. If we think of dust as something like blood, this looks like he bled himself dry."

I looked around the room again while I let the information sink in, and tendrils of fear began to creep up my extremities. If whatever had caused this man to go wild decided to come after me, what would *I* be capable of? How many people would I kill before someone managed to take me down? For the first time ever, I realized my training could be a liability, and I allowed myself to be glad that at least my magic wasn't working. However deadly I might be, the bird inside me was far deadlier, and I would have more to be afraid of if I had given in to Ray and accepted the power of his god.

Even so, I wouldn't be able to walk away and still sleep at night—not now that I'd seen this. If it was related to what I'd seen in the club last night, then this wouldn't be the end of it. *"How many more?"* the stranger had asked Gary after they'd poured blood into the clay statue's bowl. If there was only one more, it would still be too much.

"Why were you two at the club last night?" I asked, needing to confirm the connection.

Miriam glanced at Adrian, letting him take the lead.

"We spotted a vampire at the crime scene yesterday, in the crowd of onlookers," Adrian said. "He was also in the photos of the crowd at another related scene from earlier this week. And a little digging turned up Bite as his workplace."

I pursed my lips, holding in a snide remark about how I'd bet vampires wished the invisible-in-photos thing were true. Instead, I said, "His name Gary?"

"No. Reginald. The one who pulled you away last night after our chat."

So that was Gary's real name. "Yeah, that's the one I saw feeding blood to the honey goblin. You make any headway with your research on what it could be?"

"Not yet," Adrian said with a frown. "I poked around a bit before turning in last night, but there's nothing obvious in my books. At first I thought maybe it had something to do with creating mead; there's a story in Norse mythology about a special mead made by draining the blood of a man with divine knowledge and mixing it with honey. The resulting drink caused madness—and great poetry, but mostly madness. But that wouldn't explain everything, and it's a stretch."

"That might fit here," I said, gesturing at the ruined bar around me. "But no one's handing out drinks on the Metro, and that's where both other incidents happened, right?"

"Right," he said.

"Keep looking." After taking in a breath, I said, "I have a way to get in close with the vampires, try to see what they're up to." I glanced at Miriam, who nodded at me from behind Adrian, giving me silent permission to go down this road with him.

"You mean you're going to keep dancing there?" he said. "That sounds dangerous."

"How sweet of you to care, but no." I grinned. "It's more dangerous than that. The owner of the club offered me a job in security last night. After seeing all this, I'm inclined to take it."

Adrian frowned, crossing his arms in a gesture I knew had

less to do with him trying to look powerful and more to do with him trying to hide his discomfort.

"I think it's a wonderful idea," Miriam piped up cheerfully. "I'll give you a squishy to wear when you go."

"Thank you, Miriam," I said even as I groaned internally, hoping she would make it a small one. "I start tonight."

9

"CAN I talk to you for a sec?" I asked Miriam out on the sidewalk as Adrian chatted with someone who might be his boss. I didn't know and didn't really want to know; dealing with two cops at a time was more than enough for me, especially when I had to keep secrets from one of them.

Miriam turned around and came up close to me, looking strangely pleased with herself. "I can't believe they went for it!"

I twisted my face at her, taken off guard by her peppy mood after everything we'd just seen.

"I didn't think they'd agree to let me call you just because you lived with a couple fae strippers for a year, but Crane backed me up. It's good he's so sweet on you."

I crossed my arms, eyes moving towards the building we'd just come out of. "How can you be so cheerful after *that*?"

"Oh, sorry." Her expression immediately shifted to a somber one. "I didn't think you'd mind. Fae dust has an unusual effect on me." Her whole body shivered, and for a moment I thought I saw something ripple under her not-skin. "I'm very absorbent."

"Great," I said, "so you're high."

Miriam just blinked and shrugged at me. "I suppose. But I'm

still capable of doing my job, thank you. What did you want to talk about?"

My tired eyes had drifted behind her, to a man sitting at a bus stop across the street wearing sunglasses and a fluffy scarf when it was a warm, cloudy day. The bodyguard in me was still a compulsive people-watcher, apparently. I frowned, then let out a breath to refocus on Miriam.

"Even if it's not much, I need to know what you found this morning." I pointed to my forehead. "If I'm going to see Soma tonight, I don't want to go in as blind as I was last night."

"I'm sorry dear, but it will take me more time than we have to uncover anything substantial." Miriam poked me between the eyes. "It's like a swamp in there."

"Isn't that your natural habitat?" I said, despite myself. I couldn't resist.

"Don't be so literal," she told me, shaking her finger back and forth. "Your memories have been tampered with, but I don't think it was intentional. Someone did a messy number on you. Vampires are usually much more precise."

Frowning, I chewed on my tongue. That was certainly not what I'd expected. If Simeon hadn't messed with my mind intentionally, it made the whole thing more complicated. It was easier to blame him if he'd done it intentionally—to blame myself, for getting involved with him when I should have known he was trying to manipulate me. *But if he wasn't trying . . .*

I shook my head, my desire to avoid these feelings lining up with the realization that they were irrelevant here anyway. It didn't matter *why* I was missing memories; I just needed to find out which memories I was missing.

Taking a breath, I wished this realization would loosen the new tightness in my chest.

"I've got to go, dear. Do you want a ride?" Miriam asked as Adrian waved her over to their car.

"No," I said quickly, although my bank account would hate me for it. I didn't want to be in a confined space with those two right now, and I needed to figure out my next move without having to play the game of keeping Adrian in the dark about my extracurricular activities with Miriam and Dirk.

Miriam smiled and turned away from me, then turned back a moment later. "Oh, I almost forgot to give you this." She handed me a pink squishy like the one she'd put on the back of my neck at our first meeting, but this one was no bigger than my pinky nail.

"You can make them this small?" I asked, a little pissed that I'd walked around for a day with that huge one under my hair if it wasn't necessary.

"It's not ideal," she said, "but you'll need it for tonight. If they find it, they'll just think it's a wart."

I scowled but lifted my hair for her anyway, letting her press the small blob on the back of my neck.

"You're lucky you don't have to do any paperwork!" she continued, then leaned in to whisper, "With your background, the boss doesn't want you on the record until it's necessary. You're quite the liability."

"Great, thanks," I said. That was just a nice way of saying they didn't want to pay me, but I didn't mind. I hated paperwork even more than I needed money, and I didn't want to get roped into spending any more time than necessary chatting with cops.

Miriam waved at me before bouncing away to get in the car.

I picked a direction and started walking before anyone could spot me and decide to start a conversation. Stuffing my hands in my pockets, I looked around and faintly recognized my surroundings.

There was a Metro station right across the street, but after my second sighting of that creepy Noah copy last night, I didn't want to risk going down there again. It wouldn't help me to get mind-fucked by rotting, laughing children and skeletons in the walls if I didn't know how to hurt them.

Things would be so much easier if I could just drive my own damn car, but I'd stopped using it weeks ago when it had become clear just how badly Ray wanted me to submit to Popo. The volcano god had sent a horde of obsidian bunnies to haunt my ride, and I was done poking that particular anthill. The weird rabbits were there to "help" me, Ray had insisted—a "blessing"—and they had certainly been useful a few times. But just like with men, it wasn't safe to accept any help from a god who was trying to woo me until and unless I had a plan for how to escape his advances.

At this point, I still had no such plan, so avoidance was the thing.

I decided to walk to Dupont, where it might be cheaper to get a ride since there were always cars there dropping people off.

And the walk might help clear my head. I really didn't like the idea of taking Soma up on his offer without having any memory of our history. I'd already told him flat out that I didn't remember him, so he knew he held all the cards in our relationship. Maybe I could make that work for me . . . I wouldn't have to hide anything except my real reason for being there, and he might even be inclined to fill in some of the blanks in my head.

I would just have to hope he didn't have some grudge against me. If I'd done something to piss him off in my past life, he might be "hiring" me to take a trip six feet under.

A familiar scent caught my attention as my body warmed from my brisk strides.

Coffee and cinnamon.

I stopped in my tracks and looked around. This was the same block where the Sweepers headquarters used to be, before an infernal djinn had burned it to the ground.

The same block where the barista that Miriam had reminded me of had acted like she'd known me.

Could she be someone else like Soma who'd been erased from my mind? If so, she might have some useful information about my relationship with him.

Unable to remember exactly where the cafe was, I turned around to get a better bearing on my surroundings. And behind the throng of pedestrians walking past me on the sidewalk, I saw a fluffy scarf and a pair of black sunglasses that looked familiar. The man from the bus stop. Considering that the bus would have taken him in the direction opposite from where I was now walking, I doubted he'd left because it was taking too long.

I let my eyes pass over him quickly, spotting the cafe I was looking for behind him on the other side of the street. If he followed me there, I'd know for sure he was after me.

I walked past him without sparing him another glance, crossing the street without changing my speed. Then I stepped into a narrow alley next to the cafe in an attempt to separate myself from the crowds of innocent people out enjoying their Saturday. Backing myself behind a corner jutting out from the wall of the alley, I waited and watched.

It didn't take him long to appear, his dark sunglasses reflecting the glare from above into the shadows nearby. I peeked out to see him standing on the sidewalk in a moment of uncertainty before he stepped forward. Determined to follow me even when he couldn't hide in a crowd—that had to be a bad sign.

He opened his mouth to lick his lips, and I saw the gleam of long fangs—an even worse sign.

That at least explained the sunglasses. Vampires normally toted around umbrellas if they had to go out during the daytime, but the cloud cover was so dense today that hardly any sun was peeking through. Big storm coming tonight.

I pulled both knives out of my sleeves and readied my stance, listening closely.

I knew he had the upper hand even though I was the one out of sight. He was a vampire, so there was a strong chance he was old enough to smell my blood from a distance. I'd have to make the first move.

I let him take a few more steps towards me before stepping out from my hiding place and launching one of my knives at him in a smooth motion. Speed was the key here. I didn't need to hit him; I just needed to make him react.

He dodged my knife, which bounced off the opposite wall with a sharp ping. Losing his footing, he stumbled to the side. I went straight for him with my other knife in hand, my foot swiping at his knee as he tried to regain his balance. Instead he went crashing to the ground.

I pounced on top of him, knife aimed at his heart, but he was quicker than me. He leapt up, practically defying gravity, and brought his forearm crashing into the inside of my wrist.

I cursed as the bones in my wrist cracked and my knife went flying, a wave of nausea and dizziness fighting hard against the adrenaline running through my veins. I gritted my teeth against the pain and tried to keep my head.

All bets were off now that I knew this was a particularly strong bloodsucker. He might be very old, or he might have just fed, or both—either way, I wouldn't best him if I didn't fight dirty.

"Okay!" I yelled, throwing my good hand up in surrender and backing away as I lifted my head to expose my neck. "You want some of this good stuff? You can have it."

"That's not what I want," he said in a gruff voice, although he couldn't help but lick his lips in the process.

Slowly, deliberately, I brought my arm in front of me while continuing to back away. "What then?" I asked.

He followed me, step for step, eyes narrowing in a predatory confidence. "You've seen them," he said in a near whisper. "You have to die."

Cradling the wrist he'd broken with my other arm, I took a deep breath and dug my thumb nail into the palm of my hand, willing the adrenaline to win the battle against the pain so I wouldn't pass out.

I cupped my fingers around the wound to let the blood pool, still slowly backing away as I gauged the new uncertainty in the vampire's movements. He at least wasn't pouncing on me yet, a good sign.

The one good thing about fighting vampires was that their instincts became predictable once the blood lust got switched on. Without fresh blood in sight, most vampires were basically just humans with extraordinary abilities. But if you were bleeding in front of them, the human part of their brains tended to take a back seat to the predator.

And all predators were wired to go after the easiest prey.

Once I had a good amount of blood collected in my palm, I flung it to the side and splattered it all over the side of a dumpster. Drips of red shone brightly against the dull green of the rusted container, and the vampire lunged after it without thinking.

Let him try to lick it off, I thought as I bolted in the opposite direction. He wouldn't, not unless he was a braindead out-of-control botched job, but at least this would give me a tiny head start.

Sprinting to the back of the alley, I focused on the door that should lead into the back of the cafe and prayed it wouldn't be locked.

The door pulled open easily, my blood smearing all over the chrome handle. A doe-eyed stare wrapped in chef whites met me when I entered, the shocked girl holding a piping bag over a work bench covered in cookies.

"Where's the walk-in?" I shouted. She pointed tentatively to her right. "Thanks—get out of here," I said as I ran in the direction she'd shown me.

I pressed my thumb into the wound in my palm again as I made my way through the kitchen, hoping a blood trail would keep the vampire coming after me and away from any of the other tasty morsels in here.

There were only a few people working in the kitchen, but they were all frozen and staring at me rather than running for their lives, which I should have expected. I made a mental note to listen for their screams, hoping they wouldn't be drowned out by the sound of the industrial-sized mixer ahead of me, which was currently kneading dough and filling the room with loud, rhythmic thwacks.

I made it to the door of the walk-in refrigerator and pulled it open, smearing more blood on the handle. If I could get the vampire in here, maybe I could keep him in for questioning. There was an open padlock on a hook by the door, ready to secure the expensive contents of the fridge overnight.

But when I peered inside, I was met with another doe-eyed stare, this time from a cook with an entire four-tiered wedding cake in his arms. A cage with a big, juicy snack in it for the vampire was not what I wanted right now.

"Fuck," I muttered, turning my head back as I heard a scream from behind me.

I just barely managed to get out of the fridge and close the door before the vampire rushed at me from across the room.

My body moved without my brain thinking.

I stepped out of the way as he lunged at me and grabbed his arm from the side to redirect him, using his own momentum to guide him down towards the mixer with the bread dough.

I thanked all my stars that the safety guard was open. His head went right in the bowl and got whacked by the dough hook, which quickly worked his blood into the lump of dough.

Eyes wide, I took the opportunity in front of me and wrapped my arms around him, the good one over his torso and the bad one between his legs. Careful not to put any weight on my smashed wrist, I lifted his backside to dunk his head further into the mixer before he could get a grip on anything with his hands.

His screams were muffled by pink dough as the bottom of the hook made quick work of the soft skin underneath his chin. It wasn't long before whole chunks of his face had been torn off as his skull was crushed by the thick metal hook backed by an impressively powerful motor.

When his body stopped thrashing in my arms, I breathed out and took a shaky step back.

The mixer hadn't *exactly* decapitated him . . . but honestly, it looked like it was good enough. Taking the head off was the only way to kill a vampire without burning him to ashes, and there were still some pulpy parts of head attached to the torn-up neck, but . . .

Yeah. Good enough.

I moved to wipe my hands on my pants, a reflexive motion to try to wipe the violent scene in front of me from my mind. But with a bleeding palm and a fucked-up wrist, that wouldn't end well, so I stopped and folded my arms in front of me instead, one supporting the other.

I heard chattering behind me and turned to see the redheaded barista from before eying me sternly with her hands on her hips.

"Trying to make me a vampire loaf, is it? I doubt that will go over well." She turned to the doe-eyed cook beside her, who had gone frozen and white as she stared at the mess at my feet. "Go tell everyone we're closing for the day, Ira. Problem with the gas lines. No need for anyone to call the authorities; I've got everything sorted."

Ira didn't move, just kept staring at the dough she'd probably planned on baking before I'd gone and dumped a vampire in it.

"Chop chop!" the redhead said with a snap of her fingers, and Ira bolted.

The barista sighed and turned back to me.

"It's nice to see you again, love," she said with a smile. "But you could have called."

10

THE KITCHEN QUIETED as the redheaded barista stared me down, hands still on her hips. It was the same English woman Miriam had mentioned last night. I only wished I could remember her name.

"Sorry about the . . ." I tried awkwardly to fill the silence, but the mess in the mixer had even me at a loss for words.

"Are you going to clean that up?" the woman asked.

"I . . ." I glanced down at my mangled wrist, which hurt like an absolute bitch now that the adrenaline from the fight had started to wear off. Plus, I was apprehensive about touching a dead vampire without knowing what the phoenix might do. "I can call the cops," I said, reaching for my phone with my good hand.

"No!" She said it so harshly I froze, eyebrows raised.

"It's fine, they're my friends. I'll tell them you had nothing to do with this."

"That's not the issue. Do you think anyone in their right mind would come here for tea and biscuits again if word got out we had a dead body in the kitchen?" She shook her head slowly, bringing her shoulders along with it in an exaggerated motion. "Not a chance."

"Hmm," I grunted. She had a point. Although the fact that she'd thought of it so quickly made me suspect she might not be as innocent as she looked.

"Right. Darcy?" I met her eyes, unnerved at the reminder that she had me at a disadvantage. "I really don't care who this was or why his head is in my bread." She nodded at the mess beside me, her lips twitching like she was hiding a smile. "Heaven knows I owe you that. I just want him gone."

"Hmm," I grunted again. My head spun as the pain traveled up my arm.

"Can you at least help?" she asked, eyes lingering on my wrist.

I looked down, blinking as I assessed the mangled corpse. "If you get me a towel and tie his legs together, I can carry them with one hand. But . . ." I paused to glance around the pristine space, all gleaming stainless steel and white walls. "Where are we going to put him?"

"Oh, don't you worry your murderous pretty little head about that, love." She scoffed as she started to roll up her sleeves. "I've got it under control."

I pursed my lips, watching her wrap a long piece of twine around the vampire's ankles. I wasn't used to being the useless one in the room when it came to dead bodies, and this woman's attitude made me want to like her even when I knew it should make me incredibly suspicious. "What's your name again?" I asked.

She tied a bow over the double knot she'd made with the twine and stood up to sling a dirty apron over her shoulder. "Minnie Davidson." She flashed me a cheery smile, which was quickly replaced by a stern frown. "I won't forgive you if you forget it again."

After this, I was sure I wouldn't.

. . .

THE PHONE RANG in my ear as I sat on a stool in Minnie's kitchen watching her hack the vampire's body to pieces. She'd already made me a sling for my wrist and a delightful cup of coffee, and I wasn't sure yet whether I should be terrified of her or beg her to be my friend for life.

"Hey," Dirk's voice came through once he picked up.

"Hey," I replied. "You need to take Noah and go stay with my brother for a while. Make sure you pack enough for a week, just in case. Tell the kid to bring all his homework if he wants to impress Carina."

"Hang on, what?" The floor creaked and a door shut before Dirk said, "What happened?"

"Vampire just tried to kill me. Which means they're after me too now, and my apartment's not safe."

"Frog balls," Dirk said. "Alright, but I'm going to one of our safehouses if I'm going to risk moving. Don't know your brother and I don't trust him."

"You have my kid with you, and he's not going anywhere I haven't checked out personally." I paused, gut twisting at the realization that Dirk didn't have to take orders from me. He still had to work with me, though, and I hoped he knew when to pick his battles. "I'll vouch for Ray. And I'll owe you."

"Fine," he said after a long pause, then chuckled. "I never say no to a pretty girl owing me a favor."

I breathed out a disgusted sigh of relief. Adrian had warned me long ago about how much Dirk needed to feel like the boss, but lucky for me the misogyny in him was strong. He wouldn't feel threatened by me unless I somehow grew a dick.

"Grab my green bag out of the closet," I said, emboldened. "I'll need it for tonight. Just texted you Ray's address and I'll be there in a bit to fill you in on the details." I took a breath. "Wait . . . did you say frog balls?"

"Yeah." Dirk lowered his voice to a whisper. "I think this kid can hear me through the walls."

I laughed compulsively, then went quiet when Minnie looked up at me with her mascara running from sweat and her lips parted as she took heavy breaths. Cutting through bone was hard work.

Not the time for laughter—noted, I thought. I'd tried to convince her to let me help, but she'd had none of that after getting a closer look at my wrist. Yet another reason I needed to pay Ray a visit.

"Are you having frog balls without me, Uncle Dirk?" Noah's voice came through faintly over the line, and I scrunched my brows together in confusion.

"Nope, just telling Darcy how much you love them," Dirk said. "Go get all your school stuff together; we're going on a trip." He lowered his voice and said to me, "We had peas earlier. Found 'em in your freezer and did 'em up with lots of butter."

"Ah, frog balls . . ." I said with a groan. I couldn't get Noah to eat a vegetable if my life depended on it, but apparently butter and humor were magic ingredients.

Dirk was quiet for a moment, and I thought I heard a woman's voice muffled in the background.

"Is someone else there?" I asked, my good fist clenching. If Dirk had invited a stranger into my home without asking—and with Noah there—I would kill him no matter what the Guardians had to say about it.

"Nope, just the TV," Dirk said quickly. "Gotta go, see you soon." He hung up on me before I could yell at him and left me frowning, which Minnie at least seemed to approve of.

Shaking my head, I tried to put Noah out of my mind. He'd be with Ray and Carina soon, and I at least trusted them to keep him alive.

I sent off a quick text to Kat, asking her to cover my shift tonight, and she responded just as quickly that she'd love to. I'd been training her at the bar lately, and she was the only one I trusted not to burn the place down who wasn't already working tonight.

With that taken care of, I ran my finger over the dark screen on my phone, tempted to text Adrian about what had just happened. Miriam would already know because of the squishy she'd put on me earlier, but she'd keep it to herself unless I said something.

It didn't feel right to keep this from the cops, but Minnie would probably try to hack me to pieces next if I told. And I still needed to ask her if she knew anything about Soma. She was the only link I had left, with Miriam unable to pick through my brain today.

Soma . . . I frowned, eyes glazing over as I sank deep into my thoughts.

Going to see a vampire after one had just tried to kill me didn't sound like a great plan, even without the whole missing memory curveball. But Soma was already planning on seeing me tonight, so it wouldn't make sense for him to send a goon after me beforehand. If he did want to kill me, he'd have plenty opportunity this evening.

No, it made more sense that this vamp had been sent by someone who didn't *want* me to meet with Soma tonight—otherwise, why risk going after me in the light of day and in a public place?

I blinked and turned on my phone's screen, and a local news notification caught my eye.

Someone was already reporting on the crime scene I'd just come from. Damn. That was quick. But when I looked closer, it was more than just that.

This reporter had also already made the connection between

this morning's massacre and the other incidents, and they had noticed something I'd failed to: the murderers in every case were supernaturals but not vampires. The first one had been a gorilla shifter, apparently. Yikes. Adrian hadn't mentioned that.

I grimaced as I got deeper into the analysis in the piece, which honestly read like it had been paid for by vampires as a PR move. *Vampires obviously aren't the dangerous ones, we've been focused on them too long, it's time to turn our caution elsewhere . . .* Hmm.

It only convinced me further that vampires were behind both the massacres and the missing kids, and I didn't like the idea that they might be doing it intentionally just to bring about articles like this one.

Minnie let out a long breath and wiped her forearm across her face, some of the blood mingling with her sweat despite her best efforts. She'd finally gotten the vampire all portioned out on sheet trays, it looked like. "Open the oven for me, love?" she said to me, and I obliged.

She slid four huge trays onto the four huge racks in the oven, filling it entirely with chopped-up vampire.

"Will he burn up in there?" I asked, half wondering why I'd never thought of disposing of a body this way.

"Oh no, not at all—not unless we want to fill this place with smoke and attract the fire department." Minnie laughed. "No, this'll dry him out like jerky so I can grind his bones to make my bread."

I opened my mouth, then glanced over to the empty plate where I'd been sitting, which had contained a piece of Minnie's handmade bread just moments ago, toasted and slathered with butter.

She laughed again, shaking her head at me. "Just kidding. Bones would make terrible bread. But vampire powder looks much less suspicious than hunks of meat. Once he's all dried out and pulverized, I can toss him in the bin and forget he was ever here."

She was so nonchalant about it that I had to wonder if she'd done this before. In fact, I wasn't so much wondering as I was certain. There'd been no panicked reaction to the gory dead body, no long moments of indecision—just calm, collected action. This woman had absolutely disposed of dead bodies before, and probably more than once.

I narrowed my eyes at her and did my best to cross my arms. "Your cooks, the ones who saw . . ." I nodded my head towards the oven. "How can you be sure they'll keep quiet?"

Wiping her hands clean, Minnie looked me dead in the eyes. "The same way I'm sure you don't remember who I am."

I opened my mouth to challenge her, but she cut me off with a finger wag before I could say anything.

"Hold on, love. Let me clean up a bit and then we can sit down upstairs for a chat." She turned to start scrubbing down the station where she'd been doing all the cutting, and I downed the last of my coffee, wishing I had at least some idea of what to expect.

Less than half an hour later, we both settled into comfortable cushy chairs in her studio above the cafe, where I'd seen Miriam having tea with Noah's zombie mother the last time I'd been here.

I had a fresh cup of coffee and Minnie had made herself a small pot of Earl Grey. I hadn't had a chance to look around the space before, but now that I could let my eyes wander I found myself in awe of the brightly colored canvasses all around us. Light filtered in through the windows with a more magical quality than it did downstairs, and the air seemed to have a warm golden sheen to it even though it was still early afternoon.

"We first met in London, last year," Minnie said after taking a sip of her tea.

"Where Simeon was killed . . ." I interrupted, and she gave me a brief nod.

"Precisely," she said. "You don't remember it all, I'm sure. I'm sorry, that's my fault. I can go a bit overboard on people's minds if I'm not careful. And I had less control back then." She lifted her hand to tuck a loose strand of hair behind her ear, and her fingers lingered on her earring, a gleaming black feather that looked like it might be obsidian.

"Wait . . . you're the one *responsible* for my missing memories?" My head was already spinning with the implications.

Minnie nodded, taking a long sip of tea.

"All of them?" I asked. Miriam had told me just minutes ago that she didn't think it was a vampire who'd screwed with my brain, but I hadn't even considered believing her until now—that was how sure I'd been that my scrambled mind was Simeon's fault. If that wasn't the whole story . . . I shivered, pressing the warm side of the coffee mug against my lips.

Minnie gave me a shrug. "Probably? I took a lot. But I have no way of knowing if someone else has been digging around in there too." She made a little circle with her finger as she pointed at my head. "Tell me, what do you remember from that night? When your man was killed. That's when it happened, so your missing memories should all be linked to that one."

"I remember . . ." I stopped myself and looked down at my coffee, not wanting to say it out loud even now.

Simeon and I had been in his hotel room before it happened, drinking and fooling around. Expensive whiskey and a childish game of stripping and laughter. The pinnacle of my failure—I'd given in to his charm and the nonsensical distractions that came with it, let myself break rules that should never be broken. Even if he hadn't died that night, I still could never forgive myself for that.

I cleared my throat. I didn't trust this woman in front of me one bit, but I needed her help badly. Now was not the time to get precious with the details of my past.

"I remember that I didn't see her coming, the blonde woman. And he didn't smell her. She was wearing a ward to hide her scent, and it worked even on a vampire as old as him. She didn't have any weapons, so she didn't look like much of a threat in that first moment, but she used magic . . . His head was rolling on the carpet before either of us could move."

I shook my head, trying to recall more details, but it was foggy. Like the image of Soma disappearing from my mind seconds after I'd looked at it last night, the memories around Simeon's death felt slippery. I didn't want to linger on them—I had *avoided* lingering on them all this time, since it had happened —and I'd always thought that was because of his effect on me. The vampire magic invading my brain. But now . . .

"That's all," I said slowly, shocked at the realization. "That's all I remember."

Minnie pressed her lips together and nodded, sympathy in her eyes.

"Why did you do this to me?" I asked.

"It was all a bit of a mess," she said. "Do you remember Evan?"

I nodded. Evan had been Simeon's assistant at the time— "assistant" being a polite way of saying "pet human." All vampires had them, though they didn't advertise it. The relationships were consensual and somewhat mutually beneficial, although Evan had been a strange case.

"He and I go way back," Minnie said. "He recommended me to your senator when you came to town, and I was there to offer my services."

I tightened my hands around the coffee mug, trying to process this new information without giving in to the anger welling up inside of me. It was possibly the most frustrating thing I'd ever experienced, to be confronted with this knowledge that had been taken from me. I'd never be able to fully trust what this woman was telling me because it was only a second-hand account—but it was a second-hand account of my own life. It should still belong to me.

"Anyway," she continued, "the killer fled as quickly as she came, leaving you and Evan understandably distraught. Evan attacked you, you attacked him back, and then I came after you to protect him. I only wanted to put you out for a minute to stop the fighting, but—like I said—I had much less control back then. I truly am sorry."

I went quiet for a moment, not looking at her. This was all a mess. Not just what she was telling me—which did sound like a huge mess—but the fact that I had no way of processing any of this information efficiently.

I couldn't trust Minnie. To my knowledge, we'd never met before I'd wandered into her cafe a couple months ago on my way to the Sweepers' doomed headquarters. No matter how impressive her body-disposal skills or how delicious her coffee, she was a stranger with unknown motives.

"Why are you even here?" I asked, looking her in the eyes. "In DC. If you were in London then . . ."

"Oh." A slight smile graced her lips as she absently fingered one of the pendants hanging from her ears. "I married an American. Swept me off my feet . . . you know how it goes."

I pursed my lips at her, deeply rattled by the reminder of how she *knew* I knew what it felt like to be swept off my feet in love. She had stolen the feeling from me when she'd stolen my memories.

She coughed, casting her eyes down. "I would have tried to tell you all this sooner . . . but I wasn't sure you'd want to hear it."

"Why the hell not?"

"Because I can't fix what's done. Everything I took, it's gone. Well, some small bits I remember, but that's mostly emotions—feelings so strong I couldn't forget them if I tried."

"You remember that night better than I do, though. His death. Because you were there."

She nodded, taking a sip of her tea.

"Was there another vampire there?" If the memories Minnie had taken from me were all tied to that night, as she'd said, that meant either Soma had been there too or someone else had erased him from my mind.

"No," she said. "Why do you ask?"

"Because I met a vampire last night who knew me well—very well—and I have no memory of him at all. You said all my missing memories would be tied to that night, so . . ."

Minnie let her eyes drift to the side for a moment, then narrowed them back on me. "There weren't any other vampires there, but you *were* talking about one right before it happened."

I raised my eyebrows, my chest tightening in anticipation.

"I don't remember the details," Minnie continued. "I had no context, really. But I remember it was one of the senator's rivals. A powerful vampire, back here in the States, and you suspected he meant to have your man killed."

I sat up straight, a chill running up my spine, fingers turning white on the handle of my mug. "What was his name?"

Minnie shook her head slowly, biting her lower lip. "I can't recall. It was something strange; I'd never heard a name like that before. Started with an S, I think."

"Soma?" I prompted.

"That's it!" Her eyes brightened, and that infectious smile that couldn't be real graced her face yet again. She leaned forward. "I take it this means it was all me after all? In your head?"

Maybe it was, I thought, taking a deep breath and looking

down. I didn't want that to be true, not after I'd spent so much time hating Simeon for toying with my mind.

Priorities, I reminded myself. *Soma.* Had he been the one who'd arranged Simeon's death? He had insisted at the club last night that I shouldn't blame myself for what had happened. That it was Simeon's time, and that no one could have saved him.

The words had seemed friendly in the moment, something nice to say to spare my feelings. But now they took on a sinister meaning. Soma had been confident that no one could have saved Simeon *from him.*

I stood up, only managing a curt nod to the woman in front of me before I turned to leave the room. I wasn't sure I ever wanted to see her again, despite how helpful and pleasant she was making herself appear. If she had fucked my head up this badly once, she could do it again, and that made her more of a threat to me than any vampire had ever been.

"I'll just see you next time!" she chirped at my back, and bile rose in my throat.

I swallowed, clenching my teeth against the sensation. Attackers coming at me with weapons and teeth and bloodlust in their eyes—that I could handle. But the charming manipulation, the cozying up to me while withholding information that—

No. Information was too simple a term for . . . I brought my good hand up underneath my eyelashes, where heat and wetness had begun to gather.

All I could see was the look in Simeon's dead eyes as I stared at his severed head on the floor of that hotel room. The adoration, the agony, the sorrow. The betrayal.

It belonged to me, that moment. The responsibility for it, the memories of it. The hunger for vengeance that I'd almost let myself forget.

I remembered it now.

And suddenly, I was much more enthusiastic about the prospect of reporting to my new job tonight.

My chances of making it through my first day alive had just tanked immeasurably. But if Soma was the man behind Dirk's missing kids, Adrian's murder sprees, *and* Simeon's death . . . it would damn well be worth it.

11

"That looks like it hurts." Ray peered at me over the perspiring bottle of beer in his hand.

"That's because it fucking does," I said through the old belt he'd given me to bite down on while I tried to reset the bones in my wrist.

Despite Minnie's fine attempt at a sling made with one of her aprons, I hadn't been able to hold it perfectly still in the bumpy car ride over here.

And even with Ray's help, I couldn't magic crooked bones back into place. Healing magic was useful, but it couldn't do everything. I liked to think of it as more of a fast-forward button than anything else. If a wound would heal on its own given plenty of time, I could do it quicker with magic. But give me a genetic disease or a missing organ and we'd be shit out of luck without some real doctors.

After I'd pushed the biggest offender in my wrist back into place, I tried not to yell too loudly as I gently massaged the skin over it to make sure nothing sharp was poking out. Satisfied, I held out my good hand to Ray and snapped my fingers to get him to hurry up.

His touch was better than morphine, but it only lasted a few seconds. Once the damage had been repaired and he let go, pain flared up my forearm and through my fingers. Even as I opened and closed my fist without any issues and made a circle with my wrist, it felt like I'd stuck the entire arm in a fire pit.

The fast-forward button of magic didn't work on the associated pain, but it had been a long time since I'd been hurt badly enough for that to matter.

I bit the inside of my cheek, looking up at Ray and remembering just how badly he'd been hurt a couple months ago. Not only one broken bone but nearly every bone in his body—and they'd had to break a lot of them twice after I'd jumped the gun with magic healing on him.

"How long did it hurt for you? After . . . you know." I nodded at him, and he gave me a small smile.

"Still does." He took a seat next to me at his small kitchen table and put a hand on my shoulder. "But I would have died if you hadn't helped. We'll always be stronger together."

I shifted uncomfortably in my seat, and not just from the pain in my arm. "Have you considered . . . leaving?" I asked.

"Leaving what? The god my daughter and I have worshiped our entire lives? All the family and friends we've ever known?"

"Well, when you put it that way—"

"Not that it would help," he said, cutting me off. "Our power comes from our god. Without him, we're just as useless as you and I are apart."

"Not true," I said. "I wasn't useless before you ripped the mage mark off me."

He frowned. "Do you really want to go back to that? After feeling what you can do now, with me at your side and the full power of el demonio inside us . . ." Shaking his head, he took a sip of his drink and then set it down firmly on the table. "What you were before, that's like trying to grow a tree inside a house. Not useless, but crippled."

"Maybe crippled," I said, "but at least I was free. A house doesn't have to be a cage."

The pitter-patter of little bare feet running up to us prevented Ray from needing to answer me, which was probably for the best. I turned around to see Noah hanging on the arm of my chair, an uncharacteristically somber look on his face.

"What's wrong?" I asked.

"Carina won't play with me," he whined, then looked at Ray. "You said she was taking a nap, but she's not. I can hear her moving around but she won't come out of her room."

"I'll go check on her," Ray said, getting up.

My eyebrows drew together. I hoped everything was okay. I'd been looking forward to coming here today partly because it had been a while since I'd had a good dose of Carina's sass. She might be a hot-headed bully inside a little girl's skin, but at least she was always straight with me. And she could always make me smile.

I patted the seat Ray had left, and Noah hopped up on it. Tilting my head at him, I said, "She might just want some time alone."

"I know but I don't think so," he said quickly. "She usually just says so if she wants me to go away but she won't say anything now. I even told her I got an A on the quiz and she didn't care. It's weird."

"Hey, good job on the quiz!" I said, but the glare he gave me said he didn't want praise from *me* right now. "You're worried about her?"

He nodded. "Maybe she turned into a zombie," he said with eyes cast down.

I chewed on my tongue, trying to keep my face calm. He was thinking of his mother again, who had in fact turned into a zombie before she'd gone for good. Her soul was inside him somewhere still, and we'd had multiple lengthy conversations about how no one else in his life was going to randomly turn into a zombie . . . but trauma was trauma. Only time would tell how well he would heal.

"I bet she's just busy eating something," I said, trying not to linger on the zombie idea. "You don't like to talk when your mouth is full, right?" Noah kept his head down, and my stomach rumbled at the thought of food. "Hey, where's Dirk?" I hadn't seen him since I'd arrived.

"Outside talking to the goats," Noah said.

Yeah, that checked out. I wasn't sure how Ray was keeping goats in a DC town home—maybe bribing all his neighbors with fresh cheese? But you gotta do what you gotta do to feed your daughter when she happens to be a dragon.

Noah opened his mouth to say something, then snapped it shut when a screech filtered through the ceiling from upstairs. His eyes bugged out and he hopped down from the chair, running up the stairs before I could stop him.

I followed him all the way to Carina's room, where Ray was sitting with his daughter on her bed. I delivered a quick knock to the open door, but Noah had already run in and caught their attention.

Carina looked up with a red face, tears glistening on her cheeks, and my shock hit me harder than all the pain I'd just endured in my wrist. I knew she was only a child, sure, but Carina was the toughest child I'd ever met by far. I'd never seen her cry before—and I'd seen her get attacked and interrogated by a bloodthirsty assassin.

"Why are you sad?" Noah demanded, his hands on his hips.

Carina shook her head at him and then buried her face in Ray's chest.

I walked forward and put my hand on Noah's back to get his attention. "Hey, I'm gonna take care of this. You should go help

Dirk with the goats for a while, okay?" He gave me a skeptical look, glancing again at Carina, and I whispered, "She's going to want to eat once she's feeling better, right?"

Miraculously, Noah took my meaning and nodded, then shuffled out of the room.

"Hey Carina." I knelt down in front of her, the pit growing in my gut when I saw her fingers trembling as they clutched Ray's arms. When she heard the thumps of Noah running down the stairs, she lifted her head away from Ray but didn't look at me.

I gave Ray questioning eyes, and he shrugged. "She's been like this since we went grocery shopping this morning."

Ray didn't seem nearly as concerned as I was, but then he had known Carina all her life. Maybe this breakdown wasn't as abnormal as it seemed to me. "Oh?" I said, trying to follow his lead. "Yeah, I hate grocery shopping too."

"It's dumb to hate shopping," Carina said quietly, a tiny bit of fire returning to her demeanor. "And we needed to get ingredients so I can cook for my mom tomorrow."

"Mmm," I said, remembering all the times I'd fantasized as a child about having my mom come visit me. She never had, but I could see how the imminent arrival of Carina's mother might make her feel more vulnerable. "Why are you crying then?"

"It wasn't the shopping. It was on the way back."

I said nothing for a moment, hoping she would continue on her own.

She sniffled and wiped her eyes. "I saw a kid from my class on the train, and he laughed at me."

I almost wanted to laugh myself at the idea of this little bully getting a taste of her own medicine. But with her in tears like this, there was clearly much more than that going on. And not even mean little kids deserved to be made fun of. "Like the way you laugh at Noah sometimes?" I asked tentatively.

"No." Her voice turned icy. "Like the way I laugh at my goats sometimes."

Uh . . . that took a turn for the weird. "What's the difference?" I asked, genuinely not sure.

"Noah is my friend. The goats are food." Carina licked her lips and locked her eyes on mine. "He was *hungry*."

"I'm sure . . ." I started, but then my brain put the pieces together—she'd seen a kid on the Metro who had laughed at her. Putting it like that, it seemed ordinary, but I'd also been seeing kids on the Metro who wouldn't stop laughing, and they were definitely not ordinary. "Are you sure it was really him?" I asked her. "Did you see his face?"

Her eyes grew round as she nodded and whispered, "He's a monster. And he's going to kill me. I know it . . ." She hit the sides of her head with her fists and shut her eyes tight, then went still and breathed out.

My heart pounded in my chest, nausea creeping back into my gut. A glance at Ray told me he didn't believe a word his daughter was saying. And why should he? It sounded ridiculous. But Carina had obviously seen the same thing I had—a child I knew with a monstrous face. And she'd heard the same laughter I had, the laughter that had somehow been responsible for three public massacres in the past three days.

"He can't get you here." I said it more confidently than I felt it. "Not unless you go underground."

Ray frowned at me abruptly. "What are you—"

"Did you see him too?" I asked Ray before he could finish his question. I had to be sure.

"I . . . saw a kid and heard a laugh, but . . ." He shook his head, and I gathered only Carina had noticed anything sinister about the encounter.

"Look." I turned back to Carina. "I've seen him too." Never mind that the one who kept appearing to taunt me looked like

Noah and not this kid from Carina's class. "And so did your dad. So if he comes for you, you won't be alone. But I've only ever seen him underground. In the Metro, in basements . . . You're probably safe as long as you stay up here."

"What is he?" Carina asked, already looking more lively. I felt invigorated too, and I'd bet we both had been questioning our sanity. As much as I hated that this thing was apparently haunting my niece, it was nice to know I wasn't pulling hallucinations out of my ass.

"I don't know," I said, standing up. "But I'm going somewhere tonight to try to find out."

Carina nodded and wiped her face with her sleeve. "Can I come with you? You're probably going to need my help."

That sounded more like her. I smiled. "Nope. But I do need your help to watch Noah. He's outside with your goats now—you should go talk to him."

She stood up with another nod and composed herself, detangling her arms from her father's without even glancing up at him. "Sorry I freaked out," she said, and I was struck by how much her childhood looked like mine in this moment.

A sense of duty drilled into her so deep she couldn't let herself cry over something like this for longer than a couple hours, and certainly not in the presence of adults. For this to have spooked her so badly at all, the encounter must have been truly grim.

As Carina left the room, I was struck by the urge to pull her into my arms. She really was more fragile than she looked, the armor of her attitude and her scales only going so far to protect her from the reality of being a child thrust into a world of adult problems.

She might need my protection more than anyone else.

I stood up to follow her downstairs, even more determined now to get to the bottom of whatever the hell was going on with Soma and the vampires and the freak massacres.

Ray held me back before I could leave the room. "Who else has seen this thing?"

That was an interesting question, and I realized why he'd asked it when my answer was, "Just the three of us, as far as I know."

"Ay," he said, then muttered something under his breath that I couldn't understand.

"Do you think it has something to do with . . ."

"Our family? Maybe. If it really is singling us out."

"It could be just a coincidence that I haven't talked to anyone else who's seen it." But as soon as the words left my mouth, I remembered what the vampire had said when he'd broken my wrist in the alley. That I'd have to die because I'd seen something. If that something was the creepy laughing children with old faces swarmed with flies, then I doubted many other people had seen it too.

And if that was the case, it meant Ray and Carina could be in danger from whoever had sent the vampire to kill me as well.

Still, I felt relief in my chest at the prospect that maybe *I* was the only connection between Noah and the incidents that kept happening. If it wasn't a hallucination that had me seeing him but still a vision tailored for me specifically . . . that would be better than the alternative. It would mean Noah wasn't somehow responsible for all the gruesome deaths I'd seen in the past couple days.

"Come," Ray said, breaking me from my thoughts and beckoning me into the room next to Carina's. It was set up as an office, with a small desk and a whole wall of bookshelves.

"Wow, so you moved here 'temporarily' but brought a whole library with you?" I asked.

"I also opened a new location here for my business, if you remember," he said. "But I haven't heard you complaining about that."

I frowned, realizing I'd almost forgotten about that. "Why put down roots here if you're trying to get me to go back with you?"

"Because I knew it wouldn't be easy—and I don't want to end up homeless if you never come. Worst-case scenario, I'll lose Carina. But if I build a home here, she'll at least always know where she can find me."

I chewed my tongue as I watched him poke through his desk drawer. He had assumed from the start that he would fail to recruit me, before we'd even met. Part of me knew that assuming failure would often doom a mission to fail, but there was wisdom and strength in his approach as well. Whatever I decided, he wasn't going to let it ruin his life.

He pulled a notepad out from the drawer and clicked a pen open. "Now," he said, looking at me, "what exactly did you see?" I raised my eyebrows in question, and he continued, "I didn't get much detail from Carina beyond how scared she was."

"Right, of course," I said, and then I told him everything. The feeling I was being watched by the Metro tunnel walls, the behavior of the shifter I'd witnessed go mad, the little boy who looked like Noah except for his sagging, wrinkled, leathery face, the flies swarming around it, the way the laughter echoed through the space as if it had no point of origin, the dead faces in the walls and their dead arms reaching out to pull me in . . .

By the time I was done, Ray's face was twisted in deep thought as he tapped the pen against his desk.

"Any theories?" I asked.

"Maybe," he said. "But I need to check a few things." He got up and walked over to the bookshelves, running a finger along the spines until he found what he was looking for.

While he leafed through the pages, I peered around the space. My eyes landed on a book that looked familiar, sitting on a small table by the shelves. It was the book he'd shown me when we'd met, the one that was supposed to be for the two of us.

I walked over and touched it, drawn in by the velvety feel of the blank cover, the depth promised by that texture despite the lack of visible words printed on it. When I opened it, the pages seemed shadowed in strange places, hinting at the text that was hidden beyond a magic veil. I sighed, wanting it to reveal itself to me even though I knew it wouldn't unless I pledged myself to a god who wanted to own me and joined a family I wasn't sure I wanted to belong to.

"This is going to take a while," Ray said, making me snap the book shut and turn back to him. He'd eased into a comfortable slouch at his desk, a pen hanging from his mouth. "You'll be the first one to know if I find anything, I promise."

"Got it," I said, already making my way out of the room. "I'll get out of your hair."

When I came downstairs, Dirk was in the kitchen pouring white liquid into jars from a metal pail.

"Do I want to know what that is?" I asked.

"Fuckin' delicious is what," he said. "Been a long time since I had fresh goat milk. Want a glass?"

"No," I said, but he was already pouring some for me.

He handed me the small glass and said, "Still warm." The last time I'd seen a smile so wide on his face was after he'd gotten a lap dance from extra-tits Laura at the club when we'd first met. Maybe it wasn't the tits at all that did it for him and he was just weirdly into milk.

"Eugh," I said, but I took a sip anyway, knowing he wouldn't let it go unless I did. "Eugh," I said again. It was sweet and creamy and earthy, but "warm" was an accurate descriptor and not something I would ever want from a glass of milk.

I handed it back to him, and he shrugged as he took a drink for himself. "So . . ." He wiped the milk mustache off his upper lip. "You going to tell me what the fuck's going on?"

"Has Miriam briefed you about the crime scene from this morning?"

"She has. Said you offered up your undercover services to help solve the case." He braced his arms on the kitchen counter to lean forward and shake his head at me. "Woulda been nice if you'd consulted with me first."

"Should I have called in front of them to ask permission from 'my boyfriend'?"

He chuckled. "You shouldn't have told them at all. Best to keep things separate even if it turns out we're all looking for the same bad guys. If your cover gets blown, you're really done for. No more Guardian work for you, even in secret." Turning around, he opened the fridge and put the jars of milk in. "And Crane didn't buy that, you know. About us dating. He's not an idiot, just too polite to question it."

"I—"

"So you'll need to figure out another lie to tell him," Dirk said quickly, talking over me. "Anyway, I'm coming with you tonight. Mission just got a lot more dangerous if we add all the suicides from today to the missing kids, and you need backup." His eyes lit up for a moment. "Your brother has a flamethrower I can use, in case things get hairy."

"A what?" I asked.

"You know." He mimed the act of shooting flames at enemies all around him. "Bloodsuckers hate fire and I hate bloodsuckers. What time do we need to go?"

I sighed and sat down at the table, my body suddenly anxious for that nap I'd hoped to get in before tonight. "I appreciate the enthusiasm, really," I said. "But something else just came up."

"Oh?"

"Whoever sent the vampire after me today might have my brother and his daughter next up on their kill list."

"Meaning you want me to take the kid somewhere else?"

"Meaning I want you to stay here and help protect them all." I rubbed my eyes, then lifted my hair to show him Miriam's tiny blob on my neck. "So it's a good thing I told your partner what I'm doing tonight. He and Miriam can hang nearby just in case."

"They don't have any flamethrowers," he pointed out, and I didn't dignify it with a response.

"I'm going to get some rest." I looked at my watch. "Wake me in an hour. And Dirk?"

"Hm?" he asked, a slight frown on his face.

"I'll kill you if you let anything happen to them."

"That's no way to speak to your boyfriend," he called as I walked up the stairs, holding my middle finger out behind me and unable to keep a tiny smirk off my face.

I WOKE FEELING groggy although my heart was pounding in my chest. I could still hear the flies buzzing around me even though they, like the nightmare, were gone. That grotesque face on Noah's body still beckoned to me, skeletal arms surrounding both me and Carina, this time peeling the flesh off our bones with sharp fingers. It was the pain that had woken me, and the fear. Both things I'd always been better equipped to deal with when I was awake.

My legs shook as I moved them out from under the covers and planted my feet on the floor, and I cursed the lack of control I had over my body and my emotions when I was sleeping.

It might have been worth it if I'd actually managed to get in some rest, but a glance at my phone told me it had barely been half an hour. It was just past five pm now, and I had to meet Soma in a little over two hours.

After a few breaths to get my bearings, I stood and shuffled my way downstairs. Laughter filled the air, and I stopped short on the steps, one bare foot hanging in the air while my fingers gripped the railing.

No, I thought, *not here*. But then it came again, more laughter, and it didn't echo all around me like it had underground. This was distinctly coming from the living room, and it sounded like more than one person.

I finished walking down and turned the corner to see Noah, his usual face thankfully all there, sitting with everyone around the coffee table, playing a game of some sort.

Wait, no—not everyone. Ray wasn't there, probably upstairs still researching, so who—

"Etty?" I practically yelled when my eyes managed to process the familiarity of the dark hair on the woman whose back was turned towards me.

She twisted over the back of the couch to face me and gave me a stiff smile, raising her hand in a wave. "Hi," she said. "Sorry, I was napping when you got here, and then *you* were napping, and—"

"What the fuck, Etty!" All my grogginess gone, I sped over to her and threw my arms over the couch and around her shoulders.

She stiffened for an instant before hugging me back, and my head spun with the realization that I wasn't sure we'd *ever* hugged before—and that this was probably not the best time for me to get myself covered in glittery fae dust. But I didn't care. I was that happy to see her.

"Get a room, you two," Carina said from across the table with a scoff.

I held back the urge to give her the finger only because Noah was sitting next to her.

Etty, on the other hand, just shrugged and said, "That's a great idea."

She was on her feet and hopping over the back of the couch

before anyone could protest, taking my hand and dragging me into the kitchen, where she promptly poured a cup of steaming coffee and handed it to me.

"I made a pot when I heard you were asleep," she said, and I would have been even happier to see her if that were possible. "There's fresh goat milk in the fridge."

I shook my head and brought the coffee to my lips, willing to pass on the milk for today. "How the hell are you here?" I asked once I'd taken a sip.

Etty tapped her long nails on the counter in a rolling pattern, from pinky to thumb. "I snuck out of the fae realm—that place *is* hell."

I raised my eyebrows. "Snuck out? So they don't know you're here?"

"I mean at this point they probably know I'm gone. But I hope they don't know I'm *here*."

"You hope?" I tried not to let my alarm show in my face. If Etty was a fugitive again, I wasn't sure how I felt about her holing up here with Noah and Carina and Ray. Not that I'd want her anywhere else, but still.

"It's fine," she said with a wave of her hand. "They have bigger things to worry about for now."

"What does that mean?" I asked, wishing that for once she'd just tell me something straight.

"There's been an incident. One of our kind gone rogue, used a crapton of dust and did a crapton of damage." She leaned forward a little. "I mean like *colossal* compared to my thing."

I stiffened in recognition. Could she be talking about the crime scene I'd crashed this morning?

"So they sent in a couple of equally colossal enforcers," she continued. "The kind that *never* gets out of fairyland. They needed an extra-special portal, and there wasn't time to enchant it with all the usual security. And I just . . . piggybacked a bit when they were leaving."

"Hang on, back up," I said. "These enforcers. What are they supposed to do over here?"

"Enforce," Etty said.

"No, I mean . . . The incident," I said, trying to take myself back to the crime scene. The golden eyes I'd seen in the alley outside came back to me now—could that have been one of these enforcers? "I think I know what you're talking about, and the guy's dead. Drained himself completely dry of dust and swallowed an iron doorknob to finish the job."

Etty jerked at my words, her nails halting in their tapping. She leaned back, propping herself up on the counter for support as her eyes moved to the ground.

"Sorry," I said, wishing I'd remembered just how sensitive she was when it came to iron. "Do you need—"

"I'm fine." She looked up at me again. Her jaw was shaking slightly, and I could tell she was trying not to be sick. "If he swallowed . . ." She shook her head. "If he's dead. Then they'll go after whoever made him do it."

"How do you know someone made him do it?" I asked, and she gave me her signature *"Come on, Darcy. Are you high?"* look. I almost smiled to see it.

"No one would do that. No one *could* do that on their own." She bit her lip in thought for a moment. "Humans are different. You weirdos are all about self-destructive behavior all the time. For us—when iron is involved—we just can't. He might have been able to drain himself of dust, but he couldn't have swallowed that unless someone else shoved it down his throat."

"Hmm," I said. That was interesting. I'd already been operating on the assumption that these murder-spree incidents weren't caused by troubled individuals acting of their own volition. But there was a difference between making someone go crazy and forcing them to do something specific like swallowing an iron doorknob.

Or tearing out their own throat, I thought, my mind on the shifter in the Metro tunnel. Then I remembered what I had noticed just before she'd gone wild, when I'd touched her—that it had felt like her soul wasn't all there. Not her mind, but her soul. Maybe that was how these people were being controlled.

Etty snapped her fingers in my face, a touch of glittering dust sprinkling into the air as she did it. "You okay?" she asked.

"Yeah," I said. "Just dealing with too much shit right now."

"Tell me about it," she said.

I knew she was being sarcastic, but I shook my head anyway. "I'd love to, but right now I have to go get ready to do some mystery work for the vampire who had my old boss killed."

I downed the rest of the coffee in my mug and put it in the sink before turning back to Etty, who was staring at me kind of awkwardly.

Fuck it, I thought, and I stepped forward to give her another quick hug. As distracted as I was by everything right now, I needed her to know just how glad I was that she was back. I'd been shitty at appreciating her friendship before, and I wouldn't make that mistake again.

She was startled again for a moment, but then she patted me on the back like I was a child and said, "Okay, Darce. Go have fun with your vampire nemesis. I'll be here when you get back."

A COUPLE HOURS later and after telling Ray my theory about the soul control, I walked up to the address on Soma's card armed to the teeth.

This was one thing I was glad for when it came to wearing jeans and leather now that I had no fancy professional clothes in my closet—more places to hide weapons. All my usual knives were tucked neatly into my jacket and boots, and I had a couple guns and holsters in the bag slung over my shoulder in case Soma was cool with me carrying openly.

It was a tossup, really, whether he would want me unassuming or intimidating. It depended on what exactly he needed me for. Either way, I was glad to have the thick, sturdy blade I normally left at home strapped to my outer thigh and a small axe underneath my jacket across my back. I'd needed to wear my loosest pair of jeans, and I wouldn't be able to do much back bending tonight, but it was worth it to have a realistic option in case I needed to behead a bloodsucker and no one was making bread nearby.

I smirked. What was I thinking with the "in case" nonsense? I fucking hoped I'd be beheading a bloodsucker tonight—Soma himself. The idea of finally getting my revenge for Simeon's death was like a carrot dangling in front of my head, energizing me but making it harder to focus on my official task of rooting out whatever new terror this jerk had unleashed.

I peered up at the building in front of me, wondering whether this was Soma's office or his home. It was a newer construction, rare in this part of the city, with sleek lines and dark windows that shone as if they were mirrors. I'd expected a vampire so old to spend his time in something that closer resembled an actual crypt, as Kat had jokingly called it earlier. In any case, I should be able to poke around and see what he was hiding. I'd sacrificed one of my knives to bring my mini lockpick kit just for that reason.

"Miss Pierce?" someone called from behind me, and I turned to see a black van with tinted windows, one of them rolled down to reveal only the driver.

Eyebrows raised, I walked over to the passenger side. The driver sat stiffly with his fingers tight on the wheel, wearing a dark suit and dark sunglasses. The whole thing made me feel like I was dealing with a politician and not the head of a local restaurant group, but I supposed powerful men all looked the same in the end.

"Please get in the back," the driver said, not even looking at me.

"Yep," I said. *Nothing weird about this at all.*

I stuck my head in after opening the door just to make sure it was Soma back there and not someone else who might want me dead.

It was him alright, although he had his hand raised to his eyes and was squinting against the light streaming in from behind me. *Alright, old man,* I thought. "Looks like you could use some sunglasses."

"Very funny," he said as I slid the door shut and sat across from him.

The joke was lost on me, but then I supposed at a certain advanced age, things like sunglasses must become inherently hilarious.

"I thought you wanted to meet at this address," I said as the driver pulled away from the curb.

"We just did," he said. "Now we're going somewhere else."

I nodded, already frustrated with how this was going. I couldn't see much through the darkened windows back here, and we were completely blocked off visually from the driver and his view. That was a problem, because Miriam would only know where we were if I knew where we were. So if I didn't know, I couldn't count on any backup should things go south. "Where?" I asked.

"Your first task," Soma said with a fangless smile. "It'll be a little different than what you're used to, but I'm sure you'll be up for the challenge."

I blinked, waiting for him to continue. He was being too mysterious for my liking at the moment. Too eager to give me vague answers to my questions so he could watch me squirm. If I stopped asking questions, maybe he'd stop being so vague.

He tapped his finger on his thigh, a remarkably human gesture for a vampire so old. "There's been some trouble lately, with some of the younger ones."

I tilted my head and raised my eyebrows, genuinely interested.

"They aren't allowed to create any fledglings until they're old enough, but some are getting impatient. Greedy."

I frowned, trying to guess what he was getting at. Vampires as a species still made most of their money from selling immortality—making more vampires in the process. As a business model, it wasn't exactly sustainable.

So it had to be an exclusive market, with strict rules on who could sell and who could buy. And that meant new vampires couldn't buy immortality as an investment and then go around selling it to anyone they could find to make back their money. They weren't allowed. Along with the hefty fee required, they also usually had to sign away the bulk of their rights and centuries of their lives to their appointed elders. I assumed Soma was one such elder, and he was letting me know his kiddies needed to be put in time out.

"What are they doing?" I asked.

"Selling their blood to smugglers." His mouth twisted as he spat out the words, and I found myself hating him a little less as it became clear his distaste for the subject matched my own.

I blinked, guessing what he was referring to but not wanting it to be true. "As in . . . ?"

"In bulk," he confirmed, meaning there was no way these vampires were selling their blood directly from their veins. It would be in bags, which meant it would bring nothing good to anyone who bought it.

"Oof," I said. Dirk had told me there'd been more blood on the black market and an uptick in botched jobs, and this was obviously why. If we were talking about unsustainable business models, this whole deal was even worse than what the higher-up vamps were doing "legitimately." I also supposed Soma's attitude towards it meant the mutated vamp who'd tried to kill Dirk probably wasn't one of his.

But just because he wasn't responsible for that particular clusterfuck didn't mean he wasn't the one nabbing kids or orchestrating the mass murders. And it didn't mean he hadn't ordered Simeon's death.

"So you know what that implies?" Soma asked, and I remembered it wasn't exactly common knowledge how much vampire blood would fuck you up if you tried to administer it without a live vampire on the other end. If it were, no human would buy it thinking they'd just scored the deal of their lifetime.

"I worked in a clinic when I was younger. Saw the results firsthand." I breathed out, wishing I could purge the memory from my mind. But no, apparently I could only lose memories that were useful. "Can't you just make a PSA or something? Educate people so no one's dumb enough to buy it?"

"You think that would actually work? Humans have been consuming deadly substances willfully since long before even I was born. All it takes is a shred of hope to convince them." He shook his head slightly. "No. If this knowledge were made public, it would only hurt our image as a whole. Make us seem more dangerous as a species. It's not worth it so long as we can stop the offenders."

What he said was all true, but that didn't make him right. People would always hurt themselves, but they at least deserved to know what they were getting into before going down that path. Not that it was in any way feasible for me to take it upon myself to educate the whole world.

"So . . . where are we going?" I prompted. He still hadn't told me.

"To stop the offenders," he said with a grin. "You'll handle the human smugglers, and we'll handle our people."

"Handle . . ." Heart sinking further, I frowned. I really hoped he didn't mean for me to kill anyone. I was all about killing people when they were actively trying to kill me or whoever I was trying to protect, but blood smugglers? They might not even know what they were doing. Certainly some good old-fashioned handcuffs and jail time would be more appropriate. "I'd rather not do anything illegal," I said carefully.

Soma waved a hand as if to wave away my concern. "We'll be taking them in for interrogation, of course. I'll keep you out of any more legal trouble." He raised his hand beside his face, fingers up and palm flat. "You have my word." His subtle reference to the legal trouble I'd already been mired in did not go unnoticed.

Well, then. I shifted in my seat, the handle of my axe prodding my lower back uncomfortably. I doubted anyone in this car was being entirely honest about anything tonight, but I didn't mind nabbing smugglers for Soma as long as he didn't want me to execute them on the spot.

"Okay," I said. "But where—"

A knock from the front of the car stopped me, and the driver rolled down the barrier to peer back at us. "We're here."

"Excellent. Thank you, Ellis," Soma said, then turned to me. "Come." He beckoned me towards the backseat, where he pressed a button to lighten the rear-view window.

We were parallel parked in front of a gray van on what looked like a typical residential street in DC. No street signs in sight, and I couldn't see much with the limited peripheral view.

"That's the vehicle they're expecting at the blood exchange tonight. Its driver will be here soon, and you'll be taking his place."

Great, I thought, heart sinking. It was going to be more difficult than I'd thought to dig up dirt on Soma if we weren't going to his "crypt."

That and I was starting to feel like an undercover Turducken. A Guardian agent inside a strip-club manager, now all stuffed inside a dumbass blood smuggler.

And the really fun part was that this last one might be the most likely to get me killed. With no preparation and probably little information about what the vampires would be expecting of me at this exchange, it would be a miracle if they didn't make me as a plant and kill me on the spot. Either Soma had an extraordinary amount of faith in my ability to think on my feet, or he really did want me dead. Without my memories of him from before Simeon's death, I had no way of knowing which it was.

But I'd have to see some street signs if I was driving, which meant Miriam and Adrian might be able to make it just in time to see a group of young rogue vampires bleed me dry.

At least I'll die with some friends by my side, I thought with a sigh, then slid open the side door and stepped out into the fresh evening air.

SHARP WOOD DUG into my back in more than one place as I leaned against a tree beside the blood smuggler's van. I was trying to keep a relaxed posture while tilting my head down at my phone, but with the axe underneath my jacket, I might as well have been wearing a corset.

It didn't help that I'd put on a shoulder holster for one of my handguns before I'd gotten out of Soma's car. I'd always prefer my blades for self-defense, but in the event that I needed to intimidate someone without actually hurting them, a gun would always be best.

Most people aren't nearly as afraid of a five-foot-two lady with a knife as they should be, but everyone shits their pants when you pull out a gun.

The images on my phone screen blurred as I focused on my other senses, trying to place every sound in my immediate vicinity.

The clicking gait of a small dog followed by a slight squeak in the boots of its owner, passing me on the sidewalk. The slow plops of raindrops on the leaves and branches above me as a light drizzle began to make the asphalt glisten at my feet. Windshield wipers turning on over the wet rumble of tires rolling slowly out of a parking space.

And finally, the soft chirp of the latches unlocking in the gray van beside me.

I tensed, ready to move. A man walked past me and around the car to the driver's side, his bright yellow sneakers all I could see as I kept my head down.

As soon as I heard his car door shut, I made my way to the passenger side and opened it, sliding in with a big smile and immediately pulling the seatbelt across my torso as an excuse to get my hand close to my weapon.

"Hey, cutie! How's it going?" I asked, voice dripping with honey as I looked him squarely in the eyes. I figured it was worth a shot after seeing how many men had melted in the palm of my hand at this line last night.

He stared at me in shock for a moment, and I had a feeling the friendly technique wasn't going to work when I realized he was wearing more makeup than I was. Pristinely darkened eyebrows arched up at me in disbelief as his forehead creased, and eyes ringed in black liner visibly rolled at me when he came to his senses.

"Uh uh, bitch," he said. "That shit don't work on me." He cocked his head and smirked. "Shit, even if it did . . . you gotta up your game."

Lucky for him, I was always willing to up my game. "Like this?" I pulled out my gun and held it low, aimed up at him, hoping he wouldn't look closely enough to realize my finger wasn't on the trigger.

He gulped, and his eyes flashed yellow for a moment. I could almost feel his skin crawling in the confined space. He must be some kind of shifter, and his instincts were trying to get him to fight me.

But if he shifted, I might really have to kill him. "Hey," I said, "I promise I won't hurt you."

He gave me a look that said *"Bitch, please,"* and I couldn't blame him.

"I'm working with the cops," I half-lied. "We're not after you, just need your help."

"Ah, fuck," he whined, shoulders relaxing at the realization that this wasn't going to be a fight to the death. "Man, I'm just trying to pay my bills—I'm just a driver. I don't know what's back there and I don't ask." He shrugged his arm at the back of the van, which was blocked off and not accessible from the front seats. "You gonna arrest me?"

"Not if you answer all of the nice man's questions."

"What nice ma—"

Ellis knocked on the driver's side window, and the driver snapped his head around in fear.

When he looked back at me, I smiled again as I nudged the gun forward to remind him it was there. Reluctantly, he rolled down his window.

"Please come with me, sir," Ellis said, offering the driver his elbow like he was about to escort a lady to a ball.

The driver slipped out of his seat without another glance at me, grumbling something about how this wasn't the kind of nice man he wanted to meet.

I climbed over the center console and let myself sink into the warm leather of the driver's seat, a genuine smile creeping onto my face. It had been a long time since I'd been behind the wheel of any vehicle, and this ride wasn't infested with volcano bunnies.

I didn't even care that I was on a crowded, narrow street in the heart of DC. It was nice to feel in control again, like I could go wherever I wanted whenever I wanted.

Except for right now, I remembered as a burst of static rang in my left ear.

"Can you hear me, Miss Pierce?"

Damn, that was fast. They'd barely had the driver in their custody for two minutes, but I supposed vampires were uniquely skilled in getting people to spill their secrets quickly. I flashed the lights on the van once to indicate that yes, I could hear Soma in my ear just fine.

"Good. Head to Wave and pull around to the loading dock behind the building. When you get there, ask for Mia." He paused for a moment, then added, "It's one of my establishments, but I don't know any employee by that name. So keep your eyes open. We'll be a few minutes behind."

Got it, I thought to myself as I turned the key in the ignition. I went over his instructions again in my mind while I drove, more for Miriam's benefit than my own. If I was going to be caught in the middle of a fight between vampires, I wanted to make sure my own backup was on its way.

IT HAD STARTED RAINING HARDER by the time I got to Wave, which was a trendy upscale bar and restaurant packed to the brim with beautiful people. Floor-to-ceiling windows on both the upper and lower levels made it easy to see inside, with bright lights and colorful decor downstairs and a dimmer, sparklier ambiance up top.

It looked like a fun place to be on a stormy Saturday night. As I drove by, I was struck by the thought that I'd never really been the type of person to indulge in such a thing. I'd gone out to places like this when I'd been in Simeon's employ, but I was always armed and in uniform then; with him, I could never fully relax until we were alone.

What a nice life it would be, to have enough friends and few enough responsibilities to be able to go out like these people from time to time . . . just for fun.

I shook my head, not sure I'd ever done anything in my life just for fun. Or certainly not for a very long time.

The windshield wipers on my stolen van were working extra hard by the time I pulled into the dark narrow road behind the restaurant. I took them down a notch as I slowed to a roll, trying to pick out which building it was without any of the signage or distinctive decor setting it off from its neighbors in the front.

Bright light spilled out from an open door for an instant, casting warped neon highlights on the rippling puddles in the road in front of me. A woman came out, letting the door shut behind her as she opened an umbrella and then leaned against the wall, looking out in my direction.

That might be my cue.

I rolled past her and then backed into the driveway in front of her, taking the keys out of the ignition and finding the silver one on the ring Soma had told me to look for on the ride over.

I popped out into the rain, boots splashing on the pavement as thick droplets began to soak through my hair. It wasn't too cold tonight, so it felt kind of nice.

"Are you Mia?" I asked as I approached the woman under the umbrella.

She might have nodded, but I couldn't quite tell without a clear view of her face. In any case, she sprang into action at my words, pushing herself off the wall with the heel of her shoe. With a small fist, she rapped on the door she'd just come out of, two brief but strong knocks.

Wanting to make this quick, I turned away from her with my key to open the back of the van. Hopefully I wouldn't find any dead bodies inside. I breathed a sigh when the doors creaked open to reveal two large coolers, empty except for the insulated ice packs lining the bottoms and sides.

When I turned back around, the door opened again to reveal a couple of strong men carrying a cooler of their own, which they planted on the ground before standing to stare at me ominously.

"Ah," I said, reaching into my jacket for the pouch of cash I'd found in the glove compartment of the van. I handed it to Mia, who made a gesture at one of the men after checking it.

He opened the door again to go back inside, leaving me with only two vampires—which would have been good if the light hadn't allowed me to see under the shadow of Mia's umbrella.

She might not be one of Soma's employees, but she was certainly one of mine.

Kat. I kept myself from blurting out her name, just barely, but the look on her face told me she'd recognized me as soon as I'd recognized her.

The hazards of doing business in a dark rainy alley.

Bats, bats, bats. I turned away from her quickly, bending over to open the cooler they'd left at my feet. The faster I could get the blood in the van, the faster I could get out of here and wait for Soma to take care of the rest.

Except . . . Soma was not planning anything pretty for any of these vamps, and I wasn't sure I wanted to leave Kat to that fate. At least not without having an opportunity to deal with her myself first.

Kat wasn't my favorite person—especially not now that she had agreed to cover my shift tonight and was apparently out here instead—but I didn't think she was the type of evil to be selling her blood to unsuspecting humans just to make a quick buck. She was one of the most popular dancers at the club, so she wasn't hard up for cash.

"Wait," she said from behind me just as I dumped the last armload of blood bags into the coolers in the van.

I froze, afraid to turn around. Kat might not be as trusting of me as I was of her.

"Is that you, Darcy? What the hell?"

I sighed, turning around with a half-smile and a brief wave. Kat just looked stunned, staring at me with an open mouth and not even any fangs showing. The burly vampire beside her cracked his knuckles and showed me a grin with more than enough fang to make up for Kat's.

"This not the driver you were expecting?" he said.

Kat turned her head to him with a little shake. "Well, no. But—"

It was too late for any buts.

The vampire charged at me, torso lowered to my height. I barely had time to move out of the way, and I stumbled in my haste. It left an opening for him to turn and swipe his arm around my chest, slamming me into the side of the van.

Pain coursed through my upper back as my head spun from the impact. But pain was familiar territory for me. The adrenaline had hit me now.

I smiled through my blurred vision, then leaned forward and pulled the axe out from underneath my jacket.

The vampire backed away slightly as I found my footing, but he didn't look scared.

Good.

I knew what I was doing with this thing, but I didn't want him to know that right away.

Stepping forward, I took a swing that I knew would miss, using the momentum to take me to the other side of him without giving him an opening for a counterattack.

From here, I chanced a look at Kat's face. I needed to know if I'd have to fight her too, once this guy was taken care of.

But she seemed bored almost, one hand on her hip while the other still held the umbrella over her head. If she cared more about keeping her hair dry than the outcome of this fight, I'd count it as a blessing.

I adjusted my grip on the handle of the axe in front of me while gearing up for my next move. The vampire rushed at me again before I could do anything, expertly dodging my defensive swing and bending over to grab the handle of the axe, his hands right above my own.

Well, hell. That wasn't good.

He was stronger than me without question, so he would win the battle of "grapple the weapon out of Darcy's hands" if I fought it. I didn't fight it.

I let go instead, slipping a knife out of my sleeve as I dropped to the ground and swung my body around his legs. My knife was in his thigh before he could turn around, causing him to yell and drop the axe.

I rocked my back to the ground, lifting my hips in preparation to kick out his knee from behind, but he turned around to get to me instead of leaning over to pick up the axe or remove my knife like I'd predicted. He caught my leg in his hands and twisted.

Sharp pain ran through the leg straight to my gut, making me queasy as I bit down on my lip to keep from screaming. I did my best to open my lungs and relax my muscles. It would be harder for him to injure me seriously if I wasn't so tense.

But it didn't matter. He dropped down on top of me, releasing my leg only to kneel on it, and he grabbed my wrist when I tried to push myself up, bringing it to his lips as he pinned my other arm down with his left hand.

His fangs sliced through the delicate skin on my inner forearm, paralyzing me more fully as his saliva entered my bloodstream. I gasped, not in pain but in shock.

Even after all my history with vampires, this was the first time one had managed to sink his fangs into me. Simeon had never dared, knowing it would be impossible to keep our relationship a secret if other vampires could smell a blood bond between us. I'd given him a few tastes, of course, just as I had for a lucky few customers at the club last night, but never directly. Never with his fangs piercing my flesh and his saliva numbing my nerves.

Now, with the full realization of what I'd been missing, I didn't regret it. It wasn't euphoric, like so many people had said. The wound itself didn't hurt, but I could feel the suction he was exerting on my insides. My blood might as well have had tiny knives in it as it was dragged through my veins in the wrong direction. My heart wasn't strong enough to keep the blood where it was meant to be, and it was getting weaker by the second.

Cold crept into my skull through my hair, which had landed in a puddle, while droplets of freezing rain splashed onto us both to wash away the excess blood that was leaking from the corner of his mouth.

It wasn't a good sign that the rain felt like ice to me when only moments ago it had been comfortable. The longer I let this go on, the harder it would be to do anything. But what could I do? This was the second time in so many days that I'd been pinned on the ground underneath a vampire, but this time I truly couldn't move at all. Not even to open my lips and plead with Kat to step in.

And there was only one thing I could do without moving. Ray wasn't here, but everything else was working in my favor when it came to magic. I knew from experience that the bird inside me wanted me to die even less than I did—after all, I couldn't pledge myself to a god and fuel its desires if I let a vampire suck the life out of me in this rainy backstreet.

Plus, if I focused my senses on my surroundings, the energy coming off all the blinking lights was immense—reflecting in the water, fragmenting and bouncing around as the droplets rained down and jumped in the puddles. Moonlight shone down through small breaks in the clouds on top of it, creating an image in my mind that reminded me of the tattoo Carina had torn off my ankle.

For some twenty odd years, that image of the moon had given me control. My body was a tool, a conduit for magic, and the mage mark had ensured I would have no competition or distractions when it came to wielding that tool. I'd lost control without it, overwhelmed by the god and the phoenix battling to take over the reins inside me. But could I get it back?

I let my eyes blur a little to focus on the shape of the light behind the clouds, allowing my imagination to take over until I could see the full moon in my mind. I pictured the image on my skin, where it had belonged for so long, and connected the soft glow to all the other lights around me until I could not only feel the magic but pull it into my scrye.

Eyes wide, I shifted my focus to the vampire. I had never used magic as a weapon before—not while I was in control. I tried to remember what the phoenix had done to keep me from becoming a sea monster's dinner, knowing it would be easier to emulate something I'd already experienced than to come up with a new technique from scratch.

Wind, I remembered. Wind that cut like knives.

I filled my lungs, gasping air to connect to the feel of it, then closed my eyes to envision it all around me, like I was flying.

Then it was inside me—in my blood—replacing the pain of the suction on my veins with a cool energy that flowed through every inch of me before exiting my body through my wrist.

Into the vampire's mouth.

He froze, fingers digging into my arm so hard it might break again. With bulging eyes, he managed to detach his mouth from my wrist before choking. Blood spilled out over his lips as he brought his hands to his neck, releasing me in his panic.

What happened next could only be described as an explosion.

A bloodsucker bomb.

Vampire confetti.

It probably had something to do with all the blood loss I'd just experienced, but all I wanted to do was laugh when shreds of flesh and globs of gore coated me in a warm blast.

A moment later, it sounded like a tree had shaken its leaves after a big storm as the more airborne pieces of vampire came crashing down onto the wet pavement around me.

My laughter filled the air, becoming looser as the rain worked its way through the mess on my skin. It felt comfortable again, although I was still dizzy when I sat up.

Headlights shone in my eyes, making me squint, and I sobered quickly when I recognized Soma's car pulling onto the street.

Fuck. The world spun as I sprang to my feet, but blood loss was the least of my problems right now. I turned to Kat, who was staring at me unmoving from underneath her now-gory umbrella, her face still miraculously clean.

She hadn't expected me to live through the fight; that much was clear. But I wasn't sure she deserved to be left for Soma to discipline just because she hadn't been a hero and tried to save me.

"Get in now if you want to live," I yelled, pointing in the back of the van with the coolers filled with blood bags.

She was smart enough to do as I said, although I was sure I'd get an earful from her later—if she wasn't terrified of me after what she'd just seen.

Fumbling with the slippery keys only a little, I managed to shut the doors to the back and get myself in the front with the engine running.

This whole night had just turned into an unimaginable shit storm. Not only would Soma kill one of my best dancers if he found out she had been here, he'd probably also be inclined to kill me after seeing what I'd done to the other vampire. And once he realized I was running away from him, with all the blood I'd taken from the scene, I was willing to bet he'd move heaven and earth to find me.

But I couldn't think about that now. I didn't have enough blood in my brain to think about anything now besides pushing my foot down on the gas pedal and driving away, as far and as fast as I possibly could.

13

THE TOP of the leather steering wheel dug into my forehead, slowly fusing with my damp skin as I groaned over the pitter-patter of raindrops falling on the windshield.

I'd managed to drive over a bridge to somewhere in Virginia, pull into a gas station, park in the darkest corner in case Soma was searching for this license plate, and then promptly collapse as soon as the key was out of the ignition.

Kat was knocking on the walls in the back, yelling at me to let her out, and sweet sustenance was only twenty feet away through the glowing windows of the station store. My mouth was dry—my veins were probably drier—and a dark haze descended over my eyes whenever I tried to move my head.

It would only get worse the longer I waited.

Fuck it. I might not be able to see clearly or walk in a straight line, but muscle memory and sheer determination could get me something to drink.

I closed my eyes and breathed slowly, un-clicked my seat belt and felt for the handle of the car door.

Something knocked on the window right by my head.

I opened my eyes and blinked until the blur gave way to a familiar face.

My fingers pulled on the handle, letting the door crack, and Adrian swung it open.

"Sit back, it's okay," he said, curling his fingers around the back of my head and putting the edge of an open bottle to my lips.

Sweet liquid spilled onto my tongue, and for a brief panicked instant I wanted to spit it out before my thirst took over.

I swallowed, letting some of the liquid run down my chin, then brought my hands up to take control of the bottle.

"Keep it slow," Adrian said, but I barely heard him over the new pounding in my head as I gulped down the liquid, which my taste buds were beginning to register as some kind of fruit juice. "Hey." He put his warm hands around mine and broke the bottle away from my lips, causing me to glare at him. "I said slowly."

Surprisingly, I could see him clearly now. The sugar was already giving me a boost of energy, and my mind felt quicker even though I knew it would take a while for my body to physically recover.

But a tiny spark of energy was all I needed to get going. "Thanks," I said with a slight nod, and he let go again so I could take a small sip.

"Your hands are freezing."

"That's what happens when you get vampired," I said, then blinked. Okay, maybe my mind wasn't as quick as I'd thought.

He laughed, cheeks creasing upwards as he put his hands around mine again, steam from his breath warming my face.

"Miriam?" I asked, and he nodded.

"We've been following you since you left the restaurant. Lost you a couple times, too." He sounded impressed, and to be honest I was even a little impressed with myself to hear that. If the woman who had a direct link to my brain had found it difficult to follow me, Soma could only be in a worse boat. "She's getting some more provisions," he finished with a nod towards the store.

At this point, Kat pounded on a wall in the back again, metal rattling between us as she shouted, "Let me out!"

I grimaced, rolling my eyes at the question in Adrian's face. "Don't let her out," I told him.

"Whatever you say."

"Actually, let me up. I need to talk to her."

He raised his eyebrows. "Ready to take on another vampire so soon?"

I didn't want to say no out loud, so I tilted my head and shrugged my shoulders. "She saw what I did to the last one."

"Fair enough." He stepped back and offered me his hand, which I took, then steadied me after I'd hopped out of the car onto my feet.

"Thanks," I said, feeling nothing but gratitude towards this wonderful human despite the small voice in the back of my mind telling me to push him away and handle my own shit. I didn't have the energy to indulge that crazy part of myself at the moment. "Can you give us some privacy?" I said instead. "She might be willing to talk to me, but . . ."

"Sure." He gestured over to his car, parked a few spaces over from mine, and then walked away slowly. He didn't take his eyes off me until I'd managed to open the back doors to the van without immediately getting mauled by the pissed-off vampire inside.

Kat glared at me from within, sitting on one of the coolers with her legs crossed and her folded-up umbrella acting as a makeshift armrest. If she was afraid of me after what she'd seen, she was being careful not to show it.

"Kat," I said, "or is it Mia?"

"Really? That's what you want to ask?" She shook her head. "I know I didn't just get bounced around in the back of a bumpy van for half an hour because you had a burning desire to question a stripper about her real name."

"Good point." I climbed in with her, leaving the doors open, and sat on the cooler opposite her. "You got bounced around because I didn't want to see Soma tear you to shreds after finding out you've been selling your blood out of his businesses. Don't make me regret it."

Her smirk faded as the muscles in her face froze and then went slack. "He knows?" she whispered.

"He knows someone's been doing it. Tonight was about figuring out who." I paused for a moment, to let that sink in. "He'll be looking for me now. And it would be a smart choice on my part all around to let him find me if it didn't mean I'd lose one of my best dancers in the process." Yesterday, I might have called her a friend before defaulting to our professional relationship. But now . . . I honestly didn't know.

Kat let the umbrella fall to the floor with a wet thud as she lowered her head into her hands. "You're such an idiot," she said, and I couldn't quite tell whether she was talking to me or to herself. She looked up at me, solving that little mystery. "He'll kill both of us if he finds out you're hiding me."

"I won't tell if you don't," I said, trying my best to exude all the confidence I didn't feel after nearly dying in a wet backstreet at the mercy of a vampire much less powerful than Soma.

"What do you want?" she said.

"I want to know what you were doing selling your blood in bags. I know you're not struggling for cash, and I know you're not stupid enough to think that shit's going to end well for anyone."

Kat sighed, and then her face hardened as she looked at me. "It's complicated."

"Yeah, so is fucking everything in life, Kat. Just tell me," I snapped. Apparently I'd lost a good deal of my patience along with my blood.

"It's not about the money," she said. "At least not for me."

I glared at her, hoping she would continue on her own.

"I assume you know how difficult it is to get approval for a vampire fledgling?"

"In theory," I said. I didn't know what went into the approval process, but I did know not many people made it through.

"Well, I'm doing this—" She tapped on the cooler beneath her. "As a favor to someone who's promised to help me get a fledgling approved."

I pressed my lips together, trying to make sense of what she was saying. "And who is this 'someone'?"

Kat went still, her face a stone wall. "I can't say," she said. "Not out of loyalty or anything," she added before I could protest. "He's protected. By the creed of our elders."

"What the fuck does that mean?"

"I . . . can't tell you. Literally, I can't." She looked away from me for a moment, up at the ceiling of the van, then snapped her eyes back to me with a short breath in. "You know how Etty was banished back to the fae realm? Deemed unfit to mix with mortals?"

"Yeah. But I don't see how that's relevant—"

"It's kind of like that, only it's not another realm. It would be worse than death for me if I told any non-vampire."

A vein throbbed in my temple, my left eye twitching. If that wasn't the most aggravating thing I'd heard all day . . . I sighed. I wouldn't get anywhere further with her on that subject unless I wanted to torture her. And I wouldn't do that without at least seeing what else she could tell me first.

"Okay, so this mystery vampire is the one who needs money so desperately they're putting deadly blood on the market to get it?"

Kat shook her head. "It's not about the money for him, either."

"What, then? Is he trying to turn everyone in the city against vampires?"

"No," she said. "Just against the vampires they think are responsible."

Ah, I thought. Here was something that made sense. "So he's framing Soma. Making everyone think Soma is behind the blood on the black market and responsible for every human that dies from it."

"That's my guess," Kat said.

"And you're okay with being a part of that?" I shook my head, still not wanting to believe Kat was that kind of person. "Everyone who buys that shit—their blood is on your hands."

"I'm a vampire," she said flatly, showing me her teeth. "Do you feel bad about the blood on your hands every time you eat meat?"

"But you're not even eating them. You're—"

"Using their deaths to make the world better. For myself and for my kind. I don't love it, but it makes sense." She bit her lip briefly and glanced out the door before turning back to me. "I can't wait forever for fledgling approval. Well—*I* can. But the human I want to change obviously can't. For that and so many other reasons, we need new leadership. First here, and then everywhere."

I tried to keep my reaction from showing on my face, because Kat would definitely turn ugly if she knew what I was thinking. She sounded like a damn fanatic. I wanted to ask her who she wanted to change so badly that she was willing to go to such lengths to make it happen. But that would only satisfy my curiosity. It wouldn't lead me to any of the information I actually needed.

"So this vampire is looking to stage a coup," I said instead. "And framing Soma for selling bad blood is part of the plan. What else?"

"What do you mean?"

"There must be more to it." I lowered my voice. "What about the kids that have been going missing from Soma's restaurants?"

"That . . ." Kat's face went blank again. "That's just a joke."

I raised my eyebrows. "I fail to see what's funny about missing kids."

"No, I mean there aren't really kids going missing. It's only a rumor, to make him look bad."

"If rumors were all you needed to make Soma look bad, then why *actually* sell your blood? Doesn't add up."

"Look, I'm not the mastermind here. But I'd think there's a lot more to this plan than I know. Soma's so dangerous because he's not in charge of anything officially. He runs everything behind the scenes while the politicians take all the heat. So we can't just go after him through official channels . . . Honestly, I thought you were a part of it when you told me you wanted to meet him. I thought maybe, with your history . . ." She trailed off.

"You thought your boss hired me to kill him?"

Kat smirked. "I thought you'd be getting that lacy number covered in his blood." Her expression quickly sobered when she picked up on the complete lack of amusement in mine. "Anyway, no one's taking kids. We don't fuck with kids."

"Who's 'we' here?"

"Vampires. It's our biggest taboo." She sighed and slowed down her words. "We only drink from those we might change, and children are never approved for the change. Ever."

"Why not?"

"Lack of impulse control, for one. Parental mobs and pitchforks, two. I'm sure there are more reasons, but I don't really . . . It's just not done. It's been this way for longer than anyone alive can remember. None of us would ever take a child."

"Right. Okay. Well . . ." I shifted my weight as I felt myself wanting to slump over in exhaustion. "*Someone's* taking kids.

Parents reporting them missing and everything. So whatever you think is just a rumor . . ."

Her forehead creased. "That's not—"

"It is, I promise. So what's the rumor? What have you heard?"

For a moment, Kat said nothing. But I could tell the thoughts were working behind her eyes as her face darkened and she slumped over to match my posture. "I've heard he's taking them prisoner, keeping them alive, feeding on them . . . and experimenting."

"What kinds of experiments?"

"I don't know. It's hard to imagine. I just thought it was supposed to sound gruesome—"

"Where?" I asked, cutting her off. My head was starting to feel light again, and I needed another drink but didn't want to take it in front of Kat.

"Underground," she said quickly. "Near Bite, where a few of his properties are clustered."

I pressed my lips together and swallowed, trying to keep control of my body as my mind made the connection.

The Metro station Noah and I had stopped at yesterday after getting derailed by the wacked-out shifter was nearby Soma's club. It was where I'd first seen the child monster pretending to be Noah, and it was a different station within walking distance where I'd seen it the second time. Not to mention that underground *in* the actual club was where I'd seen Gary bring someone else's blood to the honey-covered statue.

Could that have been blood from one of the missing kids? Were they somehow using them to take over the minds and souls of the people who had gone on murder sprees? I remembered the man I'd heard asking Gary *how many more* . . .

Fuck. If they'd done one last night, and one the night previously, then it stood to reason they'd be doing another one tonight.

I gritted my teeth and stood up in a crouch, then hopped out of the van and gestured for Kat to stay put. I still didn't know what I was going to do with her, but I did know I wasn't going to get any sleep tonight.

Those kids were underground somewhere near the club, and I was going to find them before another person died.

14

I WATCHED the dark neon lights shine briefly through the wet car window in front of me as Kat made her way into our club.

As far as I knew, Soma hadn't identified her, so she should be safe lying low for a while. I wasn't sure if she deserved to be safe after what she'd done, but I could figure that out later—and in the meantime, she was the only one I trusted behind my bar on a busy Saturday night.

The earpiece Soma had given me had fallen out during the fight, and I didn't have a phone number for him, so I couldn't call him to tell him where the van with the blood was. But I hoped I could eventually get by with the excuse of being too almost-dead-by-vampire to drive the thing where he'd wanted me to. It was at least partly true.

"Let's get her home now," Adrian said to Miriam, who was driving the police car while I tried not to fall asleep in the back seat.

"She doesn't want to go home," Miriam said, not taking the car out of park. She turned her head to look at me. "Darcy dear, you need to be able to walk and talk for yourself if you're going to pull this off tonight."

Bitch, I thought. *I was just resting my eyes, didn't ask you to talk for me.*

Miriam let out a huff. "Well—"

"I'm fine," I said, annoyed for the first time in a while that someone else could hear my unfiltered thoughts. "Sorry. Thanks. She's right." I sat up and cleared my throat, then took a sip from my third bottle of fruit juice. "Got a tip from Kat. She says Soma's been taking kids and keeping them underground near his club. I think it's connected to the blood they're feeding that statue, and all the murders. Gotta go save them now." I was fudging Kat's words, but I couldn't tell Adrian I'd already known about kids going missing before talking to her. I'd gotten that information from Dirk—from the parents of the kids who had run to the Guardians for help finding them.

Adrian rubbed his eyes before looking back at me. "That's . . . not something that's going to happen tonight. Even if you weren't so desperately in need of some rest, we couldn't go looking for these kids based on one tip without verifying it. I'd need to figure out who they are, connect them with missing persons reports, and then get a warrant."

"That's why it has to be me," I said. "I don't need to do any of that. And if I wait, another one might die."

I could hear how crazy I sounded, how hypocritical. Going in anywhere half-cocked was a bad idea for more reasons than just red tape, and it was true I didn't know nearly enough about the situation to justify this kind of thing yet. If we were just looking at another night like the previous two, after which we'd wake up to the aftermath of another murder spree by another unlucky soul, I would be going to bed right now without a fight. Because I didn't have a clue how to stop that, sure, but also because it wasn't a child in a cage somewhere about to be tortured or killed.

"I draw the line at letting kids die when I know where to go to save them," I said. Had I recently developed a soft spot when it came to little kids who'd been separated from their parents? Maybe. But Noah would have that effect on anyone with even half a heart. I pushed myself to sit up straighter. "Miriam, got any squishies that can help me out with some adrenaline?"

"No," she said with a cutesy scoff. "What do you think I am? A pharmacy on legs?"

Kind of. "Okay," I said before she could protest further, "I'm going to need some coffee then."

Adrian turned away from me and got quiet, which was a little unsettling, but Miriam took the car out of park and drove away from the club, leaving me to watch the fading neon sign in silence. I felt myself drifting off as the club got smaller, and the next thing I knew, my eyes snapped open to see a cup of coffee in front of me.

I tried to resist rubbing my face as I pulled myself up to take the cup, which Adrian was holding while glaring at me from above.

Steam caressed my face as I pulled the lid off, and the scent immediately made my stomach rumble. When I took a sip, my confidence climbed a little in an attempt to match my determination. My body had been through much worse than this, and I was reasonably sure I could still count on myself to perform in this state.

"We're going with you," Adrian said, crouching down beside the open car door to get to my level.

I raised my eyebrows over the cup of coffee. "What about all that stuff about verification and warrants?"

"Oh, we're not going after any missing kids—we don't know anything about that. We'll be chasing a suspicious armed woman who's doing something reckless. And if she leads us to some kids who need to be saved, well . . ."

"Got it." My lips curled into a smile. "Thank you."

"I'm not doing it for you," he said, and I frowned.

My head snapped back to the confusion I'd felt at seeing him so unbothered by my fake relationship with Dirk. Was this confirmation that he'd lost whatever interest he'd had in me? "I didn't think—"

"I have no idea what you're thinking," he said, cutting me off. "I just want you to know I'm not the kind of person to run around doing stupid things for . . . to help you."

"So you think this is stupid?"

"No, that's not what I . . ." He ducked his head and rubbed his forehead before continuing, "That's not what I meant. My point is I *don't* think it's stupid. I'm doing it because I don't want anyone else to die tonight." He opened his mouth to say more and then stopped, shaking his head a little.

I wanted to ask him what else he had to say to me, but I didn't like the look in his eyes. Even though he was agreeing with me, there was something making him uncomfortable. Not the usual kind of uncomfortable, either. He wasn't fidgeting, not nervous. He was still, firm—mind somewhere else as he stared at a spot of nothing to my left.

"What is it?" I finally asked, curiosity getting the better of me.

His eyes snapped back to mine, hard and clear. "I know there's something you're not telling me. All of you," he added before I could protest.

I just stared at him, the lip of the coffee cup pressed against my face as my brain went into panic mode.

"It's obvious you know more about these missing kids than Kat told you," he went on, "or you wouldn't be so determined to go after them tonight. And you can't really expect me to believe you're dating Dirk. I mean . . ." He looked down for a moment. "Miriam never tells me everything, and that's fine. She knows too much about everyone to go around spilling secrets without good reason. But you?"

Dirk was right, then. Adrian had known we weren't really dating. Fuck—why was I focusing on that right now? "I—"

"No," he said, waving a hand at me. "I get why you've been avoiding me, and that's fine too. But this . . . Do you not even trust me? Do you think I'm so incompetent it's not worth cluing me in on information relevant to this case? I'm not out here doing this for fun, Darcy. I'm a professional, and I *am* good at my job. Only I can't do it properly if the people I'm supposed to be working with make a habit of lying to me."

I lowered the cup of coffee, its scent suddenly unwelcome as a queasy feeling came over me. I wanted to look away from Adrian, but I forced myself to hold eye contact. Because he deserved for me to be straight with him or because it was the best way to *convince* him I was being straight with him . . . I wasn't sure yet.

He trusted me. That was the worst part of all this. He trusted me and my decisions even when he knew I wasn't being honest with him. Part of me couldn't help but think that made him a massive idiot—but I didn't want that to be true. I'd never had anyone put that kind of trust in me, and in this moment, my exhausted, dehydrated soul wanted to be worthy of it.

But it wasn't even a matter of whether I trusted him enough in return to tell him the truth. If I told, Miriam would know immediately. Even if I took off the squishy now, she'd know. So I'd have to assume the Guardians would find out. And then they would fire me all over again for blowing my cover, even if there were no obvious negative consequences of Adrian knowing. That was how it worked.

In covert work, precautions like this had to be airtight. Secrecy might not matter too much on *this* job, but what about the next?

I sighed, wishing for more brainpower than I had right now. But it didn't come. And it didn't matter, because in that moment

Miriam opened the door and plonked into the driver's seat with a box that smelled like fresh donuts.

"Shall we?" she said.

Adrian didn't look away from me, and I could see the disappointment in his eyes. He had to know Miriam was only helping me avoid this confrontation. I almost wished she wouldn't—but what could I say to him besides asking him to keep trusting me? The smartest move would be to make up a new, better lie he might actually buy, but I couldn't bring myself to do that right now.

"Yeah, let's go," I said.

He stood up and shut my door without another word, and the empty feeling inside me that my roommates had left me with months ago grew a bit stronger.

"Got any cream filled?" I asked, and Miriam passed me a bundle of soft, sugary dough wrapped in thin paper.

Donuts weren't as filling as friends, but for tonight they would have to be good enough.

"YARGH!" A sharp pain shot through my wrist as I used Adrian's pry stick to remove the bars over the window at my feet. It would have been easier for him to do, but my fingerprints needed to get on it in case we needed to pretend later on that this was all my doing.

I stood up and shook out my arm, circling my wrist to try to remind my nerves it wasn't actually wounded.

Miriam handed me her light-pink hounds-tooth jacket, then plucked a pin from her fine hair and shook it out until it framed her face like a plume of bright feathers. It had stopped raining, and the moonlight shone down from between the clouds into the otherwise dark alley we were standing in.

I'd been uneasy about this plan at first, but Miriam's doll-like figure was obvious underneath the silky white tank top tucked into her maroon pencil skirt. She was even wearing heels. Of the three of us, she was by far the most likely to go unnoticed in the basement of a strip club.

Even though I'd been down there before, I looked like absolute hell tonight, so it had to be her sneaking in first to scope things out. Adrian and I would follow when she gave us the all-clear.

"The dressing room is straight ahead, the stairs are to your left, and the room with the statue is to your right," I said, trying not to fidget.

"Mmm hmm, I'll figure it out," she said in a dainty voice. Then she slid open the small window on the side of the building and morphed into a human-shaped glob of pink jelly. She collapsed in on herself quickly, slipping down through the window like liquid into a slimy puddle on the bathroom floor.

"Yuck." I grimaced, averting my eyes as the puddle turned back into Miriam. That couldn't have been necessary; now that I'd removed the bars, she would have fit through the window just fine in her human form.

"I love it when she does that," Adrian said from behind me.

When I turned to look at him, he had a childish grin on his face, like a little boy who'd just collected some sort of swamp-monster trading card. Seeing it made my lips quirk up unexpectedly, and I held in a chuckle.

"Hm?" he said, turning to me. "You say something?" His smile was gone, and mine faded quickly along with it.

"Nope," I said. Then I tossed him Miriam's jacket.

He caught it and slung it over his shoulder without a pause, the textured pink fabric at odds with the sleek lines of his dark gray coat. It looked ridiculous, but the color suited him, and I caught myself staring at the warm tones in his light hair and the slight flush on his lips.

Luckily, something else quickly caught my eye behind him. I stepped to the side to get a better view and saw a woman in a suit walking towards us through the shadows.

Her red hair was slicked back in a long ponytail, which swung from side to side as she approached, and her dark olive complexion shone under the moonlight with a surreal glimmer that reminded me of Soma.

I tensed. She must be an old-ass vamp to be looking like that. Even Simeon had looked perfectly human when he didn't have his teeth out, and he'd been older than most other vampires I'd encountered.

"What are you two doing out here?" she asked, her stance setting off a few more alarm bells in my head. She kept her arms at her sides, elbows only slightly bent, subtle tension making its way to each fingertip. Not only was she ready to draw a weapon at a moment's notice, she was calm and controlled enough that I could count on her knowing what to do with it.

"Who's asking?" Adrian said as he turned to her, and my eyes bulged. He'd picked a bad time to suddenly not be the nicest person around.

"Club security," she said. "This area is off limits to guests."

I broke out into what I hoped was a panicked laugh, then let my legs wobble like they'd been wanting to do since I'd gotten out of the car. I closed the distance between me and Adrian with a stumble and fell into his arms. "I'm so sorry," I said as best I could with my face squished against his coat. "It was my first time here and I couldn't . . . I got a little jealous when she put her . . . you know . . . in his face."

"Can you give us a minute before we go back in?" Following my lead, Adrian wrapped his arms around me and gave me a condescending pat on the back.

I fought the urge to relax as his steady heartbeat and warm chest tried to lull me back to sleepiness. Twisting my head to peek at the vampire, I saw a look of utter disdain on her face. But her posture had softened, which I'd count as a win.

"Fine," she said. "But if you're still here in—" She stopped, eyes narrowing on something behind us.

I twisted my head in the other direction, looking where she was looking as I pulled myself slightly away from Adrian.

The bathroom window. It was still open, and pretty obvious we'd ripped away the bars.

By the time I turned back to the vampire, she had pulled a baton from her belt and was holding it out in front of her, legs apart and bent, ready to pounce. I supposed the weapon was for appearances, mainly—and because vampires preferred not to cause any bleeding unless they were hungry. This one could probably rip our heads off our shoulders with her bare hands, but she wouldn't want to make a mess. "On your knees, now," she said in a tone that was calm and terrifying all at the same time.

She brought her free hand to her face, and I recognized the motion immediately. She had a communication device on her wrist, and she was about to call for help. We'd be way beyond fucked if she did that, so I stopped midway to the ground and sprang forward at her instead.

I knew how to fight an opponent who was stronger than me, and I had to assume the same principles would hold even when the magnitude of strength was completely insane.

With a quick spin, I brought my leg up and kicked the outside of her wrist, causing her to drop the baton. Not an ideal target for my first attack, but that baton would give her a huge advantage in being able to reach me before I could reach her. And after this, she would react quicker to anything I did.

Keeping a healthy distance, I circled around to put Adrian on the other side of her, drawing a small blade with one hand while holding eye contact.

She only smiled at me, long fangs suddenly protruding from beneath her lips.

Bats. It might have been necessary for me to attack, but in doing so I'd given this vamp explicit permission to eat us.

Once I had Adrian almost behind her, I moved forward with my knife aimed at her heart. Not because I thought I had any chance of making that shot, but because I wanted her distracted while I shot out my leg again and the sole of my foot crashed into her knee.

Vampires were strong as hell and didn't feel much pain, but body mechanics were body mechanics, and a blown-out knee would impair movement for a while even if she couldn't feel it.

I heard a crunch before quickly retracting my leg, and the vampire let out a low growl as she stumbled to the side before picking herself back up and fixing her eyes on me. The fangs were still out, but the smile was gone.

Now I'd made her mad.

She rushed at me with clenched fists, not limping nearly as badly as I'd hoped. I braced myself with my knife held up. If I could get it in her heart before she did too much damage to me, she'd be stunned for at least a few minutes. And if I couldn't—well, then I was probably fucked anyway.

The knife pierced her skin but glanced off a rib as she grasped both my arms. But she didn't tear them off me like I'd expected. Instead, she put her face close to mine and then released one of my arms to touch her hand to my cheek.

Her fingertips were icy cold, and I could feel them shaking as her lips parted, eyes softening for a moment in what looked like horror before everything hardened again.

"It's you," she whispered. The way she said it, I couldn't tell whether she thought I was some long-lost sister or someone who had killed her long-lost sister.

Was this crazy vampire yet another person who'd been wiped

from my mind? Maybe . . . But if that was the case, why hadn't she recognized me earlier?

Whatever her deal was, I didn't want to wait to find out. With the arm she had released, I reached across my body for the long blade that was strapped to my thigh. I almost got it up to her neck, too, before she came to her senses and grabbed my arm again.

This time, the cold from her fingers crept through the leather I was wearing. When I looked down, I saw ice crystals tearing through my jacket and snaking up my arm like vines.

My heart pounded faster than it had all day.

Not only was this vampire wielding non-vampiric magic—which I'd never heard of before—it was *ice*. The same kind of magic the Sweepers and their assassins had all but pelted at me like a barrage of deadly snowballs just months ago. The same kind of magic used by the assassin someone had sent after me just before all that, to make me think it was the Sweepers who had killed Simeon.

And here was a vampire—one obviously connected to Soma—using that same kind of magic against me now.

Rage clawed at my insides, much stronger than whatever fear I'd been feeling before now. I was used to putting my fears aside in situations like these, but I didn't have as much experience when it came to fighting people who had personally pissed me off.

I unfocused my eyes to get her face out of my mind and searched frantically around me for the electric tingle of magic I'd managed to take hold of to kill that other vampire.

But it was weaker now, not only because it had stopped raining but because I couldn't tilt my head up to see the moon without offering this vampire my neck on a silver platter. Still, I strained to pull everything I could into my scrye, knowing I couldn't fight her with anything else in the position she had me in.

The cold was paralyzing, crawling its way up my arms and over my shoulders and down my spine now to my legs.

The vampire's smile inched closer to my face, fangs long and gleaming, taunting me for whatever grudge she had against me that I'd forgotten. Until she jerked suddenly, blood dripping out from her lips as her grip on me faltered.

The ice held, still pinning me to the brick wall behind me, but the vampire slumped to the ground as a red stain bloomed over the white fabric on her chest.

Behind her, Adrian stepped forward cautiously with his gun held in front of him. His eyes on the vampire, he crouched down to turn her towards him.

Her eyes were the only thing that moved, shifting about in a panic—he had managed to shoot her in the heart, stunning her where my knife and I had failed.

"Adrian," I croaked, my chilled lungs not allowing me to speak loudly. "Use that . . ." I tried to nudge the long blade I'd dropped with my toe. "Cut off her head before she recovers."

Not even looking at me, he shook his head, then ripped the vampire's shirt away from her chest to reveal the wound he'd made. Blood continued to pulse out of it, but I could see the skin was already beginning to heal.

"Hurry!" I yelled, but he still didn't acknowledge me. Instead, he pulled something out of his pocket, what looked like a small metal disk, and placed it over the vampire's wound. He pressed down on it, causing her eyes to bulge in shock, and my own shock nearly matched hers when tiny metal legs emerged from the disk to dig themselves into her flesh, stopping both the bleeding and the healing, as far as I could tell.

"What the hell is—"

Adrian's piercing glare stopped me as he finally turned his

head up to face me. I'd never seen him so . . . intense. Was he pissed at me for some reason?

He turned away from me then, taking a few long strides before bending over to pick up the baton the vamp had dropped at the beginning of the fight. He brought it over to me and proceeded to whack me with it—okay, it was probably more accurate to say he was whacking the ice I was trapped in, but it still felt like he was taking out some frustration directed at me.

After enough of the ice had cracked away, he stopped, and I managed to pry myself loose.

I let out an involuntary groan when my right shoulder pulled away from the wall, and when I reached up to touch the area, my fingers came away bloody.

"You're fine," Adrian said. "The bullet just grazed you. See?"

I turned my head where he was pointing and saw the bullet in question lodged in the brick wall right at the top of where my shoulder had been.

Thank fuck that vampire had been so much taller than me.

"What is that thing?" I asked, eyes locked on the metal object he'd stuck over the vampire's wound.

"New trial procedure for immobilizing vamps," he said. "DSC technology."

I blinked. "They're experimenting with new technology?" That was certainly out of character for the department that had been nothing more than a bad joke for the past two decades. I wondered if the Guardians had been doing anything similar. Maybe, and maybe Dirk just thought I was so much of a badass that I didn't need any super-cool anti-vampire gear to get the job done.

Yeah, probably not.

"They're experimenting with a lot of new things," Adrian said. "And now I know why none of them involve partnering with overly violent civilians."

Frowning, I rolled my shoulders while I tried to process his words. Me, overly violent? Okay, I could maybe give him that.

A civilian, though? It was technically true, but it still stung. "Is that why you waited so long to shoot her? You had that thing all along . . ." I shook my head, gritting my teeth. "She could have killed me nine times in that fight."

"Nine times? Are you a cat now?"

"You know what I mean."

Fuming, he took a step back from me and seemed to stand up even taller. "I'm an officer of the law," he said. "I can't just attack people preemptively to get myself out of tricky situations, and you can't either if you're working with me."

I fought the urge to cast my eyes down. He had a point, but that didn't mean he had the right to be scolding me like this.

"You know you're the one I technically should have shot?" he continued. "You were the aggressor. She was just doing her job, and perfectly legally. So we'd better hope her boss is up to something even shadier than what you just did and won't want anyone asking questions."

"I think that's pretty fucking likely," I snapped, trying not to yell. "Or I wouldn't have done it."

Taking a deep breath in, I calmed myself. Certain emotions had always been easier for me to suppress than others, and anger was one of the others. But as much as it threw me to see Adrian the gentle giant pissed off, neither one of us could afford to let our emotions run wild tonight. Not here. Not while we had a job to do.

"We shouldn't be discussing this where she can hear," I said.

Adrian looked down at the vampire, who was still frozen in place except for her wildly shifting eyes. Despite his towering frame and the blood still on his hands, he looked vulnerable all of a sudden. A slight shift in posture, a releasing of tension in the muscles of his neck.

Without another word, he bent over and lifted her in his arms. Her limp body hung over him as he carried her effortlessly over to the other side of the alley, where a few crates were stacked along the wall. He set her down gently, making sure her limbs were straight before arranging the crates around her.

When she was fully hidden from view, he marched back over to me and placed a firm hand on my lower back, guiding me away. We walked past the window and into the shadows, where he took his hand away and faced me.

"I shouldn't have lost my cool," Adrian said. But when he looked up at me, I could see the frustration still in his eyes. Somehow, it made my stomach flutter now that my own anger had worn off. "It's just you're always doing this—putting me in situations where I'm tempted to break the rules and risk my job. And I can't afford to do that. Especially when you won't even give me all the facts."

Ignoring the jab about my keeping information from him, which was perfectly valid, I glared up at him just as hard as he was glaring at me. "No one's forcing you to do what I say. You can always say no. Use your own judgment. I won't blame you."

"That's the problem," he said, taking a step towards me. "You fuck up my judgment. I don't know what's right and what's wrong half the time when I'm with you." His face was close to mine now, his breath on my forehead. He reached up with a hand and touched his fingers to a loose strand of my hair, then halted the motion with a jerk.

Disappointment filled me. I wanted him to touch me. Even though he'd just given voice to my own deepest fear, it sounded ridiculous on his lips. I wasn't using any mind-control magic on him. We were both human adults capable of making our own decisions, regardless of how much I really fucking wanted him to touch me, and apparently regardless of how much he wanted that too.

I reached up and caught his hand before he could lower it, then used it to pull him closer. My other hand snaked up behind his neck as I lifted myself up on my toes to reach his face.

My lips pressed against his, a soft and warm respite from the remnants of melted ice still soaking through my clothes. For a moment, he didn't move. Then he tensed, the hand I'd caught weaving into my hair as his other hand curled around my waist.

He pressed me forward, further into him, and I stumbled because he was too damn tall to be pulling that move. Our lips broke apart and our eyes met, my heart stopping briefly with the new unwelcome fear that this moment might be over before it had even begun.

But then he bent down slightly and slid his hands behind my thighs, lifting me up as I braced my hands on his shoulders. My legs wrapped around his waist as he pressed my back into the brick wall and caught my mouth again with his.

Heat rushed through me, in a way it hadn't for a long time. The adrenaline from the fight gave way to a different kind of energy tingling through my nerves. Different and so much better.

I parted my lips to let him in, my hands moving up from his shoulders to his neck. He tasted like coffee and rain, a burning hearth in the middle of a thunderstorm. I forgot everything else, losing myself entirely in the feeling, wanting nothing more but for him to be *closer* even though he was already pressed against me so hard I could barely breathe.

Something screamed at me from deep inside my brain. As wonderful as this felt, I had a job to do tonight, and I'd kissed this man for a better reason than just that he'd been asking for it. Blinking, I fought my way back to my senses.

Adrian must have felt me tense. He broke his face away from mine but kept it close, still gripping me tightly and not letting me down.

I gasped in air, sharing his breath as I took back control of my frustrated nerves.

"Now," I said softly once I could speak. "I'd very much like to go chop the head off that vampire you left paralyzed over there before someone finds her. What do you think about that? Right or wrong?"

"Wrong," he whispered, still in a daze.

I smiled and tapped my palm lightly on his cheek, getting him to refocus his eyes on mine. "Great, see? You're capable of disagreeing with me no matter how hard your dick is."

He kissed me again, though not with the same abandon, laughter vibrating in his throat as he eased me back to the ground. His amusement died quickly though, replaced by a look of uncertainty.

"Are you going to kill her anyway?" he asked.

"No," I said. "I'm capable of compromise."

He nodded, then turned his head towards the crates hiding the vampire in question.

"Look," I said, and he turned back to me. "I get that you have to play by the rules. Really, I've been there. But reality likes to play dirty, and sometimes you have to take risks if you want to survive. There's no rulebook that will tell you when that's the case. If you stop to think, it'll be too late." Adrian wasn't trained in the same way I was. He wasn't trained to put the mission above the law—he *was* the law. And while his devotion to coloring in the lines was admirable in a way that made my chest tight to think about, it would get us both killed if he didn't know when to let it go. "She was about to call for help, and I couldn't let that happen," I finished.

He took in a deep breath and shook his head. "She wouldn't have killed us."

"But she would have thrown us out. We would have had to

abandon Miriam, and I couldn't live with myself if a child down there died tonight because I wasn't willing to start a fight."

"Okay seriously, what aren't you telling me about these supposed missing childr—"

The clacking of sharp heels on the pavement beside us made him stop. I twisted my neck, half expecting to see the vampire back up again, but instead it was Miriam peering at us with her hands on her hips.

"Very rude," she said as she stepped forward and reached her hand behind my neck.

I almost laughed when I realized she was going for the tiny squishy I'd forgotten she'd put there earlier, but then she pinched me in her effort to pluck it off.

"Ouch."

"You deserve it and more," she said as the squishy reabsorbed into her fingertip. "Making me party to all that." She waved her hand in a circle that seemed to encompass me and Adrian and everything we had just done. "And while I was doing your dirty work, no less."

She jiggled a bit in anger, but it was easier for me to not laugh this time. Now that she was back, all I wanted was to get on with what we needed to do.

"What did you find?" I asked.

"Another way in, lucky for you." Sighing, she walked past us, snatching her coat off Adrian's shoulder as she went. Heels clacking down the alley, she lifted her hands to pull her loose hair back into a tight bun. "Follow me."

15

Miriam turned a corner and then stopped right in the middle of a dark backstreet. She adjusted her glasses and tapped a heel on the ground, then turned to beckon us over.

"Here we are."

It wasn't until I was standing next to her that I saw the manhole cover on the ground. "There's a way through the sewers?" I asked.

"They're *in* the sewers," she said. "I found a way in from the club's basement, near the room you told me about. A trap door. Well hidden, but water calls to me when I'm in my fluid state."

"You found the kids?" I asked.

"No, I only went far enough to find a way in for you two."

"Great." I dropped into a squat on the ground, eying the cover. I'd done a lot of unpleasant things in my days as a bodyguard, but diving into a sewer wasn't one of them.

Before I could wonder too hard about the logistics, Adrian leaned over in front of me and held out his hand. "Knife," he said.

Part of me wanted to lecture him for being so presumptuous. I didn't hand out my knives on demand to just anyone. But then, at this point he wasn't just anyone. And I didn't want to waste any more time.

I gave him my dullest knife, the backup of my backup, and watched him use it to pry up the cover so he could get a grip on it.

He lifted it easily as I tucked the knife back in my jacket, making a mental note that while he may not be the quickest in a fight, I had to give him points for brute strength.

I peered down into the dark hole beneath my feet and pulled out my phone, turning on its flashlight. I could see the ladder rungs leading down now, but not the bottom.

Oh well, I'd see it once I got down there.

"I'm going in."

My boots hit the ground with a splash, and I held my phone up to cast light through the tunnel I found myself in. Red brick walls curved over me, with peeling paint in some spots indicating they'd stood here many years. Probably built with the city itself, centuries ago, and then modified over the generations.

It didn't smell nearly as bad as I'd expected, all the rain from this evening's storm having diluted the sewage. Distant drips punctured the silence as water continued to trickle down from above. But when I took a step forward, water rippling out beneath my feet, a familiar peal of laughter overtook all other sound.

With a frown, I turned around to see Adrian get to the bottom of the ladder behind me.

"Hey," I said to him. "Did you hear that laughter?"

He shook his head. "Seeing anything?"

"Not yet . . ." My eyes fixed on a figure that looked like Noah in the distance. Even now, my heart jumped into my throat before he turned around to show me his hideous face. *It's not Noah*, I reminded myself. But I still couldn't bring myself to tell Adrian how much this evil apparition looked like my kid. When I opened my mouth to try, nothing came out, and instead I said, "Have you come up with any ideas on what we might be dealing with?" I knew Ray was working on it as well, but he hadn't called me since I'd left his place and he wasn't here right now.

"Kind of." Adrian stepped forward to meet me. "I couldn't find much lore about creatures made of clay, except for golems. I wouldn't have thought that fit, except the word means 'body without a soul.' And you said that's what it felt like when you touched the shifter, right?"

"Kind of," I said. "She wasn't completely empty, but not all there. Maybe like her soul was outside of her body but not gone."

"So close enough?" he asked.

"Probably," I said, although I wasn't sure.

He nodded, easing up next to me into a careful stride through the dark space. "Anyway, I had no idea what anyone could be doing with golems to bring about all this, but there's a common idea throughout mythology from cultures all over the world—that gods created humans by molding them from clay. So then I thought, what if this is all someone's experiment to create a new species?"

"Hmm . . ." I remembered the article I'd seen, the one that had me convinced vampires must be behind all this if they were the only ones unaffected. What would vampires want from a new species? The only thing I could think of was food. If they could have a new source of food separate from human society—*Farmed people*, I thought with a shiver—it would solve a lot of their problems and allow for nearly limitless growth.

"What are you thinking?" Adrian asked as I heard Miriam come up behind us.

She walked past us without a word, and I told them about my vampire conspiracy theory as we followed her down the tunnel. It all sounded more ridiculous aloud than it had in my head. "It's kind of a stretch," I said when I was done. "And if that's what this is, the experiments are pretty damn inefficient."

Adrian shook his head. "Maybe they're trying to create soulless people who can function without going crazy, like living blood bags, and the murders are all just unintended side effects?"

That didn't feel right to me, but I had no better ideas. "Maybe," I agreed. "If it is a golem we're dealing with, how do I kill it?"

"That's the tough part," he said. "There are a few stories of them being smashed to pieces with success. But then there are others where you have to find the source of what's animating them. It's usually a word of power, carved into the clay or written on a piece of parchment. The only consistency I found is the concept of reversal. Destruction is the reversal of creation—so find out how it was created and reverse that."

"Like throwing the ring into the fires of Mount Doom," Miriam said cheerfully in front of us.

I had no idea what she was talking about, and neither did Adrian by the look he gave me. But I got what he was saying. Not that it would help me any. The visions of creepy children I'd been seeing didn't seem like they were corporeal enough to be smashed to pieces, nor their laughter. And the rest of it was too vague to be of any immediate use.

Miriam held up her hand as we came to an intersection of tunnels, and we stopped behind her. Water settled beneath our still feet and drips echoed through the space.

After a moment, she ushered us to follow her down the tunnel to the right. But just as I moved to take a step, the soft laughter echoed towards me from the left.

I turned to the sound and drew my gun, figuring it wouldn't hurt to *check* on the matter of just how corporeal my visions were. Just because they flitted in and out of existence at the drop of a hat and no one else could see them didn't necessarily mean they couldn't bleed.

But I saw nothing there. It was only the laughter again, and it made me feel like I was walking into a trap. Whatever was making that laughter knew I was here, and it didn't care enough to do anything to stop me.

"What is it?" Adrian asked.

"I hear it again." I lowered my gun. "Let's keep moving."

A few minutes later, Miriam stopped at a hole in the wall, crumbling bricks surrounding a dark void where once there might have been a door.

She turned to me with a small wave. "You first."

I moved forward and shined my light into the void, which revealed another ladder of rungs leading down.

"Be careful," Miriam said softly as I stepped over the crumbled bricks. "This is as far as I got. They could be just down there."

With a scowl, I turned off the light on my phone and put it away. I didn't want to announce my presence to anyone who might be waiting at the bottom.

As quietly as I could, I felt for the rungs, fingers gripping the wet, rusted metal as I lowered myself into the darkness.

After a few steps down, my sense of up and down twisted into a confused state as if I were underwater. I closed my eyes to try to help my brain process the darkness, a tiny signal that I was in control of it, even though I wasn't.

I only opened them again when the toe of my boot hit something solid.

A soft light glowed from behind me as I planted my feet on dry ground. It was comforting for an instant, before I remembered that this far underground, light had to mean people.

Pulling out my gun again, I moved through the narrow tunnel towards the light. After a quick bend, it opened up to an enormous cavern, and I stopped at the entrance to scope it out.

At first glance, it almost looked like an old zoo. Or a prison. Cages lined the edges of the space, metal bars intertwining around empty cells.

But when I looked up, I recognized the same stone pattern on the domed ceiling that graced nearly every Metro station in DC. Another glance around and I recognized old structures that might have once held station maps next to stone benches in the middle of the cavern.

This used to be a train platform. I didn't know there were any stations that had been permanently closed, and I wondered just how long this place had been sitting here, hidden, before Soma or whoever his rival was had decided to turn it into a dungeon.

A faint cry caught my attention, and I craned my neck to peer further into the space. My fingers squeezed the handle of my gun harder than I would have liked when I saw what had made the noise.

It was a child, strapped up on what looked like some kind of torture device, shirtless and shining with sweat. Squinting, my heart sank as I recognized his face.

Brady, I thought, remembering the smiling picture his mother had shown me what felt like ages ago. My jaw clenched as I struggled to make sense of why anyone would do this to someone so small and innocent.

I wanted to run out there right now and help him down, carry him away from all this and back to his family. But a rough hand on my wrist brought me back to reality. I turned to see Adrian behind me, forehead creasing as he moved his hand over my fingers, which were still gripping the handle of my weapon way too tightly.

He shook his head and I softened my grip, putting the gun away. Yet another reason I preferred to use blades—they worked just fine no matter how angry I got.

I peered out again, attempting to assess the situation. It

couldn't just be Brady alone on this empty platform.

Sure enough, now that I was seeing slightly less red I could make out the figures of a few people milling around him. They looked human, which meant they were probably vampires.

"I see three bloodsuckers," I whispered to Adrian, "and one kid. The others are probably close." He nodded, and I cocked my head as I looked behind him. "Where's Miriam?"

"Tapped out," he said. "She's not cleared for field work; just getting her to do the recon was a stretch."

I frowned. *Not cleared for field work, my ass.* If Miriam was working for the Guardians, she must have more field training than Adrian. But he wouldn't know that. Nor, I supposed, would her official employers.

"Okay," I said. But I was already pissed that this secrecy bullshit had cost me a team member when we were outnumbered by vampires. "Got any more of your vamp stunner things?"

Adrian shook his head. "I was only issued one."

I sighed as he stepped around me to peer out at the station platform for himself.

After a few moments, he turned back around. "I only see two. We should try to get closer without them noticing. We might be able to sneak the kid out without a fight."

I put my hand out to stop him before he could step out into the light. "Fine, but if they see us—you shoot as soon as you get a clear shot." Adrian had good aim, better than mine in circumstances like this, and I needed to know he wouldn't leave me hanging again.

He paused for a second and then nodded, hopefully realizing that in this scenario, our lives were unquestionably on the line.

Drawing his weapon and holding it low, he stepped out slowly and I followed. The lights were mostly mounted up on the walls, so the shadows all along the empty cells provided us decent cover.

That was, until we reached a cell that wasn't empty. I stopped in my tracks as soon as I saw it, reaching out to touch Adrian's shoulder so he would stop too.

Two small bodies lay along the cell's floor, with another sitting upright against the back wall. One child was standing, hands curled around the bars, her fierce eyes locked on mine.

I put my finger to my lips, and she gave me a nod, then turned around and sat down. My head spun as my brain registered the significance of the number of children in there. Four. Five counting Brady.

Dirk had told me eight kids had gone missing under the same suspect circumstances, which meant there were three that should be here and weren't. Three children gone—three mad murder-spree incidents.

I dug my fingernails into my palm, wishing that I could have been wrong about the connection just this once.

As Adrian and I crept up to the occupied cell, the children on the ground looked up at us while the one that had been standing made some sort of hand signal at them.

They were dirty and disheveled, unsurprisingly, but at a glance they at least looked well fed and hydrated. That shouldn't be too surprising either, considering they were being held captive by vampires, who would want them plump and juicy. The thought made all the fruit juice in my stomach threaten to come back up.

Adrian fingered the lock on the cell door as I swallowed.

"Can you pick it?" I whispered, eyebrows lifting.

He nodded, then held out his hand to me. I reached into a pocket and pulled out my portable lock pick set, glad I'd brought it with me even if I hadn't been able to poke around in Soma's crypt. Unless this *was* Soma's crypt . . . I shivered at the thought.

I wanted to ask Adrian why such a law-abiding officer like him had learned to pick locks, but now wasn't the time.

Instead, I said, "You handle this; I'm going for the kid."

I could tell from the look in his eyes he didn't like that plan, but he nodded anyway and went to work on the lock.

I continued to creep forward through the shadows, making my way closer to Brady. If I could position myself close enough, it still might be possible to wait for the right moment and get him out without alerting any of the vampires. But if not, then at least I would pose a distraction that would help Adrian sneak the other kids away.

As I crept forward, I counted only two vampires around Brady, like Adrian had said. Where had the third one gone? Once I got close enough, I moved from the shadows and crouched down behind an old bench near the center of the platform.

One of the vampires was brushing Brady's hair back while the other smeared his bare arms with something liquid. Like they were preparing a sacrifice.

The poor boy looked terrified, his face scrunched up in an expression that told me he would be sobbing if he had the energy to do so.

When the vampires were done, they moved away from Brady. And as they turned around, I noticed something strange on both of their necks. Narrowing my eyes, I realized I was looking at scarring—two identical scars. These vampires looked like someone had slashed their throats and then stitched them back together crudely. Were they even vampires at all, or zombies?

Or vampire zombies, I thought with another shiver. Not that I had any idea how that would work.

They stood guard with their backs to Brady, as if they knew someone like me was just lying in wait. Damn. If they weren't going to move, I wasn't going to be able to sneak the kid out without a fight.

I craned my neck back to check on Adrian, not wanting to attack without backup if I didn't have to. He was still working on the lock, as far as I could tell. I couldn't see him too clearly from here.

I pulled out my gun and leveled it against the stone of the bench I was hiding behind, figuring my best chance would be to stun one of the vampires while I still had the element of surprise. Then at least I wouldn't be outnumbered. But to pull it off, I'd have to shoot him directly in the heart, and at around thirty feet away my aim was just not that reliable.

I'd had a lot of training, yes, but no one could be amazing at everything.

My heart pounding, I did my best to line up the shot. My target wasn't moving, which made it a little easier. But my hands were shaking, and after all the blood I'd lost earlier and the sleep I'd missed out on last night, steadying them seemed impossible.

Exhale and relax, I told myself. With my lungs emptied and my arms as steady as I could manage, I tensed my index finger to squeeze the trigger.

Footsteps echoing through the cavernous space made me stop.

I inhaled slowly, finger loosening. If I'd had a chance, it was gone now that the third vampire was back.

I grimaced when I saw who that third vampire was.

Gary. Or Reginald. Or whatever the fuck his name was. The same vampire I'd seen pouring blood into the clay statue's bowl the night before.

Judging by the knife in his hand and the way he was making a beeline for Brady, he was after more blood for the same purpose right now.

Screw it, I thought. I wasn't going to sit here and let that kid get cut open, no matter how bad my tactical disadvantage.

I let out my breath again and squeezed the trigger.

The vampire closest to me jerked back, a spray of blood scattering out behind him and partially misting Brady with red. Time stopped as I locked my eyes on his chest, almost disbelieving that I'd actually hit his heart. My aim was always better when I wasn't thinking about it.

When he went down and stayed down, I swung my weapon around to see if my luck would be miraculous enough to let me get two this way.

The other guard vampire was already rushing towards me, so I emptied my magazine into him hoping for the best. None of my rounds hit the sweet spot.

I dropped the gun and reached for the sturdy blade at my thigh, then stepped to the side and swung without thinking, amazed yet again when it slid through the vampire's neck like butter.

That's not how that's supposed to work. I should have at least felt more resistance from all the bone and muscle and connective tissue that made the neck one of the hardest parts of any humanoid body to cut through.

But his head toppled off his shoulders and bounced on the bench, leaving a trail of blood on the cracked stone floor as it eased into a roll and then finally stopped, right at Gary's feet.

The vampire's body slunk to the ground like jelly as Gary stared at me, mouth agape.

"Birdie?" he asked, then shook his head in distaste and turned his back to me, bringing his knife to Brady's arm.

I almost paused, shocked that he would be so unafraid of me after watching me take out the two vampires next to him. But I didn't have time to wonder what he was thinking.

I stepped up on the bench and leapt over it, rushing at Gary. Something tackled me from the right, knocking me to the ground before I could make it.

Blood dripped onto my face as my attacker loomed over me, from the gunshot wound I'd made not even minutes before. Damn, he'd healed fast.

But he was weak from the injury, and the agony at the back of my head told me it might be bleeding from hitting the ground. The vampire's extended fangs and glazed-over eyes seemed to corroborate that assumption. He didn't even bother to hold me down as he went for my throat, all teeth and snarls and hunger.

I brought my knee up into his gut and shoved him off me, only to see Adrian finally running towards the fight with his gun drawn.

"Get the kid," I shouted as I gripped my blade and struggled to pin my attacker down like he should have done with me.

I didn't have much leverage, but he didn't have much sense at the moment, so it wasn't as difficult as it should have been to position my knife over his throat and slice down.

Just like with the other vampire, the blade went through his neck—through the grotesque scar—like butter. His head didn't roll away with a satisfying flare, but my knife ground against the stone floor. I'd severed it completely. It was so easy I was almost tempted to pinch myself.

I stood up. The world spun as I tried to focus on my surroundings. Yep, I'd definitely hit my head. A gunshot sounded nearby, shocking me back to something resembling clarity.

But if Adrian had tried to take out Gary, he had missed. The extravagantly dressed vampire was still hovering over Brady, blood dripping down the boy's arm and into a chalice like the one I'd worn at the strip club.

Motherfucker.

I must have growled audibly, because Gary snapped his head back at me and went pale—paler than he already was, which was an amazing feat.

After dipping his head down to look at the chalice full of blood, he pulled it away from Brady's arm, covered it with his hand, and bolted.

I almost lurched to run after him, but Brady was still bleeding, and I couldn't leave him like that.

"Hey," I said breathlessly as I ran up to the scared boy. "It's gonna be okay."

I tried to force a smile as I tore off a strip of fabric from the bottom of my shirt, then wrapped it tightly around the cut on his arm. He just stared at me blankly, disconnected, still breathing heavily. I didn't blame him.

"Come on," I said, undoing the straps keeping him in place. "I'm taking you home."

But before I could pick him up, someone grabbed me from behind and tried to sink their teeth into my neck.

Not again. I thrust my elbow backwards into my attacker's gut. It made enough of an impact that I managed to turn around to face him—the same vampire I'd just beheaded.

My brain struggled to process what was happening even as my body instinctively reached for my knife and took his head off again. It was just as easy as the first time, but this time the head fell off the shoulders and rolled away on the ground like it had with the first vampire.

I stood there frozen for a moment, staring at the body, wondering yet again if I was dreaming. *The only way to kill a vampire is to decapitate or burn.* This was what I'd always been taught, what I'd found to be true in practice—what everyone knew.

And yet, just now, it hadn't worked. I'd left the severed head still next to the neck on the ground, and it had reattached itself. The memory of how the scars had looked on these vampires' necks flashed in my mind, and I wondered if both of them had been decapitated before by someone else.

The idea created a deep pain in my chest, even before my mind could make sense of the implications.

If only I had picked up Simeon's head and put it back on his body, then maybe—

I stopped myself, feeling the heat of the emotion start to overwhelm my consciousness as blood rushed to my face and my eyes stung.

Now was not the time for whatever this was.

I had a scared, bleeding kid to get to safety, along with all the others Adrian had let out of the cage, and—

Where the fuck had Adrian gone, anyway?

He'd been running up to help me, last I'd seen. And then I'd heard the gunshot.

A quick glance around showed me nothing, so I turned back to Brady and held out my hand as the heat of guilt and sorrow inside me turned into a sinking feeling of dread. "Can you walk?" I asked the boy.

He nodded and took my hand, stepping forward on shaky legs.

I started to lead him back the way I'd come, only to hear grunting noises coming from behind the same bench I'd used for cover.

Damn it. I leaned down to get close to Brady, pointing over to the tunnel I'd come from. "Do you see that shadowy hole in the wall?" I whispered. He nodded again. "Good. Go run over there and wait for me, and I'll take you home."

He didn't exactly run, but he at least started making his way over there, freeing me to see what was going on behind the bench.

When I stepped around it, I saw Adrian on the ground, grappling with a vampire that was even bigger than he was. A vampire with a gunshot wound in his shoulder. Adrian had missed the heart. And with a blink, I realized they weren't so much grappling anymore. Adrian was already caught in a headlock, the veins on his forearms jutting out as he struggled against the other man's grip.

He made eye contact with me briefly and then passed out, his arms going limp. The vampire lifted his head as his fangs came out, and my heart stopped.

The blade I'd just used for so much beheading dropped out of my hand, clattering on the stone floor with a loud echo and making the vampire look up at me.

His fangs disappeared as his eyes caught mine, both of us unmoving in the mind-fucking time warp this hellish cavern had become.

"Simeon," I said, the name tinged with a new level of spite.

And there it was, the fierce smile lighting up his broad face. Most people looked younger when they smiled, but not this man. Instead of becoming jaded over his long years, he had become more joyful, learned how to experience happiness more fully.

Even in the most royally fucked of all fucked moments, like this one, he had the carefully cultivated determination to let himself enjoy it.

It was the thing I'd loved most about him when we were together, the thing that had made him irresistible to me. I'd grown up thinking happiness was weakness, because for me it always had been, and it was intoxicating to see such powerful evidence to the contrary.

It was the reason I'd let my guard down in the first place, the reason I'd failed to protect him, because he'd sucked me in and made me believe that if he was strong enough to be happy, then I could maybe be the same around him.

I'd tried my damnedest to put that smile out of my mind since his death. Seeing it now, with his arms wrapped around the neck of someone I cared about, it made me hate him even more than I'd loved him before.

"Darcy," he said, letting Adrian fall to the ground as he got to his feet. "How I've missed you."

16

Simeon's voice was different than I remembered. Still deep and powerful, but raspy instead of rich. And as he walked towards me and my eyes fell on the ragged scar at his neck, I realized his vocal cords must have been permanently damaged when his head had come off.

"It was you," I said, wanting to step back as he came closer. "With Gary, bringing the blood to that statue in the club. I didn't recognize your voice when I heard it then."

His fingers reached up to brush against his throat, as if he'd forgotten it had ever been cut. "I recognized the sound of your heartbeat," he said, moving his hand from his neck to my chest.

I could feel the icy cold of his palm through the thin fabric of my shirt, and my heart beat faster despite my inner protests.

"You knew I was there," I said.

"Of course. But Reginald did not. And he would have made sure you were killed if you had seen me."

"I . . ." I blinked. He'd been protecting me. When it had always been my job to protect him. But he'd never really needed me for that, had he? Even when I'd thought I'd failed, he was still alive. He must have known all along that he wouldn't die, even with his head rolling on the ground. I gritted my teeth, trying to keep the stinging from my eyes. "I saw you die."

"Yes, well. I suspect that was the point," he said with a small smile. "Soma wanted me out of the picture. He disagreed with too many of my policies but couldn't oppose me publicly because it's imperative for our kind to present a unified front." He sneered, his voice taking on a mocking tone I'd never heard him use. "If we can't make peace amongst ourselves, how can we possibly live in peace with humans?"

I reached out and touched the scar on his neck, working to stop my muscle memory from taking over when it wanted me to grasp him fully, press myself against him, never let go again. The scar was soft, too soft, where once those muscles had been powerful and thick. "But this?" I asked.

"A secret." He brought a finger to my lips, smiling as he shushed me. His voice became a rough whisper. "We are weakest here, but we can still heal if put back together again."

"Why is that a secret? If I had known, I—"

"It was decided long ago," he said. "Even before we were in the public eye, so hunters would think they had killed us when they had not. A survival tactic." He shrugged. "But to keep this secret, we had to hide. Any one of us with the scar had to live underground for centuries, until his existence had been wiped from the memories of the world and it was safe for him to return. Reginald is one such example."

I drew my brows together, confused. Maybe this nonsense was what Kat had been determined not to tell me. The best-kept vampire secret I'd ever encountered . . . But when Simeon said Reginald he meant Gary, who didn't seem old enough to have been hiding underground for centuries.

"He is old, but he is weak," Simeon said, correctly guessing my thoughts. "Beheaded as a young thing for his own foolishness. He will never be an elder like Soma."

"And you . . ." I narrowed my eyes at him, my brain finally starting to catch up to this new reality. "You've been in hiding this whole time? If you had just told me, I could have lied for you—put your thick skull back on your shoulders and pretended it never happened and fucking dressed you in fancy scarves."

I stumbled over the last few words as my throat tightened and too much blood pooled behind my cheeks. As I said it, I felt the desire aching in my bones, the longing to go back and do things differently. To stay with him. The feeling might have been easier to ignore if I'd still thought he'd fucked with my head and taken my memories, but now that I knew it was Minnie who had done all that . . . I only had myself to blame for becoming so vulnerable around him.

He let out a soft chuckle, which turned some of my longing into anger. He could have stayed with me, and he'd chosen not to. All my suffering after his death had been completely unnecessary. Even as close as we'd become, Simeon still hadn't trusted me with his life in the end.

"You're a fucking coward," I said. "After everything you worked hard for, all the changes you wanted to make, your big plans to make it easier for everyone to live together without violence . . . What? An elder throws a tantrum and you just bury yourself and play dead?"

"Not exactly." He grinned a little wider as his eyes wandered around us. "I have new plans now."

I raised my eyebrows, not sure whether I really wanted to know what those new plans were. The man in front of me here might have the same exuberance as the man I'd loved, but there was something off about him that I couldn't quite place.

"An elder throwing a tantrum means more in my world than you could understand. I could have worked around Soma in the public eye easily—but in private? He has command of resources I couldn't dream of, the support of a network of elders who would never betray one another. If I hadn't submitted as I did, he would have come after me with fire the next time. A permanent death. There would have been no way to stop him, even for you."

I thought again of what Kat had said, that she was working for a vampire who was trying to remove Soma from power, to overthrow him and become an elder in his place. "Are you the one flooding the markets with bad blood?"

He waved his hand in the air. "That was only a distraction."

"From what?"

"Dying was a wake-up call," he said, eyes distant even as they stared into mine. "I realized I would never get anything done if I had to forever bow to the whims of the elders." He paused, focusing on me again. "I watched you, you know. I saw your pain, your determination to seek justice for me. I knew you would find me eventually, so when I heard rumblings of an organization wanting to kill you . . ."

I stopped breathing for a moment, head spinning with the change of topic and what he was implying. *"You're* the one who sent the first assassin after me?" The assassin who had looked like a possum, who had wielded the ice of the Sweepers' god and worn the same ward of the woman who had beheaded Simeon. The assassin who had made me think the Sweepers had ordered Simeon's death until their leader had told me otherwise.

"I wasn't sure if it would fool you, but I had to try. And in doing so, I found my true path."

I swallowed against the feeling of betrayal, not liking the way he'd worded that. And when he lifted his hand and began to produce ice crystals at the tips of his fingers, I knew why. No one in the world had ever talked about finding their "true path" who wasn't either a religious fanatic or a bullshitter. The Simeon I'd known had been neither, but this wasn't the Simeon I'd known.

I finally took a step back, unwittingly moving away from the magic I knew a vampire should never have command over. "You're a witch," I whispered.

"Not yet." He stayed where he was, allowing me the distance I'd put between us, and somehow that made me all the more uncomfortable. "I haven't finished proving my worth to my new god."

"What . . ." I tried to remember what Ray had said about the god in question, the same one that had backed the Sweepers before abandoning them. A god of ice and death, one who wouldn't stop until the whole world was cold and dark. "What exactly are you doing to prove your worth?" My voice shook. Deep down I'd already guessed the answer, which sent the heat that had been building behind my eyes finally spilling down my cheeks.

"Sacrifices to the abyss." His eyes wandered around us again, and I finally allowed myself to realize that Simeon had been the one to take the kids—he'd been the one causing the recent underground murder sprees. I still wasn't sure how, but that didn't matter much to me anymore.

My fingers twitched. I wished I hadn't dropped my blade when I'd seen him. Nothing much mattered to me anymore except the knowledge that he had to die. For fucking real this time.

He must have seen the coldness in me, because he finally stepped forward, his expression softening. "It's not pleasant, but necessary," he said. "With the power of a god behind me, I can finally stand up to the elders. Come back into the world. Be with you again." He reached out and took my hands as he finished, and I shivered at the cold of his touch, much colder now than it ever had been before.

"And then what?" I pulled my hands away. "This god won't stop until everyone is dead—everyone. Maybe he'll take a liking to you and your kind because you're already all cold and dead, but he won't support your plans for finding balance and peace with humans. He'll want me dead, too."

"That isn't what he wants," Simeon said, but I could hear the weakness behind the words and wasn't sure how much he believed them. "He won't want you dead if you join me. Darcy . . ." He lifted his icy hand to my face, letting the crystals melt and mingle with my tears as he brushed my cheek with his fingers. "You'll always be mine."

Stepping forward, he brought his face close to mine and touched my forehead with his, like he had done so many times before. I used to love how it made me feel grounded, connected firmly to him and his exuberance in a way that wasn't over-whelming.

Now it just made me want to peel the skin off my face and throw it in an inferno.

I shut my eyes so he wouldn't see the loathing in them, slipping a blade out of my sleeve with my right hand as I curled my left behind his neck. His lips touched mine, and I tried to focus on the familiarity more than anything else.

We'd done this a million times before. I knew exactly how it would feel, how he would move, the shape and size of every part of his body underneath my hands.

So I didn't have to see or feel to know where his ribs were as I pushed my knife between them into his heart.

Searing pain pierced my sides as Simeon went still, paralyzed against me, his weight threatening to knock me over. I let out a short scream at the unexpectedness of the sensation, the panic of not knowing what was hurting me.

I tilted my head down, where red crept into my blurred vision. Small splotches of blood, spreading slowly out from under the sides of my jacket towards my belly. Simeon's strong fingers had dug all the way through the leather, his sharp nails poking holes into the soft skin at my waist.

His last movement before I'd immobilized him, grasping me tight in his clutches. If not for the knife in his heart, I imagined his next movement would be to tear me apart.

Gasping at the pain, I pried his bloody fingers away from my sides one by one. He stared at me the whole time, eyes still projecting dominance even as he was entirely at my mercy. As long as my knife stayed in his heart, he would be. I lowered him to the ground as gently as I could, laying him face down so as not to dislodge it.

Even without his eyes on me, I could feel his gaze linger. His assurance that I would join him. That he still had my love. That I would always be his. And I was, as much as I wanted to hate him entirely. My skin crawled with my love for him, which I couldn't dig out of my insides like I had dug out his fingernails.

He would always have it. And that horrified me more than any notion I'd once had of him using his magic on me and fucking with my mind.

Before I could second-guess myself, I snatched my sturdier knife from where I'd dropped it and cut through Simeon's neck.

But obviously, that wouldn't be enough.

I had the urge to keep cutting, to mutilate his corpse and dismember him the way Minnie had done to hide the body of the vampire who had attacked me outside her cafe. I had no way of making fire at hand, but if I could turn him into vampire confetti . . . I didn't know if it would kill him for good, but it would make me feel better.

I closed my eyes for a moment and breathed in, licking the nausea away from my lips. Then, working quickly, I took off my jacket and slipped off the ripped gray t-shirt underneath before putting the jacket back on.

I couldn't even feel the pain in my sides anymore, although the cuts were bleeding freely, red liquid now trickling down to seep into my jeans. The smart thing to do would be to use the fabric of my shirt to staunch the wounds. But I needed it for something more important.

I laid the shirt on the stone floor and used the sole of my shoe to roll Simeon's head onto it, careful not to touch any part of him with my bare skin. If there was ever someone I didn't want the phoenix to revive . . .

Breathing out, I picked up the corners of the shirt and tied them into the sleeves, making myself a neat little severed-head pouch that was quickly turning red.

I might not be able to burn him to ash or turn him into confetti just yet, but the least I could do was make sure his head stayed separated from his body in the meantime.

My mind spun for a moment with the wild feeling of a world turned upside-down, my greatest aim now to keep Simeon dead instead of protecting him. Then my fingers tightened over the knot on the shirt as my eyes landed on Adrian, who was still lying unconscious where Simeon had dropped him.

A new lump formed in my throat at the sight of him, and I rushed over and dropped to my knees beside him. My fingers found their way to his neck as I rolled him to the side. Closing my eyes, I pressed firmly and let out a small cry when I felt a pulse.

The relief was overwhelming, almost as much as the fear that followed it. He looked so vulnerable lying there, for all intents and purposes asleep, and I wanted intensely to protect him. From what, I wasn't sure. It didn't matter.

All it did was meld the idea of him in my mind with the last man I'd wanted to protect—the one whose head was currently dripping blood through my t-shirt.

The fear I'd let go of earlier was replaced with a new one, a far less rational one. That anyone who inspired this feeling in me must be a monster, or would become one eventually. Even if for no other reason than the power they had to make me suffer.

Peals of laughter bouncing off the stone around me didn't help. All they did was conjure an image of Noah with a monster's head, whether real or imagined, to drive the point home.

Were they coming after me now, finally? Was this what it felt like to go insane? Would I cut off Adrian's head in a minute after losing control of myself, like the shifter I'd seen lose control on the train?

I shook my head, resisting the urge to slap myself across the face. Simeon may be dead-ish, but Gary had gotten away with Brady's blood and still needed to be stopped.

Brady. I needed to make sure he and the other kids got to safety before I could do anything else.

I squeezed my eyes shut tight, trying to regain control of myself. As much as I'd practiced putting my emotions aside to do what needed to be done, those emotions weren't usually so hugely personal. But I would only feed into the feelings if I let them stop me now. It would only prove that I was right to be so wrecked.

My cold gaze fell on Adrian as I opened my eyes. I'd have to leave him here for now, because he was a lot bigger than Dirk and I wasn't sure I could move him anywhere that would be worth the risk of me damaging him further in the process.

I ran over to the hole in the wall, slight relief filling me with every step I took away from Adrian even as the blood dripping from Simeon's head followed me in a crimson trail.

When I peered in, Brady was nowhere to be seen. Thinking he might have climbed up the ladder, I walked up to it and shined my phone light around.

Nothing.

And to make matters worse, my phone had no service at all—so I'd have to leave Adrian for real if I wanted to call for help.

"Brady?" I yelled as loud as I dared. The sound echoed around me, deeper but more muffled here in the enclosed wet space.

"He's safe, not to worry," Miriam's voice called back from above. "They all are. How's it going down there?"

My eyes narrowed. I wanted to punch that woman and hug her all at the same time, but I supposed I should be getting used to that by now. "What the fuck, Miriam?" I said. "Get your pink jiggly ass over here already. Adrian's down, so you don't have to worry what he might think."

"Well, there's no need to be rude abou—"

"Wait," I yelled as she lowered a pointy heel down the hole. "If you have any signal up there, call Dirk and tell him to bring me a fucking flamethrower. We're going to need it."

17

MIRIAM POKED and prodded Adrian's unconscious body, her lips pursed.

"What did you do to him?" she asked finally, looking up at me with a disapproving glare.

"I didn't—" I started, then sighed. "He was grappling with a vampire. I thought he just got choked out, but maybe he hit his head?"

"He's breathing just fine," Miriam said as she produced a handful of healing squishies.

I looked away, the sight of that blue jelly bringing back memories of when I'd been high out of my mind on it. I hadn't let her put any on my sides, even though she'd tried when she saw the blood dripping from beneath my jacket.

When Miriam clapped her hands, I looked back to see little bits of squishy in various places on Adrian's head, his temples, his throat, behind the ears . . . Then she tore open his shirt, popping the buttons off to reveal his bare chest, all hard muscle and alabaster skin shining with sweat.

I looked away again, heart pounding, trying to banish the sudden urge to run my lips over those muscles. After everything that had just happened, the thought sent an aching lump into my throat.

I was trying to swallow it down when Miriam threw the shirt at me, still warm. "You need to at least stop the bleeding," she said, then scrunched her nose at me. "Are you okay?"

"Yeah," I mumbled, clearing my throat.

I tore Adrian's shirt in half and wrapped both pieces around my waist, trying to achieve even pressure over the wounds. Miriam was right. If I let myself lose too much blood again, I'd be even more useless than if I let her make me loopy with those squishies.

"Can you help me move him?" I asked. "We can't wait around here for him to wake up."

"Mmm hmm," she said. "But not up that ladder. I have my limits, you know."

"Let's just get him to the entrance. It's dark; he'll be hidden in case any more vampires come through."

Miriam nodded, but not without letting out a huff of reluctance as she slipped off her shoes.

We were both panting by the end of it, as we tried to put him down gently against the crumbling brick wall without hitting his head again.

"Why are humans so dense?" Miriam whined, leaning her forehead against the wall as she caught her breath. "He's not even that big."

"I mean, he's pretty damn big . . ." I said, then shook my head. Adrian was all muscle and Miriam was all jelly, so I shouldn't be surprised by her complaints.

"I'm not talking about his fuck stick," Miriam said to me sternly.

I grimaced, too taken aback to tell her that I hadn't been talking about *that* either.

"What?" she said. "Isn't that what you call it these days?"

"Come on," I said, not willing to continue this conversation. "I need you to take me back to the club basement. You said there was a trap door somewhere?"

Miriam grumbled a little as she hobbled back the way we'd come, her bare feet nearly slipping in the trail of blood I'd left from Simeon's head. "Are you going to carry that thing with you everywhere?"

"Only until I can burn it."

She slipped her shoes back on, red staining the pink suede where her feet touched the edges. "This way," she said.

We walked across the old train platform, eerie in its complete emptiness even though I was sure it would have been worse had the cages been full of prisoners. The unmoving escalator led us up to an area where passengers would have once stopped to put their tickets through machines, but now the tunnel leading up to the outside world was blocked by cement.

Someone had closed this place intentionally, neatly. Once again, I wondered what its history was and how it had fallen into the hands of the vampires in hiding.

But Miriam led me off to the side, to a service door that opened up to another ladder of rungs. This took us up to another sewer tunnel much like the first, except this one had a short ladder leading up to a trap door, just like Miriam had said.

I set Simeon's head carefully behind the bottom-most rung of the ladder, where it wouldn't get swept away by water and should at least be safe for a little while.

Then I climbed up and poked my head through the floor of the strip club's basement, finding myself in the hallway near the door that led to the statue room. This must be where Gary and Simeon had come from when I'd heard their voices and had to hide quickly before.

The hallway was empty, so I went ahead and climbed out, reaching back to give Miriam a hand.

I patted my pockets as we approached the door to the statue room. Adrian still had my lockpick set. But as soon as I tried the door handle and found it locked, Miriam liquefied behind me and slid underneath the door.

A moment later, she was opening it for me from the inside, looking every bit as perfect as she always did—except for the blood on her shoes.

The smell hit me before anything else. That sweet, rotting stench seemed even stronger than it had before. I gagged as flies buzzed around my head, skin crawling almost as much as it had at Simeon's touch.

The statue stood before us in the center of the room, still covered in honey that was shiny in some places and crystallized in others. Gary was nowhere in sight, but the bowl clutched between the statue's spiny clay fingers was filled with fresh blood.

And this time, some of the blood was dripping out of the statue's mouth, splashing into the full bowl. I stared at it for a few moments, expecting it to overflow, but it never did. Must be on some kind of magical loop, like a gory garden fountain.

"Well?" Miriam asked. "What are we doing here?"

"I need to destroy this thing."

I tried to remember what Adrian had said, that it might be some kind of golem. Smash it to pieces, I remembered that. What else?

"Reversal," I mumbled, stepping forward to get a closer look at the statue.

There were symbols inscribed on its chest. Strange pictures. Some looked like animals, and some I couldn't make sense of at all.

I walked around the thing once to make sure I wasn't missing anything, then pulled out my littlest knife and leaned in close, holding my breath.

I wasn't the greatest artist, but I hoped it was the thought that counted. Underneath the symbols, I began to carve copies of them in the opposite order.

Reversal.

It seemed stupid and obvious and way too easy, but it was the only thing I could think of. If Adrian were conscious, he would probably have had a much better idea, but he'd gone and gotten himself knocked out by my ex-boyfriend, so honestly the imaginary version of him scolding me in my head could go fuck himself right now.

So could the laughter that was trickling into my ears from the walls around me, growing louder with every stroke of my knife.

I had to grip the statue with my left hand to brace myself in order to push the knife into the clay, and by the end of it my fingers were covered in the sticky, foul-smelling honey. Flies crawled over my hand as I stepped back to eye my handiwork, which seemed to have done nothing.

But then the monstrous version of Noah I never wanted to see again flickered to life in front of me, its grotesque smile full of flies, its little perfect chubby hands reaching out for me.

They passed right through me, stabbing me in the gut like ghostly icicles.

I gasped, frozen in pain, vision blurring as skeletal faces and arms began to form in the walls around me. They stretched out towards me, and I felt myself somehow stretching out towards them, although I couldn't be moving.

It was only when I felt the energy in my scrye turn cold that I realized they were trying to take my soul.

This must be what it felt like, then. For everyone who had gone mad. A monstrous child and his army of dead things all reaching into my body at once and rooting around while I stood helpless, violated, aware of parts of myself I'd never even acknowledged that would never belong to me fully now because these *things* were scratching them with their cold, bony fingers.

I pulled back, bracing myself the only way I knew how even though I wasn't sure it would do anything.

My fingers twitched.

Maybe.

Hopefully.

No, probably not. It was like I was made of clay, like the statue before me, and not flesh and blood and bones and nerves and magic.

I could only watch myself float slowly away, inch by inch, as they dragged me out of my body and towards the walls.

A crash halted everything.

Then pain took over my world. Every nerve in my body screamed at me, like someone had injected acid into my veins and then thrown me over a bonfire. The agony flooded my senses so completely that it took what felt like an hour for me to realize it must mean I was back in my body.

I hadn't known what this felt like, but I knew what it looked like from my time in the healing clinic. It had been my job to guide loose souls back into their bodies, keeping dying patients alive just long enough for the other healers to save them. It was part of what had driven me to leave, the clear agony in the eyes of everyone whose soul I'd forced back into them.

But none of those dying jerks had told me it would hurt this bad. Sure, maybe that was because they'd passed out from the pain and then I'd avoided them forever after, but still.

I didn't have the luxury of relinquishing consciousness right now. I wasn't in a cushy bed surrounded by family and flowers and teddy bears—I was in a vampire dungeon with some kind of monster trying to kill me.

Pushing at my senses, I tried to focus on anything outside my body.

There wasn't much. Something hard and cold against my back.

Had I fallen down?

Something soft touched my neck, easing the pain just slightly in that spot, which only made it feel worse everywhere else.

Why couldn't I see?

Oh. Because my eyes were squeezed shut so hard that my cheeks were beginning to cramp.

I did my best to crack them open. The thing touching my neck was attached to a blurry lump of pink and blond and rhinestones.

"Miriam . . ." I might have croaked before focusing on what was behind her.

A shattered mess of orange clay amid a pool of blood. Like the statue had been a water balloon she had popped.

The lack of any immediate threat did me in before I could say or think anything else. Nothing to kill, nothing to fight, nothing to fucking stay conscious for.

One more blink and I was gone.

Soft drips of cool liquid landed on my forehead as bright lights assaulted my brain. I would have shut my eyes if they weren't shut already.

"I can call a car for you, ma'am," someone said in a gruff voice.

I worked my jaw, trying to take enough control of my mouth to ask who the fuck was talking to me when another voice replied, "No, thank you. We'll be just fine. Our friend is on the way."

Heavy footsteps walked away while others passed in front of me with light giggles and chatter, cars beeping and heels clicking and tires squealing.

I managed to crack my eyes open.

Blinking, I recognized the street just outside of Soma's club. I was sitting propped up against the wall near the entrance, out in the open for anyone to see.

Panic raced through me for a moment before my spent body quickly shut down any thoughts I might have had of moving.

I groaned in frustration. Gary was still out there, and he would have me killed in a heartbeat if he saw me here in this helpless state.

Not to mention that Soma himself probably had me on a kill list, too, after what I'd pulled when I was supposed to be working for him. Sure, he might thank me and be my friend for life if he knew I had just stopped his old rival from trying to use an ancient god to overthrow him and all the other vampire elders . . . but he didn't know that, and I wouldn't blame him if he didn't ask.

Miriam's face dropped in front of mine as she leaned over, her lips pursed.

"Can you walk?" she asked.

Oof. What a question.

"What happened?" I countered.

She sighed, hands moving to her hips. "I dragged you into the bathroom, cleaned the blood off, and then asked a bouncer for help carrying my drunk friend." Twisting her mouth into a smirk, she added, "It helped that you're not really wearing a shirt. You look a bit worse for wear, but it is the middle of the night."

"Before that," I said.

She shrugged. "You said you needed to destroy the statue, but then you started carving pictures into it. Then you just stood there for ages. I tried to talk to you, but it was like you couldn't hear me. So I did it myself. Smashed the thing, and then . . ." She waved her hand at me. "You were out."

I leaned my head back and knocked it against the wall, wincing when it hit the same spot that had been hurt in my fight with one of the zombie vampires. That small pain was a good sign, though. My noticing it meant the other pain was diminished, the soul-traveling pain that had set fire to every nerve in my body at once. That it hadn't lingered was a small blessing.

"We need to get away from here," I said, and then something Miriam had mentioned clicked in my brain. My arms felt like lead as I lifted them to my chest, patting the bare skin peeking through from under my jacket.

I wasn't wearing a shirt.

The panic did a better job of lighting my insides this time, my head starting to feel clearer and limbs starting to feel less like stone as I remembered *why* I wasn't wearing a shirt.

"Yes, I know," Miriam was saying. "Hence the question of can you wal—"

"Where's the head?" I snapped.

She made an exasperated noise. "Where you left it, I imagine. I wasn't going to bring that into the club." In a mocking high-pitched voice, she continued, "Ohhh, sir, can you help me please? My friend is so drunk she decapitated someone. Isn't that funny?"

Damn. "I need to go back to get it," I said, but then I felt my phone buzzing in my pocket.

Remembering that I hadn't had service the entire time I'd been underground, I pulled it out and glanced at the screen. I half expected to see some snarky text from Dirk making fun of me for needing his flamethrower after all.

Instead, the screen was filled with notifications from Ray.

Missed calls, voice mails, and one text message. I opened it.

The kids are missing.

No, I thought. *We found them.* I looked up at Miriam. "What did you do with the kids we saved?"

"Brought them to the nearest police station. They'll be fine."

I narrowed my eyes at the phone. I was missing something. I read it again.

The kids are missing.

The kids. Ray didn't even know about the missing kids I'd been after, so—

Noah and Carina.

"Fuck."

"What is it now?" Miriam crossed her arms, looking for all the world like she was trying to put to bed a child who had just eaten a whole bucketload of candy.

"Noah and Carina are missing."

She looked at me blankly.

"They were after her—Carina. The same things that just knocked me on my ass. They were trying to take my soul, like they did to all your murder-spree perps. If that happens to her . . ."

Miriam clicked her tongue. "How much damage can a little girl do?" she asked, and I would have laughed if the reality weren't so sickening.

"She's a *dragon*," I said.

"Ah, that's right. Well—"

"I have to go after her. Can you go back and get the head for me?"

Miriam raised her eyebrows.

"You should probably check on Adrian too," I said. "I can't . . ." I shook my head. If Noah had gone missing with Carina, then his life was in danger as much as hers. Maybe more. I couldn't do anything except go after them.

"Of course," Miriam said. "Just . . ." She brought up her hand and produced another pink mind-reading squishy like the one she'd taken off me earlier in the night. "Don't do anything private," she said as she stuck it on my neck.

"I won't." I assumed that by private she meant sexual. But even if Adrian weren't lying unconscious underground right now, I wasn't going to be giving in to that temptation again anytime soon.

Miriam shivered, a twisted frown on her face. "Don't think about that," she said, and I realized I'd been remembering the moment she'd interrupted earlier in the night. "I don't want to think about him like that."

"Neither do I," I said as I managed to stand on wobbly legs.

The look she gave me told me she didn't believe me at all.

I gave her a nod and then called Ray as I headed towards the Metro. There was no avoiding it now. I had to assume the things had gotten to Carina before Miriam had smashed the statue—and I had to hope that meant there was no more danger of them stealing my soul now that it was smashed.

If I was wrong about that, I was probably fucked no matter what.

The phone rang in my ear while I turned the corner of the club, and I paused as I caught sight of the alley where Adrian and I had waited for Miriam outside the basement window. The crates were still stacked up where he'd left them, and I couldn't resist walking over to see if the vampire was still there.

If she was, I would kill her. She had come at me with ice magic, which meant she was probably working with Simeon and his god. At this point, leaving her alive was a risk I wasn't willing to take, regardless of what Adrian thought.

I pulled out my neck-slicing knife as I stepped over to the crates, the phone still ringing.

Tensing, I readied myself to deliver the blow before rounding the corner.

But when I got behind the crates, there was nothing on the ground besides gravel and blood.

"Fuck," I said as the phone clicked in my ear.

"What the hell took you so long?" Ray snapped at me over the line.

"No signal," I said. "What happened?"

"Everything was fine until her mother called and told us she would be arriving early. Carina was so excited . . . I told her not to, but she went into the basement to get a piece of glass she'd been saving as a gift. Noah must have gone with her, and when they didn't come back up again . . ."

I groaned. That girl was so fucking reckless. I had told her specifically to stay out of the basement, and she'd been scared enough the last time I'd seen her that I'd naively thought she would listen. But she was still just a kid, as much as she tried hard to make me forget that, and I couldn't fault her for being excited to see her mom.

"Darcita," Ray said, but the nickname didn't hold the same affection it usually did. Not with such a somber tone in his voice. "I know what did this."

My heart raced. "You found something?" I asked. "In your books?"

"They are creatures from old México, soul-stealing spirits that guard the land. We call them los chaneques. They appear in the form of children with the faces of old men, and there are some accounts of landowners controlling them through a clay statue made with honey and the blood of young children. I don't know how or why they ended up here, but—"

"The god must have brought them," I interrupted. In the back of my mind, a part of me deflated with the realization that Adrian had been wrong about the whole golem thing—that no "reversal" technique, however clever, would have worked to stop these creatures if Miriam hadn't stepped in and smashed the statue. Next time, I'd default to the smashing first.

"What god?" Ray asked.

"The one who loves ice and death, who took over the Sweepers before they were destroyed. You said he was your god's rival."

"Itztlacoliuhqui," Ray muttered. "Of course. He is using them to form a connection to this land. If he does that—"

"He's putting down roots," I said. Just like Ray. This god was determined to spread death as far as he could, and Washington, DC was a logical place to start for any evil mastermind wanting to take over the world. It made sense that he would want to gain power here before making any more moves.

"There's a ritual," Ray said, his voice hard. "To get back Carina's soul, if they have it. I'm gathering the materials, but we can't do it without her. I need you to find her."

"If I do find her, and she's . . ." I trailed off, not sure how I should phrase it. *If she's raining down dragon fire on a bunch of innocent civilians* wasn't something that seemed right to say to her dad. "If she's out of control," I said instead, "do you have any tricks I can use to restrain her?"

He paused for a moment, and I could hear him tapping his fingers on something hard. "Fire," he said eventually. "It will weaken her."

"Fire," I repeated, confusion evident in my tone. "Against a dragon?"

"All dragons are not the same," Ray snapped. "Carina is descended of the dragons created by Quetzalcoatl in the third age of the world. The land had become an inferno, and the people needed wings to escape it. Their breath is as hot as the air currents they rose up on, but they cannot stand to be burned."

"Got it," I said, even though it sounded batshit crazy.

"Dirk is already on his way to you with my flamethrowers." Ray's tone was cold; I could practically hear the terror he must be feeling, knowing that his weapons were going to be used on his daughter instead of the vampires he'd sent them out for. "He left before they went missing, so he doesn't know."

"Okay. I'm going to be underground looking for her, but

Miriam will know where I am. Call her when you have what we need for the ritual."

"I will," he said, then paused. "Be careful."

I knew he meant for me to be careful not to kill his daughter, but it was still a touching sentiment.

"I will."

I NEVER THOUGHT I'd be so happy to see Dirk when he sauntered over to me with his cocky grin across the street by the Metro entrance and tossed me one of the flamethrowers he had slung over his shoulders.

Or at least I assumed it was a flamethrower. It was packed in a patterned cloth sack that would have been more appropriate for garden tools than weapons, but I supposed that was the point. We couldn't just walk around in public carrying these huge weapons openly without running into unnecessary trouble.

I peeked inside to make sure it was what I thought it was, and it didn't disappoint. I didn't know if all glass artists had flamethrowers lying around that were so obviously meant to double as weapons, but I was glad Ray was apparently into multi-purpose tools.

After what he'd told me about dragons, I realized it was probably an intentional precaution. Not necessarily meant to keep his daughter in line, but maybe in case her mother decided to try anything unsavory.

"Where're the bloodsuckers?" Dirk asked, and I shook my head.

"Already dealt with for now. We're going after Carina and Noah." I ignored his skeptical look. "Come on. I'll fill you in on the way."

Without another word, I made my way down the escalator, doing my best to use my words and not my fists on the awful excuses for people who had decided to stand on the left side instead of the right.

I didn't know exactly where Carina was, but I could guess. The chaneques had gone after her specifically, even though there weren't enough people in her basement at home to make a scene like the others they'd orchestrated. They had wanted *her*, either because they knew how much damage she could do in the right circumstances or because they knew she was a follower of their god's rival—most likely both. Now that they had her, they needed to bring her to a place where she could be deadly, and that place probably needed to be underground.

The high-domed ceilings of DC's Metro platforms offered the only underground spaces I could think of where a dragon would have room to fly. And Ray lived further north on the red line, so I was willing to bet we'd run into the kids if we just got on the red line here and headed in their direction.

I only glanced back once to make sure Dirk was following me, and he was red in the face by the time we made it to the train platform.

"Slacking off at the gym?" I asked him once I'd halted, nothing to do now but wait for the next train.

"I almost died yesterday—gimme a break."

Fair enough, I thought, although I'd almost died earlier in the night. But Dirk had apparently been on leave before all this started, and I wondered if he'd been taking advantage of his role as my handler to get himself some down time. The phrase *all bark and no bite* crossed my mind as I watched him catch his breath. That was what Adrian had said about him when we'd met. I hoped I'd be able to count on him to not get himself killed by my niece.

The train rushed in at that point, and my heart sank as I realized just how many people were getting on along with us. I'd expected it to be nearly empty at this time of night, but trains would stop running soon and plenty of Saturday-night party goers wanted to get home cheaply while they could.

Except if I was right, they were headed towards the jaws of a hungry dragon rather than home to their beds.

I told Dirk everything Ray had told me while we sped through the tunnel, then gave him a rundown of what had happened with the vampires since I'd last seen him.

"Damn," he said when I was done, letting out a low whistle. "You're really not good with men, huh?"

I narrowed my eyes at him. "That's your takeaway from all this?"

"I mean, it's fuckin' great to know we can't kill suckers by taking off their heads—we might get a pay bump for that."

"Glad you've got your priorities straight," I said bitterly, wondering for the umpteenth time what Etty saw in this man. Then a chill ran through me. "Wait—how do you even know this had anything to do with me and 'men'?"

"It's in your file," he said with a smirk. "I think the higher-ups knew about your little affair even before Miriam got her squishy on you. You didn't really think you could keep something like that a secret?"

I shifted my weight, knowing he was referring to the Guardians even though he was being careful to watch his language in this public space. And no, I hadn't really thought I could keep it a secret. But somehow it was harder to face the fact that it wasn't, now that the whole "affair" with Simeon had been turned on its head and my emotions were raw.

Luckily, I didn't have to say anything else on the subject

because the train pulled into the next station at that point. Peering out the window, I searched for signs of Carina and Noah. But everything seemed normal here.

It wasn't until the doors opened and I heard a faint scream in the distance that I jerked into motion, yanking Dirk out of the train with me.

"What are you doing?" he complained. "I don't see them here."

Neither did I. And as I frantically scanned the crowd of people moving on and off the train, I started to wonder if I'd made a mistake.

But when the train pulled away, I turned around and spotted two small figures on the opposite platform.

My whole body relaxed involuntarily at the sight of them. Carina was still in her human form, and Noah was still alive. I didn't doubt that they were in immense danger, but at least I wasn't too late to save them.

I hadn't realized until now just how terrified I'd been that I would get here to find them both already dead.

Still, I had heard a scream. And the people around them on the platform were giving them strange looks.

Carina ducked her head into her hands and let out a little screech like the first one I'd heard, and Noah came up beside her to put his hand on her back.

I wanted to yell at him to get away from her, but he wouldn't understand. His friend was distressed, and he wanted to help her. Of course he did.

When Carina started to grow claws, blood dripping from where they scratched the skin on her scalp just like the feline who had lost control on the train yesterday, I knew there was only one thing I could do.

I leapt down onto the train tracks, running across in wide strides and trying not to step on anything that looked electric. By the time I'd made it to the other side, Carina had spotted me with wild eyes. Those eyes recognized me, but it wasn't my niece behind them anymore.

"Darcy!" Noah yelled as Carina's black wings unfolded around him. "Something's wrong with—"

His words broke off as Carina took flight, Noah still clutching her shoulder. His legs dangled in the air for a moment before Carina's tail grew to its full size, catching him inadvertently and allowing him to get a better grip on her back.

I was still fumbling with getting the flamethrower out of its sack when she'd flown so high up there was no way I could reach her anyway.

The people on the platform mostly stopped moving when she flew up, all gaping with their phones out, as if this were a fucking circus show and not the beginning of a massacre.

Dirk was still on the opposite platform across the tracks, but he'd already gotten his weapon out and let loose a burst of fire at Carina as she flew over him.

The flames barely singed the tips of her claws, and she only flew higher in response. Dirk locked worried eyes with me, gave me a nod, and then turned around and ran up the nearest escalator to get to the raised walkway. He'd have far less lateral mobility up there, but if she flew near him he might be high up enough to get her. Good thinking.

Except there were only two of us, and I didn't like the odds of both of us taking such a passive approach. Not with all these dumbstruck onlookers and Noah still clinging to Carina's back—especially this late at night when he should already be in bed. The kid was laughing now, not understanding what was going on and probably just excited that Carina had finally decided to take him flying. But I knew how tired he must be, and I wasn't sure how long he would be able to hold on.

What could I do?

I narrowed my eyes at Carina, my flamethrower at the ready.

When she started to swoop down, I ran towards her and shot up a burst of fire. But she had only swooped down far enough to let loose her own fiery breath, and her range was better than mine.

Screams echoed through the space as the scent of charred flesh wafted towards me. And when Carina flew back up, leaving three crispy bodies in the wake of her fire, the dumbstruck onlookers turned into a panicked mob.

Through all the screaming and the running and the pushing, I could hear Noah now sobbing in the air from Carina's back, his laughter gone as he pleaded with her to stop.

He could probably make her stop, I realized. He might have done so already if I hadn't lectured him earlier on not using his magic without consent.

Carina swooped down again. I started running towards her until I realized she was headed straight for me.

I turned on my heel and leapt out of the way as heat blasted me from behind. I landed in a roll, but the heat wasn't gone when I stood up. I reached back to find flames licking at the ends of my hair.

It was still damp from all the rain and blood it had been soaked in tonight, thankfully, or my head might have already turned into a torch.

It was impossible not to remember the last time I'd had flames thrown at me, when I'd been fighting Salma the outraged ifrit on the rooftops near Minnie's cafe. But then, I'd been protected by the magic wind of the phoenix; it had blown the fire away before it could touch me, letting the heat roll off me like water rolling off a duck.

I'd also had wings then. And as much as I hated to admit it, they would be really fucking useful right now.

Noah let out a tiny scream as Carina swerved in the air to dodge a burst from Dirk's flamethrower, and I stopped breathing. All the resolve I'd had when it came to Ray and his cult of a family and the sinister strings attached to the power of his god—it all melted away in one instant when I heard the panic in the cry of that little boy.

I ducked behind a pillar, all my muscles tense and my stomach turning as I closed my eyes.

I didn't have the first idea of how to pray to a god, but I hoped it was the thought that counted.

As counterintuitive as it felt, I tried to tune out of my surroundings, imagining myself in the obsidian cave I'd been transported to when I'd first touched Ray. He had said that was where they went when they needed to communicate with Popo.

I remembered the pain of the intensity of the magic, before the cave had tasted my blood. I remembered the glittering facets of dark glass surrounding me, and the incessant chirping of the horde of rabbits herding me out to the cave opening, where they had shown me a vision of Becca and all the other burning souls in Salma's private hell.

A warm tingle enveloped me, and I opened my eyes half expecting to be engulfed in Carina's fiery breath.

But I was still safe behind the pillar, everything the same except for the little black bunny perched on my knee.

It let out a chirp as I reached out to it, and then it bit down hard into the meaty part of the palm of my hand.

I sucked in my lips to keep myself from yelping, watching the blood well up and absorb into the shiny black stone as if it were a sponge.

The pain was gone in an instant as my scrye swelled, my nerves tingling with the magic glancing off the dark surfaces around me. It was so tempting to relax into the familiar feeling that had been a constant part of me for as long as I could remember before it had disappeared entirely. I'd tapped into it hours ago, under the moonlight and with the blood being sucked from my veins, but it had been so fleeting and such a struggle.

Nothing was fighting me now, and this current coursing through me felt like home.

I touched the rabbit's head in thanks as ephemeral wings sprouted from my back. I didn't even mind the pain that came with them this time, now that I knew what to expect. Rather than excruciating, it was a signal that it had worked—that I could lift myself in the air and have a fighting chance of stopping Carina before it was all too late.

The bunny hopped away and disappeared into the shadows, its job done. I tried not to worry about just how much of my soul I'd signed away in that encounter.

However much, it was worth it to save the kids.

I gripped the flamethrower as the wings lifted me up, trying to think about where I wanted to go rather than the mechanics of how I would get there. I still hadn't had much practice flying, so I would need to trust my instincts.

Carina hadn't spotted me yet, and my best shot would be to approach her from behind. I sped over straight to her, pointing the flamethrower at her tail.

My heart pounded seeing how close Noah was to my target. But the fear in his eyes dwindled when he turned his head to look at me.

I blasted Carina's long, spiky tail with fire, dodging as it lashed from side to side in response. She roared and snapped her head back at me, and I deflated with the realization that just getting her tail hot wouldn't be enough to subdue her.

I swerved to the side, thankful for my awkward jerky flight pattern that made it harder for Carina to anticipate my movements. The flames she breathed at me only grazed the edges of my wings.

Not knowing what else to do, I darted towards Dirk, who steadied his flamethrower in my direction. Neither one of us could best this dragon on our own, but together she would have to choose which one of us to kill first. Hopefully, I could use that moment of distraction to make sure she wouldn't kill anyone.

I tried to lower myself steadily to Dirk's level as I made my way towards him, and I could see in his eyes that he thought I was insane. If he had to shoot fire through me to get to the dragon before she could get to him, he would do it. I shook my head at him and hoped he could trust me.

When I was only a few feet away from him, I slowed for a moment so Carina would think she had me. Then, as she opened her mouth and her hot breath warmed my wings, I dropped my flamethrower and lifted myself straight up to double back behind her.

She tried to follow me with her neck, but she was a lot bigger than I was and couldn't maneuver as quickly even though she was by far the more experienced flier.

Instead, she let loose her breath in a flurry of flames that went over Dirk's head and under my feet, and his stream of fire landed directly on the smooth scales of her underbelly.

Her screech pierced my ears as I dropped down behind her and reached out my arms for Noah.

"Take my hand," I yelled.

He hesitated for just a moment before unlatching one of his arms from around Carina's neck. And in that moment, Carina started to fall.

Noah's fingers slipped away from mine, panic setting in his eyes as he fell away from me.

I tried to dive down for him but ended up spinning in a tight circle instead. *Turns out diving in the air is not the same as diving in water.*

Taking a breath, I corrected myself, telling my wings to fold so I could lean forward more effectively. It must have worked, because I found myself hurtling towards the ground.

Carina was still flapping her wings, a futile effort to stay in the air, but it meant she was falling slower than I was.

I would need to time this perfectly if I didn't want to crash into her and do more damage than necessary to all three of us at once.

I tensed the muscles in my back as I locked my eyes on Noah, feeling for my wings and readying them to open. My arms reached out again, this time aiming to grab him under the shoulders like I did every night before I dropped him into bed. It was what Becca had always done, even though he was already far too big for it.

He seemed to understand and relaxed as I neared him to hook my arms under his. My wings opened as soon as I had him, and I hugged him close while I watched Carina fall away from us and hit the ground with a thundering crash.

I struggled to lower myself to the ground slowly, Noah's weight making it more difficult than ever to control the wings. And when I finally set his feet down on the platform, which was now mostly empty, he ran over to Carina and knelt beside her.

She was motionless as he moved his hand over the scales on her neck. I breathed a sigh of relief that she was still in her dragon form, which meant she was still alive.

But when I got closer, I could see her claws beginning to twitch and the tip of her tail beginning to slither across the ground.

"Noah," I said, my hand on his shoulder. "She's going to start hurting people again unless we stop her. Can you do what you did at the police station yesterday? Make her feel calm?"

He looked up at me. "But you said I shouldn't do that unless she tells me it's okay."

"I know, but this is a special case. She's not herself right now." I racked my brain, trying to think of a way to explain things quickly without telling him to just do it because I said so.

"There's a monster controlling her," I said as her wings went taut and her eyes opened, just as wild as before, "and monsters don't get a say in how we stop them."

He thought for a moment, eyes shifting away from me, before he nodded and turned back to Carina.

Steam snorted out from her nostrils, and I tensed as Noah lifted his hand to put it on her snout. Would she incinerate him before he could gain influence over her emotions? Would his magic even work on her now that the chaneques still had their bony fingers clutched around her soul?

She opened her mouth as his fingers touched her, but instead of a burst of fire, her tongue slipped out lazily and hung over her bottom jaw. Then she began to shrink.

Her scales turned over into burnt flesh, and I whipped off my jacket as soon as I saw her clothes were gone. Shredded to pieces by her shifting and then incinerated by the flames. The heavy leather I threw over her would hurt against her burns, but it was better than letting an eight-year-old lie naked in the middle of a Metro platform. Even if most of the bystanders had run away, some were beginning to filter back in now that the dragon was down. They were even giving me strange looks, not at all the kind I would expect as the one who'd just saved their lives, but that was probably because I was standing there in only jeans and a bra, with a torn-up bloodstained shirt wrapped around my middle.

At least they were keeping their distance.

All but a few. Ray caught my eye as he sprinted down the escalator, a small woman following him and Dirk close behind.

Carina sat up at this point, wrapping my jacket around her torso lazily as she stared straight ahead with blank eyes. She didn't turn to look at Ray when he knelt down beside her, didn't move when he grasped her head in his hands and planted a hard kiss in her hair with his eyes squeezed tightly shut.

"Is she . . ." he asked when he'd opened them.

"She's okay for now, thanks to Noah. But I don't know how long he can keep this up." I glanced at Noah, who seemed completely fine, and although that was good in the moment it struck me as something I'd need to worry about later. If there were limits to his abilities, I hadn't run into them yet.

Ray breathed in sharply, then slipped a bag off his shoulder and unzipped it on the ground. An obsidian blade, white feathers, what looked like dried snake skins, and a lighter were unpacked slowly and carefully. He laid them on the ground in a semicircle around Carina, then took off his own coat and handed it to me.

"Thanks," I said, pulling it over my shoulders.

But he wasn't done. He took off his shirt next, and I narrowed my eyes as he sat in front of Carina and lay down with his bare back against the cold floor.

"What are you doing?" I asked.

"This is the ritual," Ray said.

The woman who had come in with him knelt behind Carina and grasped the little girl's hands. She moved Carina like a puppet, reaching her right arm forward and curling her fingers around the obsidian blade that had been set before her.

I didn't like the look of that.

I liked it even less when Carina's arms were raised over her head, the tip of the knife pointed down. The woman took in a short breath, shut her eyes, and plunged Carina's hands towards Ray's bare chest.

I jerked into motion, gritting my teeth as I darted forward to catch their wrists before the blade could slice into my brother.

"What the fuck do you think you're doing?" I yelled.

The knife dropped out of Carina's fingers, only missing Ray because he sat up halfway to glare at me. "This is the ritual," he repeated, his words sharper now. "If you don't let her kill me, she'll be lost forever."

19

I SNATCHED the obsidian blade from the floor where it had fallen between Ray and his daughter.

"Fuck no," I said. Ray might well be right about what needed to be done, but I wasn't going to just sit here and watch my niece be forced to kill her own father unless I was sure there was no other way. "Explain."

Ray sighed and stared at me with cold eyes. "She needs to make a sacrifice."

I went silent for a moment, trying to process the implication. "Couldn't you have brought a goat?"

He shook his head, smiling at me softly. "No, hermana. Not for this."

I cringed, eyes darting to the woman grasping Carina's hands. "And who's she?"

"Vera," she said flatly, looking at me. "Nice to meet you."

I pursed my lips, not convinced at all that she thought it was nice.

"Carina's mother," Ray offered.

"The one who won't take care of her own daughter?" I asked

before I could stop myself, but I didn't regret it when I saw the daggers in Vera's glare.

"I'm taking care of her now," she said, nodding at her daughter's limp arms within her grasp.

"By making her kill her father—the one who actually feeds her and takes her to school and talks to her when she's upset and . . ." I stopped, feeling myself rambling in anger.

"This will be good for her," Vera said. "She is a dragon, and solitude is our nature. She needs to learn to do all those things for herself."

I swallowed, recognizing a dead end when I saw one. This woman was fully stuck in her ways, and I didn't think I would ever understand her perspective well enough to convince her otherwise.

"Why not you, then?" I asked, changing tack.

She gave me a questioning glare.

"Why aren't you the one being sacrificed? If you truly live a solitary life, no one will miss you." Deep down, I knew that wasn't a good enough reason to ask someone to die—but I also knew I didn't want Ray to be the one lying there on the ground.

"I am actually useful to our god," Vera said. "Unlike him." Her eyes traveled to Ray, and I followed them with mine.

He gave me a hopeless look that told me he thought she was right. It was what he'd explained to me yesterday. Without me at his side, he was powerless. And so if I didn't accept the god's power, he would have no place as a witch.

Except I just had accepted the god's power.

"That's not true," I said, moving over to him. "Not anymore."

I reached out and touched his bare shoulder with my palm, closing my eyes and opening my scrye to share with him the power of his god—*our god*, I thought with a frown—that the bunny had opened to me.

He jerked up, twisting around to look at me. "You . . ."

"I had to," I whispered. "To save her. I needed to fly."

His eyes glistened, and I hoped he wouldn't cry. I hadn't done it for the reasons he'd wanted me to, and now that the adrenaline of battle had worn off, the reminder that I'd done it at all was making me feel sick.

"Thank you," he said simply.

"What now?" I turned back to Vera. "Which one of you is less useful now that he has me at his side?"

"This is ridiculous." She glared at Ray, then said something to him in Spanish that I didn't understand.

I frowned, wishing I'd been a better student when I'd taken Spanish classes as a young child. I could usually understand the basics, but Vera's words were far too bitchy and fast and complicated for me to grasp.

Motion by the escalator caught my eye as I tuned them out, and I looked up to see Miriam and Adrian making their way down.

The anger that had my nerves on edge eased a bit when I saw him. There were bags under his eyes that probably rivaled my own, his nice coat was torn in a few places, and his hair was messy as all hell—but he was breathing and walking and conscious, projecting a sense of steady strength that made me feel like everything was going to be okay even as my brother readied himself to have his own daughter slice open his chest.

Adrian wasn't looking at us, though. His head was turned towards the crowd of onlookers, which made me turn my head as well. It didn't take me long to realize what had caught his attention.

Gary's colorful scarf stood out in the sea of dull coats. When I spotted him, I expected him to run away, but instead he seemed to be marching over directly towards us.

He pulled a gun out from under his jacket, and Adrian and I moved at the same time to close in on him.

He only got one shot off before the knife in my hands was at his throat and his arms were pinned back by Adrian, the gun dropping to the ground.

Vera growled, a bullet wound blooming red in her upper arm, which was still wrapped around her daughter. Had Gary been aiming for Carina?

"You can't do this," he said through gritted teeth.

"I can," I said, ripping off his scarf and pressing my blade into the soft scar on his neck. "And I think you know just how easy it will be."

"No—I mean *that*." He nodded at Carina. "If she takes back her soul, it will destroy everything I've built."

"That sounds like exactly what we want," I said.

"Where do you think the souls go?" Gary asked, and I stared at him blankly. "Into the land—into these walls." His eyes shifted over to the lower portion of the textured domed ceiling. "If one of them gets loose, they'll all escape."

I remembered the dead faces and skeletal arms that had stretched out to me, always from the walls, and realized those might have been the stolen souls of all the chaneques' previous victims.

"You say that like I should care," I said.

Gary's eyes widened. "I don't know what will happen," he whispered.

"We'll find out together then." I met Adrian's eyes and hoped he would understand when I said, "You should go."

Adrian tilted his head, giving me a questioning look.

"Get all these people out of here." I jerked my head at the onlookers around us, tightening my grip on the knife at Gary's throat. *Come on, Mr. Law-Abiding Police Officer, get out of my sight so I can murder this guy.* At the very least, Miriam would understand if Adrian didn't.

But his shoulders dropped as I glared at him, his mouth opening halfway before shutting again, and I knew he understood.

He cleared his throat. "Be careful."

With a nod, I wrapped my free arm around Gary to take control of him from Adrian, pressing the knife a little harder into the scar at his neck.

Adrian pulled away from us and began corralling the onlookers with Miriam, waving them away as they would do for any crime scene.

I pushed Gary forward, walking us over to where Ray was still sitting on the ground.

"I have your sacrifice," I said as I approached. "Put your damn shirt back on."

He almost smiled at me, which would have been an amazing feat considering the state of his daughter. Instead, he pulled his shirt on and came around behind Gary.

"I can take over from here," he said, and I relinquished my hold on the vampire, switching out one of my own knives for the obsidian blade at his throat. Gary let out a sharp yelp as Ray twisted his arm.

Dirk came over to me with a sly grin on his face. "That a bloodsucker there?" he asked, holding up his flamethrower. "If he needs torching . . ."

I almost felt sorry to have to deny him the pleasure. But if anyone was going to be torching a vampire tonight, it would be me with Simeon's headless body.

Ray shook his head. "No, but can you rip off his shirt while we hold him?"

Dirk shrugged and did as he was asked, grumbling just a bit in the process.

"Let's get him down," Ray said.

I did my best to help him move Gary to the ground without pulling the knife away from his throat.

Gary was whimpering now, struggling against Ray, and my blade sliced a shallow cut into his scar accidentally. Blood dripped slowly from the wound, and Gary squeezed his eyes shut as he froze to avoid hurting himself further.

There was no way out for him now.

Noah had started to sway from side to side in boredom, and Vera was way beyond antsy. She lifted Carina's arms again and swiftly sliced down into Gary's chest with the obsidian blade.

Gary let out a long whine, his teeth grinding together and his lips pinched in. Blood welled up from the cut, and Vera loosened Carina's hold on the knife until it fell to the ground.

Then she carefully directed her daughter's fingers to peel open the layers of flesh and muscle on Gary's chest, revealing the white edges of ribcage poking out of the gore. She curled their fingers around the ribs, breaking them apart two at a time as Gary jerked and grunted beneath us.

I had the fleeting thought that I hoped Carina's fingers wouldn't be crushed under her mother's strength, but I knew Carina was stronger than a human girl even when she was in her human form.

When it was done, Gary's heart lay bare, beating, vulnerable inside his broken chest. Vera and Carina picked up the obsidian knife again, cutting carefully into the connective tissue around the organ before scooping it out with their bare hands.

Together, they held it over Carina's head and squeezed, the blood flowing out into the girl's hair and down her neck.

Gary went stiff under my grip, and I let go of him, motioning for Ray to do the same. Even though he wasn't technically dead, he wouldn't be able to move with his heart no longer pumping blood through his veins.

Carina absently blinked as they set the squashed heart down in front of her.

With bloody hands, they picked up the feathers and snake skins and layered them into Gary's ruined chest cavity.

I narrowed my eyes, at this point wondering just how much was involved in this horrific ritual. I would have thought the whole bit about taking a shower under a beating heart would have done it, but . . .

Ray smiled at me as Vera pushed Carina's thumb into the lighter, sparking up a flame. "We must set a fire in the chest," he said, "for the light will guide her soul back to her."

"Mmm hmm," I mumbled, hoping I'd never again come across a monster so nasty that *this* was considered the cure for it.

Vera guided Carina in lighting aflame a single feather, then dropped it into the pile of tinder in Gary's chest.

"Feathers and serpents, a link to the god who created her ancestors," Ray whispered to me, "whose mark will always be on her soul no matter which god she serves."

The feathers curled quickly in the heat, almost melting as the flames licked over the snake skins. The fire grew higher, and soft laughter shook the walls around us.

I twisted my head, putting my hand on Noah's shoulder as duplicates of him appeared in every direction, each one grinning at me with yellowed teeth and shriveled cheeks.

With the real Noah close enough to touch, these fakes weren't nearly as frightening. But the dead faces emerging from the walls were frightening enough to make up for it.

There were so many of them—maybe even hundreds—despite the fact that there was no way the chaneques had taken so many victims already. Unless their victims carried over with them from place to place, or . . .

My insides went cold as the alternative dawned on me. Maybe they took the souls not only of their victims but of their victims'

victims. Everyone the cat lady had killed on the train, everyone the fae had killed in the bar, everyone the gorilla shifter had killed in the mall . . .

Where would they all go, now that they were free?

The air whistled as the skeletal specters flew overhead, stretching out as I'd seen them do before and then slowly turning into mist.

By the time Carina's made it over to her, it was far from horrifying. It looked just like any regular soul, hardly visible at all but for a slight sheen in the air.

It hovered before her for a moment as she looked up, slight apprehension in her otherwise empty eyes. Then it sucked itself back into her, causing her to go stiff for a second before she let out a long, piercing shriek.

Bats. Maybe I should have warned Ray about the pain.

I rushed over to her even though I knew there was no way I could help, but Ray got there first. Carina collapsed in his arms.

"She's okay. That's normal," I said, not sure if he could even hear me above the panicked words he was saying to her in Spanish.

Noah came up next to me, and I set my hand on the back of his head. "Is the monster gone?" he asked.

"Yes, thanks to you," I said.

The ground shook under my feet, tremors moving all throughout the walls and ceiling of the space as dust fell from overhead.

It seemed Carina's soul had shaken loose more than just the other souls. Gary had implied they'd been woven into the land already—into the structure of the tunnels. And if they had all come out here, in this station, at once . . .

"We need to get out of here," Vera said.

I nodded in agreement. "Dirk," I snapped, waving him over and gesturing to the vampire campfire at my feet. "Go nuts."

The glee on his face lifted my spirits, as did the sight of Gary engulfed by the plume of fire spouting from the flamethrower. The fire in his chest couldn't be counted on to burn him entirely, and I needed to make sure he was dead for good.

That taken care of, I swept up Noah in my arms and ran.

He would slow me down, the heavy thing, but not as much as he would if I'd asked him to run on his own tiny legs.

The others were already on the move, Ray carrying Carina as the dust filtering from above quickly turned into pebbles, which only threatened to get larger. I wouldn't be surprised if this whole tunnel collapsed in a few minutes.

Or maybe sooner, I thought with a chill as a chunk of stone the size of my head crashed into the ground beside me.

I ran faster, legs pumping hard as I made it to the ginormous escalators that led up to the open air. Everyone else was ahead of me, but not so far ahead of me that I wasn't worried for them as well.

Thunderous crashes sounded behind me, the vibrations so strong they sent jolts of pain through the bones in my legs as I pressed down and down and down into each step up.

I could barely see through all the dust that billowed out from behind and below, but I thought I could make out someone moving towards me from above.

Adrian? I thought as I recognized his sturdy frame. *What the fuck kind of bullshit are you doing now?* This crazy man was going to get himself killed along with us.

He didn't even pause when he reached me, just plucked Noah out of my arms and turned tail. Without the kid's weight slowing me down, I moved faster—and Adrian moved faster still with his long legs and powerful muscles.

But neither of us were moving fast enough.

The thunderous roar moved closer, the impact of each slab of concrete sending shock waves through my body from behind.

We're not going to make it.

It was the last thing I thought before the dust around me transformed into glitter.

I COUGHED into the clear air. Cold crept under my backside, and when I moved my hands they splashed in the puddle of water I was sitting in.

Noah and Adrian were beside me, the rest of the group scattered around us, everyone on their backs or asses on a wide sidewalk aboveground near the Metro station we'd just been trying to escape from.

"Etty?" I thought out loud, remembering the burst of glitter that had to be fae dust. I wasn't sure if Etty even had enough in her at this point to get us all out of there like this, but I couldn't think of any other explanation.

"No," said a sweet-sounding voice beside my ear. "But we are grateful you've shown us where to find her."

I twisted my body and got to my feet, finding myself standing before two fae who seemed to have no desire to use glamours. They were almost identical to one another, with pointed ears, rich dark skin, absurdly long nails that looked more like claws than anything human, and narrow sharpened teeth in their sly smiles.

Their heads were shaved, their bodies covered in matching

floor-length blue coats, and their facial features androgynous despite the glittering sheen over their cheeks. They both had glowing golden eyes, same as the ones I'd caught spying on me in the alley this morning.

I bit my cheek, wondering if these were the fae Etty had hitched a ride with in order to escape. The enforcers.

"Why did you save us?" I didn't even try to hide the skepticism in my tone.

"You have done us a favor, and we have done you one in turn." The fae on the right nodded at the group of people around me. "I trust seven lives are enough to fulfill any debt that was owed."

"What did I do for you?" I asked, knowing fully well I was looking a gift horse in the mouth. When the fae were involved, anyone would be stupid not to.

"Vengeance for our ravaged kin." A poisonous spite crept into the words as they spoke. They must be talking about the fae in the bar who had completely drained himself of dust in committing the worst massacre I'd ever seen with my own eyes. Who had been forced to swallow iron. Whose soul we had probably just released along with Carina's. "And leading us to this fugitive," they continued.

With a snap of their fingers, Etty appeared beside them in a puff of glitter. She looked confused for only a moment before her face fell into a sullen state I hadn't seen on her since Becca had died. The sheen of glittery dust surrounding her settled into something that looked like a cylindrical forcefield, which she didn't even try to move through. They had her trapped.

"How did you even . . ." I started before realizing it was pointless. It didn't matter how they had found her, only that it meant I was going to lose her again.

"We've been keeping one eye on you since you left the site of the ravaging. We were there, watching, in the hopes of discovering what could have done such a thing to one of our own."

I nodded, not sure what else to say, and Etty lifted her hand in a defeated wave as I made eye contact with her.

Noah pulled himself out from Adrian's grasp at this point and started to run towards her. "Etty! Don't go away again!" he yelled. I tried to hold him back, but he moved faster than I expected.

The fae didn't pay him any mind as he ran up to Etty—not until his hands broke through the glitter surrounding her and he wrapped her waist in a hug.

The fae narrowed their golden eyes at the two, watching intently as Noah took Etty's hand and led her out of the glittering cylinder, which dissipated easily in a puff of dust.

Etty's eyes were wide and her steps small. She turned back to the fae when one of them said, "Stop."

They bent over, their tall frame curving in an inhuman manner to put their face level with Noah's.

"And who is this?" they said.

I stood, shaking slightly with the sudden realization that I might lose two people to the fae today, and not just one.

"He's mine," I said, my hand on his shoulder.

The fae tilted their head up, peering at me with laughter in their shimmering eyes. "I doubt that." They reached out and touched Noah's forehead with a single finger, their long nail curving over the top of his head. "Ah," they said, "I see, he is an oddity . . . but still kin."

They stood up straight again and exchanged a glance with their partner, who had been silent this entire time. The silent one blipped out of existence in a puff of dust and then back again only a few seconds later. The first one turned back to us, just as I was contemplating whether to start running, and said, "We'd like to make a deal."

I stiffened. Making a deal with the fae was like lying down in front of a hungry vampire and opening a vein. You might have fun for a while, but they would suck all the life out of you before it was over.

Fae were more than fair in matters of accidental debt, as evidenced by their saving all our lives just a few moments ago, but that was only because they were control freaks who couldn't stand the idea of owing anyone anything nebulous.

When it came to intentional deals, they never made any that weren't somehow weighted in their favor.

"What kind of deal?" I asked, despite Etty glaring at me over Noah's head like I should know better.

"We'll let the fugitive stay," they said with a wave towards Etty, "if the child becomes hers as well as yours."

I pressed my lips together, not sure exactly what they meant. "You want us to share custody?"

"If that is what your laws call for. As long as it is equal. She should have as much claim to him as you do."

I frowned, wondering if it would be a good idea to tell them I didn't have much of a claim at this point to begin with. Noah's self-loathing ifrit father hadn't planned on letting the kid live long enough to bother specifying who should take care of him in the event of his death. And Becca had requested Etty as his caregiver in the will she'd drawn up hastily before going after her ex. I'd somehow managed to convince a judge that I was the next-best choice with Etty out of the picture, but if she were to come back, she might not need a fae deal to take over for me.

All this contributed to me feeling like I was clearly getting the better end of the deal here—and that meant I was most certainly missing something.

"Why?" I asked. But they only smiled as Etty shook her head at me.

I sighed, trying to work through the implications. Etty was powerless against these creatures, as far as I knew. She lived her life at the behest of their whims. And anyone who had control over a parent would effectively have control over their child.

It was Noah they wanted, although they weren't yet sure when and how and in what capacity. Planting Etty as his guardian would allow them to keep an eye on him, to influence him, to come back later and offer me another deal I might be stupid enough to take.

After all, I was certainly stupid enough to take this one. There was no way out of it in my head—now that Noah was on their radar, I couldn't risk that they would dig deeper and find out Etty had a case for full custody.

And as much as I knew her limitations, I trusted Etty completely. I knew that while she may technically be their pawn, she would look out for what was best for the kid. And so would I. Together, we could handle anything they decided to throw at us down the line.

"Okay," I said. "I agree."

Etty let out a breath, her eyes closed, and I couldn't tell whether it was relief or frustration, or a combination of the two.

"It is done," the fae said, and then they were gone.

I turned around to see that some of the others had disappeared as well, all except for Miriam, Dirk, and Adrian. I assumed Ray and his family were smart enough to know you should always fuck off quickly when the fae started trying to do favors for you.

"Ha haaa," Dirk hooted, sauntering over to me with a wide grin. "You got our girl back for good!"

Our girl? I thought with a grimace, but then my eyes popped wide open in horror as he grabbed the sides of my head roughly and pressed his lips hard against mine.

It happened quickly and ended quickly, not at all a romantic kiss but more the kind you would give to a puppy in training who had done a good job.

I hated it thoroughly.

"I'll make sure to give you a good write-up," he whispered close to my face before giving my arm a slap and turning away from me towards Etty.

The side eye she was giving him was almost as terrifying as the even stare Adrian was giving me.

Miriam marched over to me with a huff, reached around my neck and plucked off her squishy.

I'd had just about enough with everyone at that point, and Noah's head was digging into my side as he leaned into me with sleepy eyes.

"We all need to get some rest," I said calmly as I settled my fingers into his hair and shifted my hips so he wouldn't slide off. "Etty . . . let's go home?"

I MET THE MORNING GROANING, unable to even open my eyes under the weight of the dull, aching pain of my battle hangover.

Sure, all the individual wounds and bruises and breaks had already been healed by magic. But that didn't matter to my nerves, and it all felt a thousand times worse without the adrenaline there to distract me.

I winced as I turned over in bed and cracked open my eyes, almost wishing that Noah would wander in with his intoxicating joyful morning spirit and force it on me.

But I was alone, no little intruder beside the bed, not even any creaks or squeaks to be heard through the walls of my room.

That was new. I hadn't woken up before the kid . . . well, probably ever. And he wasn't exactly great at being quiet or holding still at this time of day.

It was weird enough that it was actually concerning, and I sighed at the teeny adrenaline boost that came with that realization.

It was enough to get my achy ass out of bed.

I pulled a robe around myself and wandered out of my room, glad at least that I'd managed to take a shower before turning in for the night. If I'd had to deal with crusty blood on my bedsheets on top of all this . . .

I shook my head at the empty living area, then poked my head into Noah's room, which was similarly empty. The bed was even made, like he hadn't slept in it at all last night.

I frowned, letting a small burst of panic run through me before I remembered it wasn't just me and Noah in this apartment anymore. Turning to Etty's room, I twisted the doorknob gently and cracked open the door.

Etty's snores washed over me like a wave of calm, a more reassuring sound even than the hiss of freshly brewing coffee. Better still was the little lump in the star-patterned pajamas lying next to her, his arm hanging loosely over her side.

Noah was awake, I was sure of it, but he was pretending to sleep so he could stay in bed with Etty a little longer. As much as I'd missed her, he'd probably missed her even more. To lose not only his mother but the auntie he'd been closest with at the same time . . . I had done my best in their place, but I'd always been more of a stranger to him, the new arrival trying to live in his home without really fitting into his life.

I knew I wasn't that stranger anymore, so my heart ached with comfort rather than envy at the sight of them snuggling.

The door creaked as I moved to pull it shut, and Noah lifted his head to look at me with bright eyes.

He moved a finger to his lips, imploring me to be quiet, before extricating himself from Etty's bed much more carefully than he needed to; that woman slept like a rock.

"I'm hungry," he said to me as soon as he was out of her room and I'd closed the door.

I chuckled, my insides grumbling, emptier than they'd been in a long time. "Yeah, me too."

Noah ran circles in the kitchen while I threw stale cinnamon rolls in the microwave and cracked some eggs into a pan. He was quiet while we ate, which I was fine with, every sip of coffee waking up more of the brain cells I would need to have a meaningful conversation anyway.

"Do you want to go see Carina today?" I asked when I'd drained my mug. As much as I wanted to stay here all morning and relax with Noah and Etty, I had a ton of damage control to do after everything that had happened last night, and part of that meant visiting Ray.

Noah was quiet for a moment, chewing a bite of cinnamon roll slowly before saying, "No," as nonchalantly as if I'd asked him whether he wanted some orange juice.

"Oh?" I hadn't thought I would ever hear Noah turn down a visit with Carina. But he had seen her murder several innocent people last night. "Why not?"

He looked down instead of up at me, putting his fork back on his plate. "I'm embarrassed."

"What do you have to be embarrassed about?" I scrunched my face up in genuine confusion, giving him a playful tap on the shoulder. "You proved to her you could fly without falling off."

But he didn't even smile. "I get it now," he said. "Why I'm not supposed to make people feel things. Even though there was a monster controlling her, I could tell . . ." He ducked his head even further. "I could tell she wouldn't like it."

I opened my mouth and then closed it, at a loss for how to respond.

"Like . . ." he continued. "You said she wasn't herself, but then I made her even less herself."

"I—" I started, but he kept going.

"It was like when Mommy was a zombie. That was bad, but then with the jellies on her, it was even worse."

It clicked in my head as soon as he said that, the point he was trying to make. I remembered how I'd felt seeing Miriam control soulless Becca like a puppet, the way it had seemed to make a mockery of her even more than what her empty body had done of its own accord.

"And . . ." he said in a dark tone, making me raise my eyebrows. "It was fun."

Ah, I thought, heart sinking even more. This was what was really bothering him. Just like his Auntie Salma and Uncle Baz, there was some part of Noah that liked controlling people. Maybe even hungered for it. But I couldn't help the feeling that if he was telling me all this—if he was aware enough to be able to put it into words and admit it to himself, let alone me—that he would be fine. At least I hoped that would be the case.

I nodded at him. "Okay," I said. "I get it. Just remember there was a monster inside Carina, and she would have died if not for you. You didn't do it *because* it was fun. I know it feels wrong, but you did a good thing."

My fingers twitched on the handle of my empty coffee mug as I watched Noah's face harden. It was no surprise he was struggling with the contradiction. I was so in over my head here, and this conversation needed far more coffee and planning to be had properly.

"That's why everyone hates monsters," I added, feeling the need to leave him with something more. "They put us in situations where there are no good choices, and sometimes it's hard to figure out which choice is less bad."

That seemed to get through to him, and he picked up his fork again to stuff a bite of eggs into his mouth.

"Now, I have to go. If you don't wanna come with me, I'm gonna need you to go jump on Etty as hard as you can." I felt a tiny bit bad about it, but I couldn't leave him here with her unless she was awake.

Noah smiled at me, his mouth still full of eggs. Then he hopped out of his seat and burst forth into Etty's room, and if I'd had more coffee in me I would have laughed at the commotion that ensued.

Fifteen minutes later, I'd put on clothes and twisted my hair into a messy knot at the back of my neck. I sent off texts to Kiri and Mitch telling them I'd be getting to the club late today; hopefully they could coordinate with each other so no one would be locked out of the building.

When I opened the front door to leave, I almost tripped over a rectangular box at my feet. It was made of aged wood, beautifully polished—definitely not something dropped off with the mail.

Curious, I brought it inside and set it on the kitchen table. Dark velvet peeked out from the inside as I opened it, and atop it lay a handwritten note.

I think you dropped this.

I stopped reading after the first line, a lump forming in my throat as I lifted the velvet to reveal what was beneath it.

The axe I'd brought with me last night and then promptly lost before I could use it to do any actual beheading. It was covered in gore despite its lack of use, all from the vampire I'd exploded outside of Soma's bar before fleeing the scene with Kat.

I sighed, knowing I would need to find a way to make things right with Soma. I hoped he would forgive me once he found out I'd eliminated his rival.

But when I picked up the axe to put it in the sink, I noticed another lump of fabric underneath it.

It was so stained with blood I didn't recognize it until I spread it out, and then my whole body filled with rage.

My t-shirt. The one I'd used to wrap up and carry Simeon's head until I'd needed to stash it so I could sneak back into the club.

The one that should still be wrapped around Simeon's head, in Miriam's possession, waiting for me to come incinerate it.

My vision blurred as I pulled out my phone and smashed my thumb over Miriam's name.

"You're up bright and early!" Miriam chirped into my ear, and I ground my fist into the kitchen table so hard I felt the skin start to rub away from my knuckles.

"The head." I managed to get it out without yelling, but just barely.

"Excuse me?" she said, but I knew damn well she knew what I was talking about. She might not be in my head this instant, but she—

Fuck, I thought, realizing just now that she *hadn't* been in my head during my encounter with Simeon. She had put her squishy on me and taken it off so many times in the past couple days that I'd lost track. I felt sick to my stomach now as I remembered her taking it off in the alley, while I was worlds away in Adrian's arms, mind still half melted from our kiss.

She'd only put it on me again when we'd parted ways, after I'd asked her to go back to get the head for me. She'd agreed, but she hadn't understood the importance of the request. For all she knew, Simeon's head was just a grotesque battle trophy I was determined to mount on my wall.

And I'd gotten so used to not having to tell her things that I'd taken for granted her willingness to fulfill my unreasonable-sounding requests.

I squinted to keep the tears of frustration from flowing as I heard Etty and Noah emerging from her room. I'd disappointed myself many times over in the past year or so, and even before that, but this was the first time I was so angry at myself that I wanted to hurt something.

"Darcy?" Miriam questioned through the line. "Are you alright, dear?"

I let out a slow, shaky breath as Noah ran into the kitchen, and I carefully shut the box Soma had sent so he wouldn't see the bloody fabric inside.

"Why is there an axe in the sink?" Etty asked from my side. I shook my head slightly before turning away from her to try to hide the distress in my face.

"Did you go back and get the head like I asked?" I said as steadily as I could manage into the phone, even though I already knew the answer. "The one I was carrying around."

"Oh, that!" Miriam said it so brightly that for a split second I almost wanted to believe she had just gotten rid of my shirt from around the head and taken it home with her in something more sensible. But then she said, "It was gone when I went back. Probably washed away in the water. I'm sorry, dear, but I couldn't waste time searching for it when Adrian was down there all alone."

I hung up on her, even though I knew I should really say something like *"That's okay, I understand, of course, don't worry, you did your best . . ."* I buried my face in my hands instead. It wasn't Miriam's fault, but it was fucked all the same.

I knew without having to be told that Simeon's body would no longer be where I'd left it. Neither would the bodies of the other vampires I'd left down there beheaded. The icy bitch from the alley must have gotten to them before Miriam had gone back, and I should just be grateful she hadn't found Adrian along with her fellow vampire witch wannabes.

At least I'd managed to kill Gary once and for all.

But Simeon was still out there. And probably still entangled with an evil god who was officially out to get me now that I'd joined forces with his rival.

Etty tapped twice on the top of my skull with her fingernail, and I looked up at her sleepy glare of disapproval. She had no idea why I was upset, but she wasn't impressed by my sullen mood.

"I know you didn't make these cinnamon rolls," she said as she stuffed a piece of one into her mouth. "They're amazing."

"That was Dirk," I said, thankful that Etty was refusing to indulge my emotions right now. I knew I could talk to her about it later if I needed to, but not now—not with Noah around. "You know he's an asshole, right?"

Etty just shrugged, licking the sweet sauce from her fingers. "I know," she said with a grin. "But assholes are fun to play with. *And* he can cook?" She let out a dramatic sigh with a shake of her head, like that was all that needed to be said on the matter.

And with that, I sat back in my seat and resigned myself to the fact that they would probably be together forever.

I blinked, eyes landing on the note that had come with the box. I hadn't finished reading it.

I picked it up, focusing on the fancy script. Underneath the first line, it read:

Be at Bite in one hour. Ellis will take you to my crypt. -S

I crushed the note in my fist, smashing pieces of crusty blood into the paper.

I'd hoped I would have some more time before I'd have to face Soma. But disobeying a clear order like this would not be a great start towards trying to repair our relationship.

"What's that?" Noah sang as he climbed up into my lap.

I winced at the pain of his sharp knees digging into my sides. Pushing the box away, I said, "Not anything good."

But Noah wasn't looking at the box anymore. He was staring straight into my eyes, one tiny hand on my cheek. "You feel sad." I could hear the emotion reflected in his voice. "Want me to make you feel better?"

Heat rushed into my face. I bit my tongue as I squeezed my eyes shut, both to keep Noah from looking too deep and to keep myself from crying.

I wasn't sad.

Or maybe I was. Maybe I was still mourning the new loss of Simeon, who had resurfaced in my life just long enough to open the wound he'd left me with and cut it even deeper.

But more than that, I was mad. Mad that I couldn't wash my hands of him yet. Couldn't stitch up the wound and let it heal. Not until I could find him and give him the permanent death he deserved.

"No," I said to Noah, opening my eyes and forcing a smile. "But thanks for asking."

I would need all this anger, or sadness, or whatever it was, to fuel me when I met with Soma. Because he might be inclined to help me go after the vampire who had fucked over us both.

I LEANED against the darkened windows outside of Bite and closed my eyes as the cool breeze ran over my bare arms. The sun was out today, and I'd taken the opportunity to go without a jacket.

For the first time in years, I didn't have a single weapon on me.

I wouldn't need any today. If things got squirrely at Soma's crypt, no amount of steel or silver could save me.

But I hoped things wouldn't get squirrely. Soma had seen me explode one of his blood smugglers with my bare hands. If he was smart, he would take my naked arms as either the white flag they were or a credible threat.

Now that I'd given in to my godly benefactor, I wasn't above taking advantage of the power that leant me. I didn't know if the phoenix's magic could turn a vampire as old as Soma into confetti, but I would damn well find out if he tried me.

A dark van pulled up to the curb in front of me.

Ellis was late, as I'd expected. Vampires always moved slower on sunny days.

He said nothing to me when I got into the backseat, and I

spent the thirty-minute drive staring into the black windows trying not to worry about the fact that I had no idea where we were going.

When the car stopped, I walked out into an enclosed garage, already sealed off from the daylight. Ellis led me into a mirror-lined hallway, which opened out into a sitting room filled with modern furniture, all elegant and simple at the same time.

Soma sat on a black couch, a woman resting across it with her head laid on his lap. Her wrist was clutched tightly in his hand and pressed to his lips.

He opened his eyes after a moment to meet my gaze, taking the wrist away and licking the excess blood from his teeth.

"Darcy. Please sit." He gestured at the white suede chair across from him. "Can I get you anything?"

"I'm good," I said, stepping forward to do as he said.

I wasn't good. Seeing him licking at his meal in front of me had turned my stomach. I'd never been squeamish about blood, but there was something about the lethargic state of the woman on his lap, so close to death and so powerless to do anything about it . . .

Nothing about that would ever be appetizing to me.

"Let's get right to it, then," he said. "I've heard our mutual friend is on the run."

My eyebrows lifted. "Friend isn't exactly how I'd put it, but sure."

At Soma's unamused stare, I sighed. I needed to ease up on the attitude and remember I should probably be begging for forgiveness after I'd run off with all the blood this man had hired me to steal.

I tried to relax into the comfortable chair before I said, "I took off Simeon's head again, but I lost it before I could burn it."

Soma dropped the wrist he'd been holding, and the woman shifted sluggishly on his lap. The frown on his face unnerved me.

"Simeon was trying to frame you—overthrow you," I continued. "I thought you would want him truly dead."

"I know." Soma tapped a finger on his knee. "And I do. But I thought you would want him alive."

I shifted my eyes, confused for a moment, before I heard Soma's words in my head. *You'll always be his.* It was what he had said to me at the club. What Simeon had always made me believe.

Ah. So that was why I was here. Soma thought I would know where Simeon was. Maybe he thought I'd been helping him all along.

I breathed out through my nose, the harsh sound cutting through the silence. "No," I said. "Not after what he's done."

"Wonderful." Soma smiled, his fangs still tinged with a small amount of blood. He tapped twice on the head of the woman on his lap. "Get up, darling." To me, he said, "I had intended this as something of a bribe, but now I hope you'll accept it as a peace offering."

I pursed my lips, not sure what he was talking about. "What exactly—"

I stopped when the woman sat up and looked at me, her glazed-over eyes meeting mine with vague recognition.

"Minnie?"

She blinked, then gave me a childlike smile. "Hello, love." Her red hair was loose around her face, long strands sticking out in every direction, her skin ashy from the blood loss.

I snapped my eyes back to Soma. "I don't understand."

"You will." He reached over and pushed a strand of Minnie's hair away from her face. "Go on, darling. Show her."

Minnie reached into her lap and pulled out a phone, pushing the button to turn on the screen. She handed it to me, and I found myself looking at a photo album.

Wedding photos. Minnie and her wife, an attractive blonde—

I looked up, my heart jumping.

"Recognize anyone?" Soma asked innocently.

I dipped my head back down, zooming in on a photo to get a closer look. It couldn't be her.

Tall, slender, light hair and light skin . . . wearing a slinky ivory gown that I couldn't help but imagine covered in blood. Simeon's blood.

It was her. The woman who had taken off his head in the first place. The assassin with the ward. The one who had taken us by surprise, whom I hadn't been able to stop.

The woman who had bested me and ruined my career in the process.

"Isn't she beautiful?" Minnie asked lazily.

I gaped at her, too shocked to respond. My lungs ached as I thought back to the way Minnie had so expertly butchered the vampire I'd killed in her kitchen, how calm she'd been at the prospect of disposing of a body, how adamant she'd been that we not involve the police.

Marrying an assassin would do that to anyone, I imagined.

"Very beautiful," I finally replied. If I'd seen these photos a few days ago, I would have said she was the most beautiful woman in the world. I would have been ecstatic to see her, to hunt her, to finally get my revenge.

Now, though, I only wanted to forget her.

I looked up at Soma again. "You want to make peace with me by offering up the woman *you* hired to kill him in the first place?"

Soma shifted his shoulders in what might have been a shrug. "Like I said, it was meant to be more of a bribe."

"For what? What do you want from me?"

"After what I saw last night, I'd like to have you on my side. And . . ." He ran his tongue over his fangs once more, his hand lifting to idly touch his throat. "I'll need you to keep our secret."

There it was. I'd almost forgotten. After I'd so easily cut the heads off three scarred vampires last night—one of them twice—

and after hearing the fear in Kat's voice as she'd tried to persuade me there was *one secret* she really couldn't tell without forfeiting her life . . .

I knew my life would be just as forfeit if I didn't agree to Soma's request.

Never mind that I'd already told Dirk the whole thing. Never mind that he might have already told the Guardians decapitation didn't really kill vampires, but it did make them vulnerable as hell.

Never mind that I was agreeing to an impossible task. I'd never let that stop me before.

"Alright," I said smoothly. "But I'm keeping this." I clutched my fingers around Minnie's phone, more for show than anything else. The Guardians might make a good spy of me yet.

"I'm glad we could come to an agreement," Soma said, his expression unreadable. He tilted his head towards Minnie. "What would you like me to do with her?"

"Put her back where you found her." I glanced back at Minnie. Even with what she had done to my mind, and even with the proof in my hand that she had lied to me, I didn't want her dead. Not yet, at least. "I don't want to alarm her wife."

"Of course." Soma raised his head to look behind me, and Ellis stepped forward. I supposed that meant our visit was over. But then the ancient vampire leaned in, extending his hand towards me.

I took it, expecting a simple handshake. To a casual observer, a handshake was what it would have looked like. Until Soma's thumb nail sliced into the delicate skin at the top of my hand, blood welling up underneath it.

I winced as he dabbed his thumb carefully in the red liquid before releasing my hand. He brought his thumb to his mouth and touched the drop of my blood to his tongue, closing his eyes for a moment before setting them back on me.

"I'm glad to have you, Miss Pierce," he said.

I couldn't suppress the shiver that came over me at his words, which vibrated in my ribcage the way they had when I'd met him at his club.

It was intentional. There was magic in those words. The way he saw it, I belonged to him now.

I knew better than to tell him he'd better get in line.

It was afternoon by the time I got to Ray's, and my head was a mess.

The buzzing in my scrye had gotten steadily stronger as I'd gotten closer to my brother's townhouse, that effusive fire of magic charging through my nerves at the ready. It felt as unwieldy as every other weapon I'd ever touched before training with it, and I didn't like the fact that I still didn't know exactly what it could do.

On top of that, I couldn't stop digging my thumb into my back pocket to feel for Minnie's phone. It sent a heaviness through my body every time I touched it.

My own phone buzzed soon after I'd rung the doorbell—a text from Ray.

Let yourself in. Be with you soon. You can wait in my study.

I shrugged and pushed open the door, enjoying the faint smells of hot chocolate and toasted tortillas that greeted me. But the kitchen was empty, their breakfast already cleaned up and put away, so I just made my way up the stairs.

I couldn't help stopping by Carina's room to check on her, but that was empty too.

Ray's study, however, was not.

When I pushed open the door, I immediately knew why Ray had sent me there.

Adrian sat at my brother's desk, reading glasses sliding down his nose and a thick book cracked in front of him. He looked fucking fantastic for someone who had almost died last night, and I almost opened my mouth to tell him so.

But mixed feelings fought for space in my chest as I looked at him. I was tired of this, done with playing the ridiculous game of wanting Adrian and fearing him—and not actually knowing him well enough to make any of that worthwhile. It had distracted me to the point that I'd made a critical mistake and let Simeon's accomplice escape with his head.

Hell, if I hadn't been so preoccupied with Adrian's concerns in the first place, I would have trusted my gut and killed the vampire in the alley instead of leaving her stunned, and Simeon's head would have been there waiting for Miriam to pick it up regardless of how unimportant she thought it was.

Adrian lifted his gaze and took off his glasses to look at me, the boyish expression of concentrated curiosity falling from his face to be replaced with a cold stare.

"Hi," I said. "I'm . . . glad you're not dead."

"What are you doing here?" he asked me, closing the book and standing up.

"Waiting to see my brother," I said, thinking that was obvious. "You?"

"He has books here that are hard to find in this country. Mostly because they're not in English, but . . ." Adrian stopped and shook his head, his fleeting excitement abandoned. "That's not important. The important thing is I can't work with you anymore, even informally—especially informally."

"What?" I gaped at him, trying to make sense of what he'd just said. I had plenty reason to stop working with this man, but I hadn't expected *him* to be the one to want to cut contact with *me*. "Why?"

"You lied to me," he said, staring at me levelly.

"I . . ." *Fuck*. Had he somehow found out about what I was really doing behind his back with Miriam and Dirk?

"You told me all you saw were dead things in the walls, besides that clay statue." He walked towards me around the desk. "Then I asked how Ray figured out it was the chaneques, and he said it was the visions of children with old faces that clued him in." Adrian was speaking faster now, gesturing at the many books around us. "*Plenty* of dead things and clay statues in mythology and folklore everywhere—far too many to be useful. But children with old faces?" He shook his head, and I could feel the heat from his chest now as he hovered over me. "I just did a search on my phone and found the chaneques in five minutes. I wouldn't have known how to stop them, but I would have known where to go to find out."

"We did stop them, though."

"Eventually," he snapped. "When was the first time you saw them?"

I swallowed as the memory came back to me. It was right after the incident with the shifter in the train, when I was looking for Noah . . . "Friday morning," I said softly, like maybe if he couldn't hear me then it wouldn't be true.

"All those people in the bar, and the ones Carina burnt," Adrian said just as quietly. "We might have saved them if you'd only been honest with me."

"I had no idea it was connected at that point," I said in a weak voice. "I thought I was hallucinating."

"Doesn't matter," he said. "Look around you—look at your life. What makes you think it's ever a good idea to assume you're hallucinating? I promise you, you wouldn't be able to make up the kind of shit that happens to you."

He was right, and I knew it. The truth was I *hadn't* really thought I was hallucinating. I'd only hoped I was, because the chaneques as I'd seen them had molded themselves to look like

Noah. They'd done it just to fuck with me, like they'd shown Carina the boy in her class, but I hadn't known that at the time.

"They looked like Noah," I said, and that made Adrian's expression soften just a tiny bit. "I was worried . . . I didn't want him dragged into a police investigation."

"Exactly," Adrian said, sadness in his eyes. "You didn't trust me to do my job properly. You thought I would harass your kid, treat him unjustly."

"No." I looked straight into his eyes for the first time today. "It was him I was unsure of. I know you would never . . . I know he'd have nothing to fear from you if he was innocent. I was just afraid he might not be."

It felt like someone had stabbed me in the chest to hear myself say that out loud, especially after I'd witnessed how disciplined and kind and self-aware Noah had been about his abilities throughout this whole nightmare.

Adrian looked like he could see that horror in my face, like he knew that I knew what I'd just trotted out as my defense made me even worse than what he'd been accusing me of.

"You need to stop being so afraid." Adrian lifted his hand as he said it, like he wanted to touch me, then put it back down when my eyes shifted towards the movement.

I swallowed. "I know that now."

"Do you?" he asked. "Or were you planning to never speak to me again, even before this conversation?"

I took in a deep breath and pressed my lips together, looking down. I knew this man was smart, yet still I was surprised he'd picked up on my unease despite the limited amount of time we'd spent together since our encounter with Simeon. He couldn't know all the history there . . . but then, I supposed he didn't need to.

"Some fears don't go away easily," I said.

Adrian's fist clenched briefly, and then he brought his hand up swiftly to take hold of the side of my face. I couldn't stop myself from leaning into it, remembering the way his fingers had felt curling through my hair with his lips on mine.

He lowered his face until his forehead was almost touching mine, then stopped. "Since when do you give up on anything just because it's not easy?"

I closed my eyes, not wanting him to see just how right I knew he was.

Then he was gone, cool air replacing his hand on my face, and when I opened my eyes he was halfway to the door, book in hand.

I'd like to think I might have asked him to stay if I hadn't seen Ray standing in the doorway, watching us.

But I didn't, and he left without another word.

RAY HAD the grace to say nothing as he led me downstairs to his basement, where he had apparently been holed up for the last hour or so with Carina and Vera.

The space was unfinished, wood rafters running overhead and pipes visible. Dark, dusty, walls lined with boxes. It was the basement of a normal person, except for the obsidian shrine in the center of everything.

Sharp, jagged pieces of black glass brought me back to the cave and the magic and those damn rabbits—back to the decision I'd made to accept this god's power, which I supposed was why I was here today.

I tried to clear Adrian's words out of my head, eyes landing on Carina as she smiled at me too wide, showing her teeth to an unnatural degree.

I narrowed my eyes at the loose t-shirt she was wearing, not at all her style. "What's with the getup?" I said, and her fake smile went away instantly.

"The burns," Ray said to me softly, which only caused me to deepen my frown.

"I can heal them." I moved to go to her, but Ray put a hand on my arm to stop me.

"Burns on a dragon cannot be healed with magic," Vera said from behind Carina. She put a hand on her daughter's shoulder, causing the girl to wince. "She will bear these scars for the rest of her life, a reminder of what she has done."

Whoa. I gritted my teeth together, wanting to admonish this woman, tell her that it wasn't Carina who had killed anyone last night. She couldn't be held accountable for anything she had done without her soul, and she shouldn't be made to feel ashamed for it.

But I could see in Carina's eyes that the damage had been done long before I'd arrived, and fighting about it wouldn't get me anywhere now.

"Why are you even here?" I said to Vera instead.

"For you, of course," she replied. "They thought I could convince you to accept us, but it seems you didn't need much convincing."

I nodded, letting steam out through my nose while I held my mouth tightly shut.

"We've contacted Popo." Ray stepped in between us as if his presence could cut the tension. "You've been ordered to report to the mountain, to officially swear your oath."

I tilted my head. "The mountain?"

"The volcano, in Mexico," he said. "The physical embodiment of our god's divine spirit. You must visit to prove to him you are loyal."

"Just me?" I asked. "I thought we needed to stick together."

"For now, he wants us to stay in DC, and I can't leave my business unattended."

"In case the icy death god tries to gain a foothold here again?"

I asked, but in the back of my mind I also wasn't sure I could leave *my* business unattended. How long could I keep asking other people to cover for me before Baz realized I wasn't running the show anymore?

Ray nodded. "He's tried twice already. We have to assume there will be a third time."

"So you should go as soon as possible. I return tomorrow," Vera said, then threw a stern look over to her daughter. "And I'm taking Carina with me."

Ray and Carina both stiffened when they heard her say that, Carina's little hands balling into fists and Ray pinching his lips tight.

I wrinkled my forehead in confusion. "I don't get it. You got what you wanted—I'm officially a member of Team Volcano Witch. Doesn't that mean Ray and Carina can stay together?"

"Theoretically," Vera said. "But Carina can't stay in this city after what happened last night."

Ray's face went slack, his shoulders falling. "If the law isn't looking for her now, it's only because we have friends on the inside," he explained. "As soon as witnesses identify her, there won't be anything Detective Crane can do to keep her out of prison."

I nodded slowly. They made a good point, and it was true that Carina couldn't stay here. But that didn't mean she had to go straight back to Mexico, and it certainly didn't mean she had to go with her mother.

"I can take her with me," I said. "Give her a few days at least, to say goodbye and pack her things. I can keep her out of handcuffs until then."

Ray and Vera exchanged a look, but Ray spoke before Vera could voice any complaint. "If that's what Carina wants," he said.

Carina's mouth fell open, and then she let out a squeal. For the first time today, the bright expression on her face looked real. "Hell yeah!" she said. "I'll start packing now!"

She ran up the stairs, and I followed her after getting the okay from Ray. It had been a while since I'd talked to Carina alone, and it had been a while since she'd seemed like herself.

"Road trip! Road trip! We're going on a road trip!" Carina sang loudly as she threw clothes around her room.

"Uh," I said, "I was thinking we'd just fly."

"What, because we both have wings now?" Carina scoffed and threw a flowy orange skirt at my face. "Yeah, and any human can run a marathon with no training because they all have legs."

"I meant on a plane," I said as I peeled the skirt off my head and tossed it on her bed. She was getting on my nerves already, but I couldn't deny it was good to see her spirits lifted. After what she had been through last night, it was an absolute fucking miracle to see her spirits lifted.

"I don't do planes," she said, going still for a moment as a shadow moved over her eyes.

"Okay . . ." I held back a comment about how silly it was for a dragon to be afraid to fly.

"Hey," she said, her brow furrowing as something seemed to dawn on her. She came over close to me and whispered, "We're not really going to the mountain, are we?"

I grinned, my smile opening into an actual laugh as I saw her eyes brighten with my reaction.

"Nope," I said, only a small part of me worried at how easy it had been for this little girl to read my intentions. "At least not right away."

She leaned in and bounced up and down, looking like she might breathe fire on me if I didn't tell her my actual plan right this instant.

I shifted my eyes to her door and chewed on my tongue for a moment, unconsciously fingering the spot on my ankle through my jeans where my tattoo had been before Ray had made Carina rip it off me.

I wanted it back. And I had a tiny hunch—which was growing steadily by the second—that Carina might want one too.

"Get ready, little dragon," I said as she bit her lip. "Cause we are going to California."

Carina pressed a pillow into her face and screamed into it, falling onto her bed and kicking her legs up in the air in her excitement.

Laughing, I let myself fall next to her, finally finding the contagious joy I'd been looking for when I'd woken up this morning.

I'd have to find a way to make sure the club didn't implode without me for a while, because I might need this road trip just as much as she did.

It might be exactly what I need, I thought as I pulled Minnie's phone out of my back pocket and brought up the photo album again. This time, it sent a fluttering through my chest.

I'd scrolled through the whole thing while Ellis had driven me back. Wedding photos had given way to everyday life, couple's selfies turning into individual ones as it became evident the blonde half of the equation had to travel frequently for work.

An assassin's life couldn't be easy.

At the very bottom, the most recent set of pictures had backgrounds I recognized instantly from my childhood.

Dusty brown hills with hazy air and strong sunlight, palm trees shooting up into the sky as ocean waves lapped behind them, the distinctive white lettering of the Hollywood sign making the deadly woman posing in front of it look like just another tourist.

The bitch was in California. And if she had already killed Simeon once . . .

Maybe she could help me do it again.

AFTERWORD

Thank you for reading Awakened Abyss!

I hope you enjoyed it, because Darcy's story is far from over . . . I currently have five books planned for this series, and Book 3 is coming soon.

To stay up to date and be the first to know about upcoming releases, join my mailing list or connect with me on social media. You can find me here:

https://www.erinembly.com

(Psst . . . If you sign up for my newsletter, you'll get a free novella about Minnie and Darcy to read right away!)

Want to make an author's day? Please consider leaving a review! Even if it's just a rating or a few words, it will be a great help.

I'm a new author, and every review counts.

Till next time, happy reading!
Erin

ACKNOWLEDGMENTS

Thanks so much to my amazing team of beta readers:
    Nikki Dekeuster
    Wendi Adams
    Sam Rooney
    Katheyer
    Stephanie Mirro
    Pat Walsh
    Sue Walsh

You've helped me make this story much more enjoyable than if I'd tried to go it alone, and I'm immensely grateful for your input!

9 781734 457018